Praise for

Relentless Aaron

"For an incisive look at a man's inner thoughts and feelings as he juggles multiple sexual encounters, look no further than Relentless Aaron's (*Extra Marital Affairs*) new novel. In capturing the emotions of pure sexual release and introspective debates on being true to women, this author is unparalleled…a matchless combination of sensuality and naughtiness." —*Library Journal* on *Single With Benefits*

"[A] self-publishing street lit phenomenon."
—*Publishers Weekly*

"Gripping." —*The New York Times*

"Relentless Aaron…is seriously getting his grind on." —*Vibe*

"It's very real. He's an excellent writer, with good stories and good suspense." —98.7, KISS FM

"A pure winner from cover to cover." —Courtney Carreras, *YRB* magazine on *The Last Kingpin*

"Fascinating. Relentless has made the best out of a stretch of unpleasant time and adversity…a commendable effort."
—Wayne Gilman, WBLS News Director on *Push*

"Relentless redefines the art of storytelling…while seamlessly capturing the truth and hard-core reality of Harlem's desperation and struggle." —Troy Johnson, Founder of the African American Literature Book Club on *Push*

Also by

Relentless Aaron

Platinum Dolls

Relentless Aaron

St. Martin's Paperbacks

This is a work of fiction. All of the characters, organizations, and events portrayed in this novel are either products of the author's imagination or are used fictitiously.

Relentless Aaron, Relentless, and Platinum Dolls are trademarks of Relentless Content, Inc.

PLATINUM DOLLS

Copyright © 2000 by Relentless Aaron/Relentless Content.

Cover photograph © Donn Thompson/Getty Images

All rights reserved.

For information address St. Martin's Press, 175 Fifth Avenue, New York, NY 10010.

ISBN: 0-312-94968-5
EAN: 978-0-312-94968-6

Printed in the United States of America

Relentless Content, Inc. edition / February 2004
St. Martin's Paperbacks edition / February 2009

St. Martin's Paperbacks are published by St. Martin's Press, 175 Fifth Avenue, New York, NY 10010.

10 9 8 7 6 5 4 3 2 1

DEDICATIONS

To my readers:
I appreciate you inviting me into your lives, your homes, and your bedrooms. Thank you for adopting my words into your consciousness, and for spreading the word about my true objective: to totally take the literary world by storm.

To my fellow authors:
I appreciate you who blazed the trail before me, as well as those of you who are the "first movers" in the game. As we fine-tune this machine of urban fiction, I hope that we strive for even greater accomplishments time after time. And let us realize that there should be no competition in the world of storytelling, since every voice has the right to be heard and acknowledged. In this multibillion-dollar industry of publishing, may the best man/woman win the brass ring, but let us all maintain harmony, passion, enthusiasm, and most of all, respect.

To the many book clubs:
Stay tuned! I'll never let you down! Thank you for your support.

To our sisters and brothers in prison:
I hope that this book serves as a form of release, one that is entertaining and, at the same time, inspiring. Having been where you are, I understand the frustration and tension of being away from loved ones. Here's hoping that this book is that mental escape you can use to free your mind. More important, this book, and many others that I've written, serve as clear proof that:

> What the mind of a man can conceive,
> and believe, it can achieve!
> *Please,* do *not* waste your precious time;
> do what you can, with what you have
> right where you are.

To my friend and mentor Johnny "Jay Dub" Williams: We did it!!! Thank you for keeping me focused during my stretch. You are a true mentor to me. To Tiny Wood: This content might be a little too strong for you. Don't hurt y'self! (Seriously: I'm glad you're in my corner when I've needed you most). To Julie and Family, Emory and Tekia Jones: Thank you all for your faith in me. To Renée McRae, my big sister and motivatress; Carol and Brenda, Curt Southerland, Darryl, Adianna, Joanie, Kevin, Lance, Lou, Mechel, Henry Perkins, Rick, Ruth. Thank you all!

FOREWORD

Stew Gregory is twenty-eight years old, his hunger for sex and money is insatiable, and his drive to achieve is unstoppable. He's at the top of his game.

Platinum Dolls Industries is Stew's company. Once only a small-time, amateur Internet Web page, it has skyrocketed into a major conglomerate with branches from Malibu to Scarsdale, thanks to certain investors. It's a Goliath that employs over five hundred people, most of them attractive women beyond compare.

Just when it all seems creamy, things begin to spin out of control. A girl is murdered, shot down in cold blood. Penthouses are destroyed and more women die. This is big news. It all makes for spectacular headline news. Yet the company profits as a result of the growing body count.

Ultimately, it's Stew who must solve the puzzle as to why his girls are dying. In the meantime, he's coming to grips with his own priorities regarding love and life. He faces a clear challenge: Can he still live his dreams while they're becoming living nightmares?

Welcome to Stew's world . . .

Malibu, California

ONE

Stew Gregory was out on the back terrace, about to end his twenty-minute conference call, when Timmy poked his head out of the patio doors.

"She's at the front door," Timmy said, speaking of the visitor that Stew was expecting.

Stew signaled that he'd be one moment and then returned to the call, hoping to finalize the business with his New York investors. "I'm more than certain this is going to be a healthy quarter, Lex. The moment spring kicks in, our new website features are gonna post. *Trust me* when I tell you, this shit's gonna blow your mind!"

Stew stared out at his chunk of Malibu Beach, as he listened to Lexington Roland complain. He could barely hear him, because his mind was on the beautiful clear skies, and the crystal blue water of the Pacific Ocean. The scene in Malibu was as bright as his future. As he absorbed it all, he played with his custom-made cherry-wood tobacco pipe, taking it out of his mouth and putting it back in as if he was Hugh Hefner, the black version. Imagine that.

Stew snapped out of his daze to address a comment made by his other investor. "Trent, the last quarter, the holidays especially, was a *killer.* We made *crazy* money. Ain't you mutha-fuckas *never* satisfied?"

"The holidays are always gonna be big, Stew," said Trent Morris. "This first quarter might not be what we projected."

Stew yawned, and then without another word to either of them, he hung up. "I don't have the patience for this shit," Stew said, beneath the warm sun and to nobody in particular. Then he threw the cordless phone so it flew over the railing and landed somewhere below in that vast blanket of Malibu's finest sand. "I *gotta* buy those fuckers out," he mumbled. He adjusted his robe and turned to see about the new visitor. He took a deep breath and smiled, anxious to meet this girl; a fresh piece of ass never failed to put him in a good mood.

As soon as he stepped back inside, Stew was reminded of why he'd needed to step outside in the first place. *Women.*

Altogether there were eight of them in the lounge, just off the master bedroom. They were playing Twister, having a good time and loud as shit. Stew figured they were getting juiced-up for the party later that night. He cracked the adjoining door enough to get a peek of the action. The sight was an eyeful: a roomful of half-naked bodies.

"Left foot, red. Right hand, blue," instructed a girl, wearing nothing but a thong.

On the other side of the room, another girl was holding a camcorder focused on the action. Stew smiled, amused by all the giggling and shenanigans. He closed the door quietly and made his way upstairs.

Just behind the master bedroom was another great room. It was huge, with an entertainment center and fish tanks built into two walls opposite each other. Tonya, Salt, and Dream, three of Stew's employees, were lounging on the ivory white sectional couch. They were watching *Heat* on the giant plasma-screen TV. The movie was right at Stew's favorite part, when Pacino and De Niro meet. The good guy and the bad guy, face-to-face for the first time. They can't help but respect each other. Stew stopped to watch for a minute. He could probably recite the whole scene. "*Ya know, there's a flip side to that coin. . . .*"

Stew continued on through the house. The plush, wheat beige carpet felt good under the soles of his feet. *It feels good to be me,* he thought. All this luxury was part of the world he'd struggled to create; the world of Platinum Dolls. Beautiful women surrounded him every day, usually in various stages of undress, all of them professing absolute loyalty. The girl waiting in the other room no doubt would do the same. Thinking of it all was sometimes a little overwhelming, but Stew never let it get to his head. He'd breathe deep and say "Bring it on," no matter the challenge, or how fast his heart throbbed.

Stew walked up a short flight of stairs, and seeing Timmy and Goose, both of whom were sitting at a counter with their teeth sunk into some sub sandwiches, he nodded in acknowledgment.

"How was the trip?" Stew inquired.

Both men gave a thumbs-up sign and mumbled something in response. On the opposite side of the counter there was a sunlit kitchen where Star and Dawn were preparing all kinds of goodies for the party later. Stew snuck over to steal a finger sandwich, and then shrugged and gave a guilty-as-charged expression when the two women caught him. He swallowed his food and walked on to the front door to greet his visitor.

The girl waiting for him was cute. She was wearing a red blouse, showing lots of cleavage, a red skirt, and red pumps. Her complexion reminded Stew of creamy peanut butter, and her hair rested on her shoulders. He immediately liked her, with that one loose tendril of golden-brown hair curving across her forehead. But the attitude on her heart-shaped face was another story.

"Am I at the right address?" she asked. She flipped her cell phone shut, as though she'd just tried to call everyone but the president to get some assistance.

"I dunno. Who are you?" Stew folded his arms, noticing the piercing in her right nostril and the bracelet on her wrist, which sparkled when she waved her hands.

The girl took a deep, exaggerated breath and said, "*Excuse* me? I just told some guy that my name was Misty. Did he *not* tell you?" She put her hand on her hip and struck an arrogant hooker's pose.

"Oh. Of course. Candice sent you, right? Come in."

She took another deep breath. She didn't answer, but her eyes narrowed enough to hurt somebody. Misty picked up her floral carryall bag and stormed right in, grumbling about "disrespect and manners." Stew shut the door behind her, ignoring her slight tantrum.

It wasn't until the two walked through the living room that Stew realized there wasn't anywhere to conduct this interview. There were people everywhere. The girls playing Twister, Timmy, Goose, and the girls in the kitchen, and all the girls upstairs in orientation with Stephanie. He thought for a moment.

"Follow me," Stew told Misty, finally guiding her into his master bedroom. "Put your bag on the floor. We'll talk here."

For a moment he contemplated taking her outside on the patio, but decided he didn't want to give his visitor the view of the beach, not just yet. Especially since there was no telling if he'd be kicking her out of the house in another minute or so. If she didn't lose that fucking attitude, that was exactly what was gonna happen. He'd have to wait and see.

"Sit," he told her, pointing to the bed. Then he flipped on the lights and poked his head in the other room. "Girls . . . *Girls!* Keep it down a little, would ya? I'm busy in here." Stew closed the door. The giggles in the next room were reduced to a murmur.

Left hand, yellow.

Stew turned and went to sit on the bed a couple of feet away from Misty. He studied her expression and could almost read her thoughts.

I know he ain't just gonna sit there in a robe and interview me.

Sitting there looking at her, Stew'd had just about enough of her attitude. It was time to put her in her place. "I'mma tell you from the word go. . . . What's your name . . . *Misty*? Well, Misty . . . you need to *fix your face*. Unless you wanna make a U-turn—and you'd be crazy to think I'm paying for more limos and plane tickets—you'd better fix your face." Stew propped one ankle up onto his knee and rested his hands there. Smooth. He let his words sink in before continuing.

"I'm sure Candice filled you in. But in case she didn't,

lemme do the honors. I'm Stew Gregory. I run Platinum Dolls. I call the shots. I handle the money. I produce the films. It cost me two grand to fly you here from Colorado, but I'll be quick to tell you I use that kind of petty cash to wipe my ass. Don't get me wrong though. I'm a nice guy. *Real* nice. But you *don't* wanna get on my bad side. You'll wind up back at your miserable grind, dancing for dollars."

"I-I . . ." Misty stuttered, suddenly wanting to try reconciliation.

Stew cut her off. "I'm not finished speaking." Stew stood up and walked over to the wall of green curtains opposite the bed. He pulled the drawstring so that the curtains parted, revealing a breathtaking view of golden beachfront, sparkling ocean, and blue sky. Stew looked out at the beach. His back was still to his visitor when he spoke again.

"You're sitting on a forty-thousand-dollar bed, in a one-point-three-million-dollar home, located on a piece of Malibu that you have to pay just to look at. Now"—he turned back toward her—"let's try this again. My name is Stew." He put his hand out to shake hers.

"H-Hi," his guest stuttered. "I'm Misty Summers. Pleased to meet you."

"Good. Good. Nice smile, too. Already you've got me inspired. So, you ever do this kinda work before? You ever work for a sex site?" Stew asked, but he already knew the answer.

"N No . . . but Candice told me "

"Oh. Right. No experience, I remember." It suddenly struck Stew that *this was her*. This was the girl that Candice had told him about just the other day. He had been excited about meeting this chick after all the claims that Candice had made. He'd almost forgotten about her. With so many new girls coming through the door each week, sometimes it was hard to keep track of all this pussy.

If Stew recalled correctly, Misty wasn't experienced in the sex-on-the-web business, but she *did* have talent. And wasn't that what Platinum Dolls customers wanted? An inexperienced girl? One who *thought* she had what it took and would do just about everything to prove it?

"I did get to develop *these* before the flight," Misty said. She pulled out an envelope from her bag. ONE-HOUR PHOTO was printed in bold black lettering on top of a blinding-yellow background. Misty pulled out a half-inch-thick stack of photos from the envelope. Stew took them and began to browse. As he was doing so, he remembered Candice's claims.

You've gotta see this girl's amateur video, Stew. She was in a long-term relationship with a guy—one guy who she says took her virginity. The girl's only nineteen, Stew. . . . Nineteen! But she sucks dick like a champ! I actually got wet watchin' it, and I never get wet over this shit, Stew. She's Heather Hunter, I swear—to—God. She's Angel Kelly, Vanessa Del Rio, and Midori—all in one innocent, Colorado prom queen. A winner, Stew. A goddamn winner!

Stew considered Candice's praises as he flipped through the photos. He wondered if Misty was shy, and why she had so many photos with clothing on. Lingerie. Swimsuits. Evening wear. Bra and panties. *Boring!* There was a body there, but so far Stew hadn't seen any of it exposed.

"I could've taken some better ones," Misty said, as if reading Stew's mind.

Did this Misty chick know the *real deal?* Stew was in the skin trade. He sold fantasies, the fantasies that a man imagined when he saw what Platinum Dolls had to sell; at least visually. Stew's whole game was based on revealing what was *left* to the imagination. His theory was to show Web surfers exactly what was behind his beauties, taking down their curtains of clothing and their façades of innocence.

"They were the best I could come up with on short notice." Misty went on issuing excuses. "And . . . well . . . I also have a video, if you wanna see that." Misty reached inside her bag and pulled out the tape. Stew could almost hear her saying *ta-dah,* as if this was the moment he'd been waiting for.

"I'll definitely check this out later," Stew said. "But what's better than having you—the *real* thing—right here in front of me?" Stew caught a glimpse of Misty's uncertain smile, as he put down the tape. He spread the photos across the bed like playing cards. "You got anything else for me? Paperwork, maybe?"

"Oh, yeah, right here. Clean bill of health. Dated last week." Misty with the singsong response. Again, she produced it for him like *ta-dah*. Stew took a perfunctory peek at the document. *Negative*. A doctor's signature. A medical seal on the bonded stationary. Ta-*dow*! He loved it when a plan came together.

"Good . . . good. Stand up for me, Misty. Do that little turn that you girls do . . . like you're modeling or something." Stew propped his arms behind him on the bed as he sat back and watched. He nodded with approving murmurs. "I heard you danced a little. How 'bout a little striptease. Pretend there's music."

"Here? *Now?*"

Misty looked around the room as if she wasn't sure he meant it. It was a familiar response. Stew had been here quite a few times before. He knew this to be a response to help a girl get past her nervousness.

"Here. Now," Stew said, looking straight into her eyes. "You're not shy, are you?"

Misty made a face like she could take on any challenge. She tugged the blouse up and out of her skirt. She unbuttoned it and dropped it to the floor. Then she wiggled out of the skirt.

"That's okay," Stew said, enjoying the show so far. "Leave the pumps on. I like pumps."

Misty reached up behind her back to undo her bra, and Stew watched with interest. This would help determine if she was good enough for Platinum Dolls. If her breasts sagged to her navel, or if she'd tried to put in some extra padding, this moment of truth would tell all. Misty shimmied her shoulders so that the bra straps fell off of her arms and onto the floor.

"Nice. Nice," Stew commented. "Not exactly reaching for the sky, and not sagging too much either. Just what the guys like. Go on, go on . . . Don't let me stop you."

Stew didn't want to say it, but Misty's breasts defied

gravity. He watched as she wiggled out of her panties and stepped out of them, one foot at a time—a big production he wouldn't blame her for. Clothes off, she seemed unsure of what to do with her hands.

This was where Stew came in. As if this was his practiced on-cue stage entrance, he got up and approached Misty. He knew the hairs were sticking up off her skin. If she were a cat, her tail would be straight up right about now.

"Lay back against the wall, Misty. Like you're on the beach out there . . . with the wind caressing your curves." Stew looked out of the window and gestured as he spoke.

"Like this?" Misty stretched herself like a swan on the bedroom wall.

"Yeah, that's good. How 'bout putting your arms up a little more? Show those pretty wings of yours."

When Misty did this, Stew came closer, so close he could feel her breathing . . . smell her body's scent. With his forefinger, he pushed aside the cute tendril that had been dancing against her glowing skin since she first came through the door. He ran the same fingertip down her temple, feeling a thin mist of perspiration. He smoothed his fingers along her cheek, her chin, and then her lips.

"Nice face, Misty. Colorado, huh?"

"Denver." She trembled. "Born and raised."

"You look like you could be one in a million," Stew said. "Ever meet a twin of yours? Maybe by coincidence?"

Misty let out a breathy "*Noooo . . . ,*" more a reaction and a response to Stew's caress. The tip of his forefinger made a trail to her armpits. They were smooth, almost.

"About two days' worth of stubble here. I'd hate to be the one to tell you about your grooming, but we're gonna have to do something about that. . . ."

TWO

Misty didn't answer. No excuses this time. Candice had already told her not to, and she didn't want to blow this any more than she might have.

While she was thinking this, Stew slid his finger across her skin, from one intimate spot to the next. Misty shivered as his finger brushed over her cleavage, her nipples. This was all new to her. On the one hand, she felt he was violating her, treating her no better than he'd treat a piece of fruit at the market, checking it before buying it. And yet, on the other hand, this total stranger was turning her on. Somehow, in his eyes there was the promise of good times and plentiful living . . . there was evidence of wealth and prosperity of pleasures unknown.

Oh God, she thought, stifling a gasp. *Do what he says*, she told herself. That's what Candice had instructed, and that's what she was gonna do.

"You could use some waxing, too," Stew said, toying with the stray strands of hair between her breasts.

Misty's heart could've fallen down to her feet when his finger made the speedy shortcut past her navel to her pubic area. *No he didn't!*

"And this down here," Stew said, with a pinch of Misty's bush between his fingers, "this has got—to—*go*. I know what our customers like. The hairy chicks can get a job at the Beaver Hunt website. But us? We like 'em clean shaven. Even though you're of age, customers like the illusion of youth," Stew said, while his hand followed the curve of Misty's hips, her ass, and her waist then moved up to her left breast.

Ohhh . . . Not the sensitive one, she grieved.

"I know me touching you feels foreign . . . a violation even. But one thing you should know coming into this game . . . coming into *my* game. . . . This . . . beautiful body of yours? This . . . *if* we should accept you into our family . . . this is our money maker. Almost like a bus company. We own all the buses, and you . . . You, my dear, are one of our drivers. That's what we pay you for. That's why we pay so well. Cooperation. Willingness. An open mind. That's key."

The words coming out of Stew's mouth may as well have been whispers. Misty couldn't hear a thing for all the sensations ripping through her body. Her eyes rolled in her head as he continued exploring her. At one point she wasn't sure about going through with this; at another, the sensations were absolutely *killing* her. Stew inched closer now, with his lips next to her ear.

"A little nervous, babe?"

"Mmm-hmm," Misty replied, her words trembling.

"But I don't see *how*. I heard that you were so good at what you do. So *talented,* I remember Candice saying."

Misty managed a smile. It was an uncomfortable smile, but a smile nonetheless. How was it that this guy seemed to be able to see right through her?

"Relax, baby. You've already been accepted. We're gonna make you a star. A *Platinum Doll*."

Misty took her arms down, unable to control the many emotions stacking up inside of her. "Really? *Really?*" She could hardly contain herself.

Stew felt her energy, like there was a suppressed cheer somewhere in her body, hungry to get out.

"Yeah, really. Does that make you happy?"

Misty exhaled loudly. "Ecstatic!"

Stew chuckled, amused by her response. "There's, well, something I'm curious about, Misty."

"Yeah? What?"

"This . . . this *talent* that Candice raves about. I'd like to know more." Stew backed up an inch, smooth and intimate as a lover would. He undid the belt of his silk robe. He did it nice and slow, so that when he looked up at Misty, the seduction would set in gradually, hopefully tempting her. This was his style: smooth, but outrageously direct.

Fully naked underneath the robe, Stew let the flaps fall to his sides. His bare chest moved closer to Misty, as he put his hand on the wall just by her head. He stared her straight in the eyes. "Show me your talent, Misty."

He could feel the line was crossed when Misty's eyes turned from bright and excited to deep and alluring. Submissive but a little uncertain. As if to lend some assurance, he leaned in and lightly kissed the corner of her lips.

"Think of this as your audition. Flatter me."

Misty bravely put her hands on Stew's chest. She made herself familiar with his fit and trim muscularity—his pectorals, his ripped abdominal muscles. Stew stayed in great shape, even though he didn't spend long hours at the gym. A light workout three times a week was all it took.

"Whew . . . Gee, I never . . ." Misty cleared her throat. "You are so . . . so *big*," she cooed.

Her declaration didn't surprise Stew. He knew he was *blessed*, as the women liked to say. Stew was all of eight inches, and that was *before* an erection. But while others may have had their opinion, Stew sometimes felt it to be a burden. He hadn't met a woman yet who could take him cock-strong, full-throttle between her folds. And there were just a few who could perform a deep-throat blow job. His reality was, more often than not, that those couple of inches usually went unsatisfied.

Misty was on her knees in front of him. Stew ran his hand through her hair, about to help her by applying some pressure to the back of her head. But he had second thoughts. Better to let this new girl warm to the calling on her own. An instant later, a tingle shot up through Stew's body. It was in response to Misty flicking her tongue playfully along the shaft of his penis, kissing him lightly and graduating to inviting licks.

Eventually, Stew was fully engaged, his muscle palpitating inside of her grip. She took the tip between her lips, again familiarizing herself, and soon the blow job was off to a running start. Stew figured maybe he wouldn't be kicking this woman out of his house after all.

THREE

Stephanie walked in on Misty's performance.

Stephanie Koboyashi was part Japanese, part black (on her father's side), and she had been born on a strawberry farm up above Seattle, on San Pedro Island. Her mother had been a part of the settlement there—Jap Town they called it— a place where Japanese immigrants and Japanese-Americans lived. Stephanie's father had once been a reporter, a CNN correspondent straight out of Brooklyn, when he visited the islands to cover a story of a shipwreck there. Her dad met her mother, one thing led to another, and the result was the birth of a daughter, Stephanie.

Stephanie was a fine, mocha-brown woman, with those Asian eyes and full, luscious lips. Her hair was jet black and fantastically long, and she maintained a body that could've been shaped and designed by a very talented sculptor.

Stephanie helped Stew orchestrate and manage his flock of website beauties, and generally had carte blanche to walk into the master bedroom—*any* of his master bedrooms around the country, that is—unannounced. It wasn't until she was fully in the room that Stephanie looked to her right to see just *how* busy Stew was.

Oops, she mouthed. She started to backtrack out of the room. After all, this was the boss. He probably wanted some privacy.

Even as Misty was engrossed in this (so far) ten-minute audition, Stew put his hand up, stopping Stephanie in her tracks. He indicated by hand gestures alone that she should stay in the bedroom and lock the door behind her.

Stephanie did as Stew directed. And yet she couldn't help but look into his eyes; to look anywhere else would have been too obvious, as if *she* was the one with something to be ashamed of. Now it was Stew who made eyes at Stephanie, so as to say, *Check this girl out, can you believe the sound effects?*

Stephanie nodded back at him, studying the encounter. *Does she have papers?* Stephanie mouthed. Safety came first in this business.

Stew read his friend loud and clear, neither of them interrupting Misty and the loving attention she was giving him. He hooked his thumb over in the direction of the papers and photos. Stephanie nodded and eased over to the bed. She gave immediate approval once she saw the clean bill of health. She had long warned Stew about taking sexual risks that could end his life and the dream. It didn't make sense to give up his life over a quick thrill.

Meanwhile, Stew gestured again, encouraging Stephanie to come over and stand behind him. When she did, he whispered, "Hang out for a minute. I wanna see you two together." Stew had his hand caressing the new girl's face, while he twisted his upper body to whisper to Stephanie over his shoulder. Stephanie cracked a mischievous smile and stepped back out of the way, leaning up against the wall, not far behind where Misty was kneeling.

Stew took a bolder stance now, more confident, with both hands propped on top of Misty's head. His legs locked into that chauvinistic stance while his eyes locked on Stephanie's. Yes, he was feeling cocky. Yes, he was in total control here, and *yes*, this new piece of ass just walked in the door, and within minutes, without so much as a deep kiss, the girl was on her knees, slurping on him like he was a human lollipop.

Stephanie was comfortable enough with Stew to watch this and smile that slick smile. Actually, she was proud of her boss and his accomplishments. As long as he was safe and the girl (whoever she was) was willing, she was all for him getting his freak on.

Mmm-mmm-mmm . . . you are surely living your dream, mister. You deserve this. I love you so fucking much! Stephanie was thinking, and began thumbing her own nipple as she was watching Stew reach the finishing point. She had to admit, this was a hot sight to see.

"Yes, Misty, you surely *are* talented," Stew said, looking down at his new friend. He didn't want her to stop until he . . . until the cows came home.

Stew looked back up at Stephanie, at her crooked smile and folded arms. It looked as if she was waiting her turn.

This was when Stew would remain strong. He wouldn't show the weaknesses of many men—the funny facial expressions, the buckling at the knees. And none of the sudden responses, like, *"Oh God,"* or *"Yes . . . Yes! Yes!!!"* After all, it wasn't like this was romance.

Maintaining his cocky composure, Stew saw this occasion as somewhat of a challenge. He *wanted* Stephanie to see this; for her to know just how focused he could be; how he was able to look at her, even think about whatever else, as he was experiencing his orgasm. And it wasn't that Stew needed to prove anything to Stephanie, because Stephanie had been in this very same position on many other occasions. He just wanted to exhibit his raw power. His mojo. And as the electricity rattled Stew, as it charged through his body and made his eyes wanna twitch, made him wanna black out, he kept that locked gaze on Stephanie. He accepted these surges in his body as boosts, not as the tapping of his vital resources or the expenditure of his energy. This, for Stew, was empowerment. He was the *man*!

Misty was finishing up, humming her appreciation as she milked him dry.

Stew's eyes dropped back downward. "There's no more soda in the Coke bottle, baby. *Damn!*" Stew exhaled quietly. "Candice didn't tell a lie. You *are* Heather Hunter!"

"Who's that?" Misty asked in her sexy voice, looking up at Stew as her lips left his flesh with that last suction sound.

"Never mind," Stew said, shaking his head at her innocence. "Misty, meet Stephanie."

"Oh God . . . I . . ." Misty's eyes filled with shock and fear.

"No need for words, sweetheart," Stephanie said, her words tinted by a slight Japanese accent. Stephanie approached to help Misty to her feet, while Stew closed his robe and picked the photos, the video, and the doctor's letter off the bed. He circled around to the entertainment center, close to the bedroom window, and slipped the video tape into a VCR. Stew slumped down in the leather La-Z-Boy so that he had an exclusive view of the bed, the TV, and the beachfront.

Stew could see a void in Misty's eyes. She was looking for a word from him, or an acknowledgment at least. As far as he was concerned, there was nothing to say. Meanwhile, Stephanie was fiddling with Misty's hair and checking her out from every angle.

"I told her about the waxing and shaving, Steph. You can go over that with her later. But . . . maybe you'd like to get to know her better in your own way."

"Mmm-hmm," Stephanie murmured, standing behind Misty and looking at her backside. "Nice ass, too," Stephanie said.

Misty swung her head around, her hair flinging wildly, as she followed Stephanie's movements. She was overcome with feelings of discomfort and fear. *What in the world are these people up to?* she wondered nervously.

Stew chuckled, amused by Misty's response, and fascinated by Stephanie's actions. He watched intently while Stephanie unbuttoned her sundress and let it fall easily to the floor. He smiled when Stephanie moved in behind Misty, pulling the girl back into her, until their bodies were seamless. He leaned back, enjoying the show that Stephanie was about to start. She kissed Misty's right shoulder, while reaching around with her right hand in between the young girl's legs. Stephanie tugged at Misty's hair until her head arched back ever so much, twisted enough for their lips to meet. Stew watched all this with pleasure, knowing that while they kissed, they also shared the taste of him. His juices.

"But I . . . I'm not—"

Stephanie cut her short by putting her hand on Misty's mouth. "None of us are. It's just for show, baby. Keep that in mind. Just a show to make the boss happy." Stephanie glanced over at Stew, and Misty followed her gaze. It didn't seem like he was watching, so Stephanie turned back to Misty. The two of them continued with the deep tongue kissing and touching.

Stew was busy checking out Misty's videotape, the volume turned too low to hear. On the TV screen, Misty seemed to be giving an introduction. Then she and her ex-boyfriend joined hands. That was the point where Stew turned off the TV. He'd only wanted a look at the guy. It was a *man* thing, he'd just wanted to know what she'd been working with. And in that instant, he decided the competition was irrelevant.

While these calculations and others were going through Stew's mind, he watched Stephanie as she led Misty onto the bed. Stephanie was in complete control, and it made Stew realize that she'd come a long way from the woman who left Jap Town. She'd transformed from the woman who'd vowed, *I don't wanna be Japanese,* into one who'd pledged complete devotion to Stew. She was willing to follow him wherever he took her.

Is there anywhere else in the world that this goes on? Stew wondered, as the two women became more familiar with each other. *Is there anybody out there who is as privileged as me, experiencing this freaky shit? Straight up satisfaction guaranteed? Is there anyone who can make things like this happen on a whim? Is this even in a movie I missed?*

Even if this *was* going on in some other place in the world—maybe in some hut with a sizeable harem in Egypt or Kenya or Bangladesh—*so what,* Stew told himself. *This is happening here. This is happening now, and for me.* In his eyes, nothing else mattered. It seemed nothing could go wrong. Over the next few days, they'd be busy with the video shoots, filming girl-on-girl action. Exclusive shots of virgins and nonvirgins. That's all Platinum Dolls pushed.

And after the shoots, they'd be off to Transylvania, Canada, to set up a new leg of the Platinum Dolls dynasty.

And with all of that going on, there were still seven other locations online, all of which were kickin' ass. Platinum Dolls was going strong in New York, North Carolina, Washington, D.C., Atlanta, Seattle, Texas, and, of course, Malibu. Over the next six months, Stew expected to turn up the volume and do something in the Caribbean. Maybe even in Africa. And, if he could manage it, maybe he'd set up a home close to Buckingham Palace. There seemed to be no limit to what could be done or where he could go.

The sighs, the whispers, and the soft cries continued as Stew contemplated his future. The future of Platinum Dolls. And as he turned to lose himself in the horizon, that distant demarcation between water and sky, he couldn't help but remember that he was chained to this monster that had once been only a dream. He was tied to a business agreement that he no longer wanted, handcuffed to partners whom he no longer cared for.

FOUR

By eight o'clock that night, the Malibu party was in full swing. There were twenty-five women in all, including Misty. Stephanie had taken the new girl around earlier to meet everyone and get comfortable. All the while, a video camera roamed and recorded the action.

Timmy was down on the beach, sitting in a lounge chair and watching a group of the girls play volleyball. Afterward, the crowd watching the game, and others who were up in the house, congregated outside near the campfire. They formed a *Soul Train* line so that each girl could strut her stuff, dancer or not. The boom box by Timmy's side was already pumpin' old school jams by Biggie, 2Pac, Wu-Tang, Jay-Z, The SOS Band, Michael Jackson, The Gap Band, and some unknown artists. They played club joints, too. This was the music that was familiar to all in attendance. It was music they had all heard at some point in their lives—the soundtrack of a generation.

"Everything cool, boss?" Goose asked, his muscles pushing through his T-shirt.

Stew was on the terrace, leaning over the railing, half oblivious of all the goings-on and the excitement inside and outside of the beach house. A thin crescent moon glowed overhead.

"Sure," he answered, looking over at Goose. "You need me?"

"Nope. Just checkin' on you. Hey, Steph," he said, as Stephanie came through the patio door.

"Hey, Goose. Can you get any goddamn bigger?" joked Stephanie.

Goose laughed, and then left to continue watching over the girls.

"For you," Stephanie said, handing Stew a glass of champagne.

"Didn't we already toast over the food?"

"Of course we did. But that was for *them*. This is for you and me."

Stew took the glass and gave a second look up and down Stephanie's body. She had showered and changed since the earlier activities. Now she was wearing a white evening gown that hugged every curve and left little to the imagination. Her hair was swept up into a bun. There was something so unpredictable about her; a certain something that never ceased to amaze him. But Stew usually kept those thoughts to himself. He didn't want to wear out the compliments or make her feel exclusive, although she was. Sometimes, he'd decided long ago, you just had to let a person wonder. Just had to leave them guessing. Keep 'em sharp.

"Little change in pace tonight?" Stew asked, as the two of them tapped glasses.

Stephanie eased up closer into Stew's personal space. She hooked her arm around his so that they were real close, although still able to sip. "I s'pose," she replied.

"So what're we toasting?" Stew asked.

"The most incredible man . . . the most incredible lover I've ever known—"

"You've ever known? You've had, like, two men in all your life, Steph—and one of those two is me. Stop bullshittin' me," he said, laughing.

"I know, but it just sounds good. Shhh . . . you're ruining my moment."

"Excuse *me*," Stew said, lost in the eccentricity of

Stephanie; her chinky eyes, her sensual lips, and her hair, which he loved to get tangled in, that many times fell down her back, sometimes in that single braid he liked; and other times was pulled over her shoulders to fall between her healthy breasts, such as it had earlier in his bedroom.

"I wanted to say something special to you . . . so please, bear with me. Back on San Pedro Island, my only dream was to have my own strawberry farm. I knew nothing about love, except for what my mother told me. What I knew about life was only what the elders told of. The racism . . . how Americans hated the Japanese—especially after Pearl Harbor. I began to hate myself and all that formality of doing things quietly, being docile, with a spirit of silent dignity. I disclaimed my heritage. And just when things turned hopeless—those dead-end jobs in Seattle, the bastard who tricked me out of my virginity—just when I wanted to die, you came into my life, Stew. You changed the world for me. I had new vision. New hope. True love. You are my true love, Stewart Gregory. I'd *die* for you."

"Don't say that, Steph—"

"But I *would*. If you said the word, I'd meet my eternity and I'd be happy. I'd be content that I'd spent a part of my life with you."

Stew was dumbfounded. It was a spell Stephanie had on him. Some kind of goddamn witchcraft. Had to be, because Stew just *never* got this way. He was stubborn. Tough, full of ego and ego's blood. He chose not to be mushy. Chose not to love. But here was Stephanie, giving herself to him. Again.

"Should we sip now?" Stew asked, having little else to say and wanting desperately to lighten up the moment.

They finished their champagne and Stephanie took his glass. The two embraced and shared a loving kiss.

"I *know* you love me, Steph. But we're gonna live forever. You hear me? You, me, and whatever craziness we design. Forever. And I . . . I *do*—"

"Come on, you two. Join the party." It was Leslie who interrupted the two from the adjoining terrace. The girls from inside the house were strutting out in bikinis, heading down two flights of steps to the beach. Stephanie glared at Leslie as if the girl had been smokin' rocks, to come and interrupt her moment. Stew, on the other hand, was glad for the interruption. He had almost said it. He had *really* almost said it; almost said what was in his heart, something totally against his mantra.

Fuck no, I don't love these hoes.

On the beach, close to the volleyball net, the barbecue grill, and a blazing campfire, a lounge chair had been set up for Stew. Stephanie was kneeling there in the sand beside him. Leslie was standing behind, applying lotion, massaging his neck and shoulders. Now and then she'd reach down to grab his chest and arms as well. In the meantime, there was a sort of ongoing presentation. The music set the pace with beats and rhythms, while the campfire flickered into the night sky.

> *"My name is Crystal, uhh . . .*
> *and I'm from Frisco, uhh,*
> *and I can party hard,*
> *and I can also disco, uhh . . .*
> *I like to shake my thang,*
> *and I'm a Cancer, uhh,*
> *Just say the word*
> *and I will be your private dancer!"*

And as Crystal was doing this spontaneous rapping that was going on, she was certainly shaking her thang. Her thong barely covered her pubic area, and her stiff C-cup breasts bounced happily in the bikini top. The next girl marched forward now, clapping and keeping time with the others.

> *"My name is Tuti, uhh,*
> *and I'm from Oakland, uhh,*
> *I like to party and*
> *sometimes you'll catch me smokin, uhh*
> *I live for foreplay,*

I love to travel, uhh,
but look deeply
and find secrets yet unraveled!"

Tuti's rap got laughter and applause. Stew looked back at Leslie and smiled. He appreciated all of this. Got a kick out of it, too.

"Now listen, mister! Whoa,
my name is Trina, wow!
But don't look now,
'cause this sweet black thang is on ya!"

Trina was in a hurry to dance over and climb onto Stew's lap, her ass now wiggling on his groin in a spontaneous lap dance. The crowd went bananas.

"You like my ass? Uhh,
the way it moves? Whee!
Spend some time with me
and I'll take you to school!"

Stew and Stephanie locked eyes. "I bet you planned that, Steph," he said, eying her with a grin.
"Wha? *Me?* I didn't have nothin'—"
"Yeah, right."
Not to be outdone by Trina, Sondra came over and pulled off her top. She shook her double-D's in Stew's face. But compared to Trina or Jessica, Donna or Evelyn, Misty took the cake. Misty took it all off. She came forth and simply said,

"My name is Misty, uhh,
and I'm spoken for."

Misty cut an eye at Stew, as if he would confirm that. Screams and laughter ensued, as if everyone was in on their intimate encounter. Stew in turn gave Misty the thumbs up, and the crowd of mostly women jumped up and down with approval.

Once they were done performing, they changed the tape in the boom box and all twenty-five girls broke into a five-line Electric Slide.

"You can feel it,
It's electric,
Boogie-oogie-oogie . . ."

"A lot of flesh out here, Steph," Stew said, watching the tits and asses bouncing in front of him.

"And it's all yours, boss. Anybody in particular?"

"Funny you should ask. I like Donna."

"Then you've *got* Donna."

"And . . ." Stew cut Stephanie short as she was about to signal to the girl. "I like Trina, too."

"We thought you would." Stephanie turned to Stew, her hands on her hips. "Anything . . . or, uhh, anybody else you like?" Stephanie said adorably.

"Well . . . come to think of it . . . no," Stew said, giving her a pert smile. "Send them both up. I'm turning in for the night."

"Scandalous, Stew. Really scandalous," Stephanie said.

"But you love it," Stew said, his back already to her.

"I'm in for the night, Timmy. Hold it down."

"Right, boss."

Stew gave an unconscious wave at the same time that Stephanie went over to pull both Donna and Trina out of the group dance. She took time to instruct them about the three-some that Stew wanted. Both were thrilled with the idea—the boss asked for *them*? Together? Donna and Trina hurriedly made their way toward the beach house. Stew had already stepped inside and slid the door closed, when suddenly, Trina fell backwards and tumbled violently down the steps leading up to the house.

Timmy and Goose immediately sprinted across the sand when they heard Donna's scream. "She's been shot!" Timmy yelled to Goose.

Both men looked out toward the dark waters. No boats.

No sign of movement. The sand where so much dancing had been going on may as well have turned into a sidewalk full of frozen pedestrians. The crowd of flesh closed in as one, still unaware of the true trauma that faced it.

"Carry her inside," Timmy told Goose. Then to everyone else he shouted, "Inside! Now! Get inside!" Timmy lunged up the steps as he screamed instructions. He'd never thought he'd need his gun in such a secluded place.

FIVE

Timmy charged into the house, then into Stew's room, quick as a flash. Without seeing his boss, he shouted, "Trina's been shot! Boss! *Trina's been shot!*" Timmy didn't wait for a response. Instead, he jetted for his travel bag, where he kept a nickel-plated .45 caliber, a weapon given to him by his father, a former weapons specialist for the FBI.

As Timmy was climbing the stairs, Stew stepped out of the shower, barely wet. "What?" Stew asked, not sure if he'd heard Timmy correctly. *Trina had been* . . . Stew rushed to dry himself as he approached the bedroom's picture window, his feet soaking the carpet along the way. Looking out, he realized there was mass confusion down below. He could see the people rushing around underneath the outdoor lights, all of them moving up the stairs, fearing for their lives.

"What the *hell* . . ." Stew swung around, pulled on his robe, and ran into the leisure room, where the Twister mats were still on the floor. He could hear Goose's orders.

"Keep 'em movin' . . . Upstairs! Everybody, *upstairs!*"

Stew muscled past the assorted house guests and employees that had already gathered in the room to see Goose kneeling on the Twister mat, his body somewhat shielding the view of one of the girls. Was that *Trina* laying on those big colorful dots? Stew approached, and for the first time ever, he saw something frightening in Goose's bloodshot eyes. As if this was something that was outside of the big man's control.

"What happened?"

"Boss . . ." Goose barely uttered the word before his attention returned to Trina's body. Trina lay lifeless on the floor, her blood creating a red pool underneath her, covering a green dot where her head was positioned.

Stew was frozen. His heart thumped mercilessly, and his mind went for a wild spin. "Who? Where'd it . . . *How did . . .*" Stew had so many questions, he couldn't get them out right. The girl's blood there on the floor injected a sense of reality into his world of excess, a hard knock that he was in no way prepared for.

"Boss, I don't know. There was a scream, she tumbled down the steps. . . . Donna was right by her side."

"God*damn*! Who the fuck has a gun out there? One of the *girls?*" There was a movement in the crowd, Timmy pushing his way through, and Stew turned around.

"Steph, take 'em up to the bedrooms. *Everybody!*" Timmy ordered. There was a .45 in Timmy's hand, hanging close to his thigh. "Boss, I'm goin' to check out the grounds. Leslie's already dialed nine-one-one."

"*Fuck!* What the fuck is happening here? I turn my back for two minutes and a girl gets shot? What type of *Crypt Tale* shit is this?"

"No time to talk, boss. Stay here, I gotta see about this. Trust me, it wasn't any of the girls." Timmy left quickly. He figured it might still be possible to catch up with whoever had done this.

The beach house sat on a plot of land shaped like a baseball diamond snug within a hill. The entrance was at a narrow edge, where shrubbery and an electronic gate led onto the grounds. Inside the gate, a driveway and a walkway snaked down a steep decline, with bushes and trees lining the path toward the house. Other than a side gate that was always locked, the house provided the only means of access to the eight hundred fifty feet of beachfront—that exclusive chunk of Malibu's coastline owned by Platinum Dolls. The wingspan of the beach was bordered by tall piles of boulders to the right, and a high cliff and mountainside to the left. There was beachfront at the foot of the ragged mountainside, but it receded in the distance and then broadened again, leading into the neighboring property.

Timmy knew the place well. He'd run the length of the beach, back and forth, in the early mornings, and sometimes, if he was in the mood, late at night. This was the routine anytime Stew took his entourage to Malibu, sometimes for two-, three-week stays. So then, Timmy's first guess (since he didn't see any speedboats, yachts, or other vessels) was that someone (perhaps a sniper) took a shot from the left, the southern most end of the beach. He started to sprint in that direction despite the dangerous darkness, cautious and alert and keeping as close as possible to the mountainside, his .45 cocked by his shoulder.

There had been no other shots, as far as he knew. No other casualties. He wondered if this hadn't been a hit-and-run. Still, he executed practiced maneuvers, pulling up beside the large rocks, taking quick evaluations from within the protective barriers provided, and then jetting off again, keeping low in a crouched run. Once he approached the farthest edge of the property, his hearing was overwhelmed by waves washing ashore and the sounds of seagulls. There was also his heartbeat, which drummed more in his head than in his chest, with a mix of fear and courage.

The rock cliff would be his last protection. And he knew that after swinging out again he would be open game—an easy target for any awaiting killer. After saying a silent prayer, Timmy whipped the full weight of his body around, both hands gripping the automatic and directing it in quick jerks left and right. Nothing. Nothing but darkness between himself and the constellation of house lights twinkling in the distance along the beach. It was too dark to look for any details such as footprints in the sand. Nothing but a quarter moon's glow to illuminate things. For these reasons, as well as what his instincts told him, Timmy came to the conclusion that someone—although he couldn't guess who—had just gotten away with murder.

SIX

Less than half an hour later, the oval driveway and part of the winding road that snaked up toward the entrance of the property were converted into makeshift parking lots for various emergency vehicles. An Emergency Medical Unit was backed up to the front door and its team was sliding a gurney into the vehicle. Trina Washington lay flat and lifeless on the gurney. She'd been with Platinum Dolls for less than eight weeks, and now she was dead with a gunshot wound to the back of the head. Next to the ambulance there were half a dozen LAPD patrol cars as well as a few unmarked detectives' vehicles. The beach house, within the space of an hour, had transitioned from a wild party with half-naked aspiring actresses, into a mass investigation with a dozen or so police officers questioning everyone. Each officer had a notepad and pen as they addressed one or two women at a time, asking them what they'd seen, what they'd heard, and what their relationship was to the decreased.

Salt was the girl that the police wanted to talk with the most; she was crying and sobbing so violently that Leslie and Star had to practically drag her to a separate room. Not that Salt was the only one distraught, because many of the girls were indeed shaken by the news that Trina—*one of us*—had been shot dead right on their private beach. But Salt had other feelings for Trina. Besides just the porn flicks or the

Internet videos, Salt and Trina had done a lot more than acting in the three videos Platinum Dolls had on the market. The two had become lovers.

"Damn, this shit is crazy!" Stew exclaimed.

"Mr. Gregory, please try and stay focused. I know this has been tragic for you," an officer said to him. "But it's important that we have the details to help solve this crime."

"Man, listen, I told you all I know. I hardly knew the girl. Can you understand that? *I hardly knew her.*"

"But according to what one of your house guests says, she . . . and . . . is it Donna? They were headed to your bedroom for the night."

Stew looked up at the cop incredulously. He couldn't believe those words came from his lips.

"*And*?" Stew said questioningly. *Is there something special about that?* he wondered.

"Well, sir, if you'd excuse me for saying, I'd imagine you might know a woman a *little* better if you two were about to engage in, well . . . ya know." The cop couldn't even look straight into Stew's eyes.

"Hey! Who's in charge'a this guy? Who's the top cop in here?" Stew was loud, and unwilling to say another word to a young cop who was obviously an imbecile. "Apparently, you don't know who the *fuck* I *am*, do you? You have absolutely *no concept* of what you're dealing with here. I'm not the subject you should be focusing on, and this is not a *Penthouse* interview. Stick to the goddamn issues!"

"Stew—*Stew* . . . relax," Timmy said as he approached. The sound in both the dining room and the kitchen had been loud with the buzz of questions and answers, a constant hum; that is, until Stew raised his voice. The hush was in anticipation of what would happen next, since Stew seemed about ready to blow his top.

Timmy brought over another law enforcement type and put a hand on Stew's shoulder to calm him down. Apparently it worked, perhaps causing Stew to think that maybe this guy was the answer, a friend of Timmy's, on account of all his pop's involvement at the FBI and what-not.

"This gentleman would like a word with you," Timmy said.

"Mr. Gregory, I'm Inspector Elliot, Malibu PD Officer; would you excuse us?" He paused long enough to watch the cop who had been interviewing Stew slither away as if he'd been admonished. "I've been asked to oversee this investigation and I thought we could cut through a lot of red tape if we talk, sorta CEO to CEO, if you know what I mean."

Inspector Elliot. The chest and shoulders of a football player, the neck of a wrestler, and silver-blue eyes that seemed able to read past most bullshit. Elliot had a clean-shaven head, and his badge was draped around his neck on a beaded chain. He wore a military-green safari jacket, matching cargo pants tucked into black combat boots, and a red ribbon on one of his pockets.

Stew led the inspector downstairs toward his bedroom so they could talk. Timmy followed the two. He figured it would be the quietest spot in the house. He was wrong. "How'd *they* get down there?" Stew asked as he looked out at the beach. There was a news crew down near the volleyball net, the campfire slowly burning out behind a female reporter holding a mic.

"Ten o'clock news," Elliot said. "I believe your house is live in folks' living rooms."

"*Shit,*" Stew said. Then he picked up the remote from the bed and turned on the TV.

"*. . . Details are sketchy right now. But you can count on us for the latest right here on NBC-four, Los Angeles. Once again, we're live at the Malibu home of Web-porn king Stew-art Gregory, where one of his actresses, nineteen-year-old Trina Washington, was shot and killed just an hour ago. Stay here for the latest. Back to you, Bill . . .*"

Stew cut the TV off and turned to look at Timmy. His dream had suddenly spun out of control, when just that evening he'd seen the world as his own. A murder. Police all over the place. The ten o'clock news. The events of the past hour left no doubt, when it rained it poured.

"See over there, Mr. Gregory?" The inspector pointed to the left of the beachfront. "We've sent a few men out with metal detectors. They found a shell down that way, over near the halogen lamps."

Stew looked to where a quarter of his beach was brightly lit with manufactured light.

"A shell?"

"I should say shell *casing*. What's left once a bullet is fired." Elliot directed the next question to Timmy. "You all don't do any type of target practice out there, do ya?"

"Of course not," Stew responded.

"Well then, we should have something here. Perhaps there's a match with the bullet that struck the girl." The inspector turned away from the view outdoors. "Any *enemies*, Mr. Gregory?"

"I'm thinkin' that nature's my enemy right now, the way everything is spinnin' on its own. It's like someone pressed a button out there and all of a sudden, my whole game is on the news."

"Good thing you mentioned that, sir, 'cause I needed to ask you about that. That is, your *game*. If there *is* an enemy out there—and I assure you, it's not nature that pulled the trigger—then we should join forces to find out who it is. Stomp 'em out. Know what I mean?"

Stew nodded.

"Can you tell me how your business works? In short, how you've become so successful?"

Stew walked over to his La-Z-Boy and Timmy pulled up a chair for the inspector. Stew sat down and took a deep breath.

"It's not really that big a number who visit the website— about two hundred thousand solid customers. But it pays the bills. We mostly make our money when viewers buy the movies we produce. Our product, so to speak, is girls. Girl-on-girl stuff, solo-masturbation scenes, and once in a while we'll throw in a guy. But this company is personality driven. Girls with personality."

"Which is something I see that you all have a lot of. I've listened in on a few conversations, Mr. Gregory—"

"Please . . ." Stew wagged his head and raised his hand. "Very, *very* few people call me that. Call me Stew, please."

"Great, Stew. It's just that . . . well, I'm just puzzled as to why someone would pick Ms. Washington. As far as I know at this point, the killer handpicked his target. That shell casing out there is almost two inches long. Know what that tells me?"

"Long distance," Timmy offered.

"Good. I see your pop taught you well," said the inspector, already comfortable with the young man. "My guess is, either someone was well equipped—maybe even a deep-sea diver with underwater gear and water-proofed weaponry. Or the guy could've come by way of your neighbor's place down the beach. They could've gotten far enough on foot to outrun Timmy here. I figure they had five, maybe six minutes after the body dropped. And one more thing, the shot wasn't heard. The trigger was pulled, the bullet traveled past . . . what? There were twenty-something people on the beach? Dancing, were they? And yet the first thing anyone heard was a scream. Donna's scream. So now . . . that tells me something else."

"Silencer," Timmy said.

"I oughta deputize you, son. You're right again. A silencer. Which makes me think that this was a heavily financed hit. A thug off the street ain't gonna execute a hit like this. This was more like a mercenary."

"A *what*?" Stew looked at Timmy for the explanation, since he seemed to be the one with the answers all of a sudden.

"That's one of them dudes that was trained real well sometime during their lives. Could be a former Navy Seal, Special Forces, Recon . . ." Timmy said.

Elliot added, "FBI, SWAT, CIA, DEA . . ."

"Point is, the guy, or maybe it was a woman, fell off from their official, lawful commitments. Probably a freelancer," said Timmy.

"Could be," added Elliot. "These people put ads in all the gun magazines, the *Soldier of Fortune,* the detectives' magazines . . . and they get hired for a bunch of under-the-table stuff. They go to work for, say, a John Q. Public and do John's dirty work. So it brings me to wonder what'd Ms. Washington ever do to anybody? Why would someone with money want *her* dead?"

"Jesus. This is deeper than I could've guessed," said Stew.

"Okay, lemme backtrack a bit. The website, the movies; has Ms. Washington been in any of these? I hear she's been with Platinum Dolls, for all of . . . eight weeks, is it?"

"Yeah. Matter of fact, her videos—we shot seven or eight so far—are some of the most requested."

"Hmm . . . sounds like a radio thing: *And the most requested song is* . . . Sorry, I digress. Please continue," the inspector said.

Stew and Timmy looked at each other.

"Well, at first we figured the popularity was due to her being the new kid on the block. But soon we realized that her performance with Salt was the reason why she, well . . . she became very good at what she does—or did. I believe they had a thing together."

"A thing. Like, a romance?"

"Mmm, more like a chemistry. Salt coulda been the reason Trina was more *into* the act, if ya know what I mean."

"Oh, I, uh, I sure *don't* know. But I'm learning."

"The bottom line . . . what I'm gettin' at is that we can hardly keep her movies in stock." *Damn, she made us a lot of money,* Stew thought. "We put her up on the website, a lot of live stuff, ya know? Auctioned her soiled panties, sold—"

"*Soiled* panties?"

"Sure. After the performance, Web surfers make bids on the panties Trina wore as she did the foreplay."

"The *foreplay*?" Inspector Elliott couldn't believe what he was hearing. What kind of world had he walked into?

"Right, we got a fifteen-thousand-dollar buyer once."

"*Fifteen thousand dollars*. A guy paid fifteen thousand dollars for *soiled* panties?"

"Absolutely," answered Stew, wondering why that was a surprise. "We had a girl once whose panties went for twenty-five grand. The Web surfer was from Hawaii."

"Goddamn freaks!"

"Exactly."

"Now I see how you've become so successful. Buy a case of panties, tell the world Trina wore them, maybe spray 'em with some kinda—"

"No, no, Inspector Elliot. Our soiled panties are authentic. I assure you."

"I can't believe I'm sitting here having a conversation about *soiled panties*," said the inspector. A moment of silence passed before he got his business face back on. Then he said, "Okay. Trina Washington. How'd you all come to meet her?"

Stew thought quietly. He didn't want to mention Candice. He didn't feel it was anyone's business. And besides, to know Candice was to have a hand in Stew's cookie jar . . . his pot of gold. Not even his investors knew about Candice.

The door opened and Stephanie poked her head in. "Stew? The officers are finished with a lot of the girls. I'm putting them to bed. Need anything before I turn in?"

"Excuse me, Inspector," said Stew. He got up to speak with Stephanie in private. "Come down after everyone's gone."

"I will. Alone?" she asked.

"Alone," Stew answered. He returned back to where Inspector Elliot was seated. "Inspector? You were asking about Trina. No, I *don't* know her background, or if she had enemies. I know she had a lot of fans. Maybe it was a stalker."

"A boyfriend—a jealous one perhaps?"

"Nope. The girl came to us out of the blue. Said she wanted to work with us. She auditioned, we liked her, the rest is, or was, history. I don't know anything about jealous boyfriends, and if Trina did, she sure kept it a secret from us."

Inspector Elliot sat there deliberating for a time. Like he was reading Stew's mind. "Long night, huh."

"Very," Stew said, sighing heavily.

"How 'bout this, Stew . . . I'll see to it that the last of the interviews with your girls hurry along." He stood. "I'll be outside with the homicide crew for maybe another hour or so, and then we'll be out of your hair. How 'bout we get together tomorrow? I'll come by after lunch. You'll be rested, I'll be rested. We'll see about a few things. Sound good?"

"Sure."

"By the way, word has it that Trina and, er, Donna, is it? That they were, how should I say, sequestered to come to your room for the night. Any chance that Salt might've—"

"Inspector," Stew said, now standing face-to-face with him. "Sex for me is business *and* pleasure, as you might've guessed. None of the girls here are jealous of who I'm with or how many I'm with. I've been with Salt, with Salt and Pepper, with Salt and Sugar, with Pepper and Sugar, with Sugar alone. . . . *You know what I'm saying, Inspector*? That's the way I play in the sandbox. Funny thing is none of my girls disagree with my lifestyle or my choices. None of them are envious or jealous. This is just the way it is. It's convenient and enjoyable for all parties involved, and each participant is always willing. *Always* in agreement. I never force anyone to do what they don't want to do. I really hope I've made that clear for you, sir."

"Very," the inspector said. "And I bid you a good evening—until tomorrow," he added and left the bedroom.

"I've been wanting—" Timmy began. A quick knock interrupted him. Inspector Elliott peeped back in.

"Oh. One last thing, sir, ahh, I mean, *Stew*. I don't know any other way to put this. I'm gonna have to ask that you and your guests make yourselves at home here in Malibu . . . at least until we get some things cleared up."

"Are you telling me not to leave town, Inspector?"

"Basically, sir. It's also for your own safety, sir. You never know. It's possible that Trina wasn't the actual target." The inspector allowed that comment to sink in before he said "Good night," and pulled his head out of the doorway.

"Damn. So now I'm like a prisoner," said Stew.

"It's just standard procedure, boss. Nothing special. As soon as they clear things up, maybe tomorrow, you'll get clearance to move freely, to travel, whatever."

"Timmy, we're supposed to be in Canada on Wednesday."

"So, that's almost a week. Let time set in, boss. Lemme work on it. What I'm most concerned about is security. I've been wanting to suggest this earlier, but I guess now's as good a time as any. I wanna beef up security. Two, maybe three more guys. Originally, I wanted an extra guy at each of our locations, but for sure I want to keep a guy here in Malibu. And I'll need an additional man to travel with us."

"You got it, Tim. Whatever you say. But can we discuss it tomorrow? I'm getting a massive migraine."

"No doubt. I'll secure things for the night . . . clean up, if you know what I mean. Anything else you need?"

Stew shook his head. He was ready to get under the spray of his full-length shower.

"In the morning then," said Timmy. And he left Stew alone.

Inspector Elliot was met by officers the moment he cleared the threshold of Stew's bedroom. They informed him about their discussion with Salt and how she was devastated by the death of her friend. Still, they were able to collect details. Their relationship was but two months in the making. Trina was from Delaware. And no, Salt was in no way jealous of Stew and Trina. Her love for Stew was "crazy strong," she'd said. And, no, there were no stalkers or fanatics that Salt was aware of. No enemies.

An officer had taken two rolls of snapshots, inside and outside the house. The shell casing from the bullet was bagged and marked as evidence. All of the witness testimonies were documented, and the rest of the beachfront had been inspected as best as could be, with further inspections set for early morning. No footprints or tire marks were found, and the mystery remained. Who had shot Trina Washington, and why?

Stew immediately sensed the difference in the bedroom, as he stepped out of the shower. The lamplight had been replaced by candlelight, and incense was burning. Stephanie was there in his bed, her body raised on her elbows, waiting. Stew smiled as best he could. The first bit of pleasure in hours, hours that felt like years.

When he was through toweling off, Stew eased down onto the bed and in-between the silk sheets. The sheets welcomed his skin and soothed him to some degree—the candlelight and incense didn't hurt either.

Stephanie was naked as well. The instant she heard Stew's tired exhale, she knew exactly what it meant. She felt much of the same tensions that he had. The loss, the stress, the anxiety . . . She sensed that this was not the time for talking or rehashing the details. Stew needed release from the frustrations that welled up inside of his mind and body, and Stephanie would be there to help him unload the weight.

She immediately cuddled up beside him and put her mouth to his. Her hands squeezed all they could manage, while her knees, calves, and feet joined in to simultaneously massage him. Within minutes she had him spread out underneath her, his arms extended behind his head into the pillows. Where her hands and limbs didn't go, her lips and tongue explored. It all progressed to a Kamanshi squat, with Stephanie working and winding on top of Stew, receiving him as deeply as her body allowed. Eventually, after a struggle, a confusion between anguish and pleasure, a blur of images and concerns racing in both of their minds, Stew erupted and Stephanie collapsed over him until both of them were caught up in that web of deliverance. Eventually, once they came down from their high, they'd still be stranded in a maze that they could not decipher.

SEVEN

Stew demanded that the day ahead of them somehow be conducted with a semblance of normalcy. "We've got to get back to business as usual. No matter what, we *always* gotta be able to bounce back from challenges," he told Stephanie, Goose, Leslie, and Timmy, in their little powwow the morning after the killing. "I know it's gonna be hard, but *life* is *hard*. So we've got to *live hard*. I didn't come all this way to forfeit the game. What, because one of my batters dropped out in the second inning, I'm supposed to close up shop? This may sound hard and callous but we have to replace the batter and step up to the plate. The game must go on," said Stew.

Stew studied their eyes for any hint of drifting, for some loss of faith. But he saw none. They understood, and that was what he wanted—loyalty and devotion despite the challenges.

"Now, of course, we'll see to it that Trina's body is laid to rest in the most respectful, most honorable way, because frankly, that could've been any of us out there on those steps, hit by that bullet, and laying in some morgue right now. *Any of us*. So we'll treat her as we would want to be treated. And, of course, we'll be taking greater precautions now. Maybe we've been taking all of this success for granted. Maybe we've been too relaxed for the kind of money we're making; the kind of impact we're having on the industry. Who knows? We could be a threat to our competition. Maybe . . . well, I don't wanna get into speculation now. This isn't a time for that. Timmy has brought up a thing about tighter security, so we'll have that. We're still expecting two new girls today, so we're not at a loss for talent. In the meantime, we cooperate with the inspector, we tie up loose ends, and we continue to succeed. Agreed?"

They answered in unison. "Agreed."

Around noon, hours after Stew's orchestrated team huddle, Barbara, director of the Malibu branch, was handling the rush of phone calls, while Stew was escorting Inspector El-liott through the upper floors of the beach house. There was the floor where the girls slept; two or three to a room. And then there was the third floor where business was conducted.

"This is known as Studio A," Stew said. "Two cameras are set to capture this side of the room, the couch, the bearskin rug, and the window bay."

The lush rooms he referred to were decorated with throw pillows and stuffed animals, and everything was styled in light pinks and blues, with a theme of bright-red hearts.

"Two cameras also pick up the other side of the room— basically, the bed." The bed was mostly pink and white, with silk pillows and a teddy bear–printed comforter.

"While we're doing the walk-through nothing is live. However, we expect to be delivering a live Malibu feed over the Internet by, say, one o'clock."

"Oh . . . don't let *me* interrupt things."

"Actually, you're not, Inspector," said Stew. "This is the routine every day—at least for the past three years it's been."

"You mean, you live here in Malibu? I thought you were a summer vacationer."

"No. Six of one, and a half dozen of the other, sir. I'm kind of in and out. I'm here, yet I'm not. I have a number of homes like this one. But this one is where I can live it up. Get that whole family feel: barbecues, parties, house guests, the whole bit."

"And where *else* would you call home?"

"Atlanta, New York. Actually two in New York. Then I have

leases—apartments, really—in North Carolina, D.C., Houston, and Seattle."

"Jeeze. How do you keep track of all these places?"

"To tell you the truth, we're about to pick up a few more. Canada's next on the list. See, Inspector, my homes are also places of business. As we speak . . . *Here*, why don't I show you?"

Stew walked from Studio A into an adjoining room where there was various computer equipment, a few desks where women were busy on telephones, two vanities accessorized with makeup and hair-care products, and racks of lingerie against the adjacent wall. There was also a couch and a table full of sex toys, dildos, handcuffs, leather restraints, and whips.

"Whoa! Who uses *this* little doodad?" asked Elliot, although what he held up was anything *but* small.

"That's actually two dildos in one. You know, for two women—one side for each."

"Oh, I get it. As if there's a man inside each girl."

"Right."

"But there's really no man at all."

"Exactly," Stew said, as he politely took the toy from the inspector. The toys needed to be kept as sterile as possible. "We're gonna make you a sex expert yet, Inspector."

Stew led his visitor to a computer terminal. There were four of them, all occupied.

"You online yet, Suzie?"

"Just logged on, boss. Haven't typed a word yet."

"Good, good. Let me use your terminal for a minute. I wanna show our guest here our website."

Suzie maneuvered the mouse ever so slightly, the curser gliding across the company's home page up on the bright computer screen. "Already up and running for you, sir," Suzie said, and then she swiveled around and got out of her chair.

"Thanks, babe."

As Stew sat down to navigate around PlatinumDolls.com, Elliot bent down to get a closer look.

"Was she here last night? I don't remember a Suzie."

"No, Inspector. Actually, none of the girls you met last night are up on the site yet. All these women you see help with the behind-the-scenes operation. The business end."

"Very involved up here. You'd think a website was just some dweeb sitting in front of a computer screen," said the inspector.

Stew chuckled in response. "Okay. This is the Platinum Dolls home page. The photo you see is upgraded every ten seconds. It's a camera shot of our New York studio—the Bronx actually. Since they're three hours ahead of us, things are already kickin' over there. That's Brenda there in the still frame."

"Go, *Brenda*," Elliot said. "Is that a bathing suit or a string of dental floss?"

"It's a bathing suit, Inspector. You'd see the same thing in *Sports Illustrated.*"

"Yeah, but . . . She don't hardly have . . . I mean, she's damn near naked."

"That she is. Let me take you around the nation," Stew said, clicking the mouse as fast as he spoke. He'd done this more times than he could remember and could probably go through the motions with his eyes closed. "This is the scene in our other New York studio. Who's this, Suzie?"

"Ahh, that might be . . . Sheena. Yeah, I'm thinkin' it was Maria, cuz she has black hair, too. But no, that's definitely Sheena," Suzie said.

"Okay, and as we see, Sheena looks delicious in her turquoise thong and servant's apron. They do a lot of pretending, the girls. They pretend to be nurses, maids, teenyboppers, and even cops."

"You don't say."

"And here's Judy. Hey! What's up, Judy!" Stew was speaking to the computer screen, being humorous. "Judy is in Washington, D.C., and, mmm-mmm-mmm, she's got her whole belly dancer outfit on. Straight out of a king's harem, huh, Inspector?"

"Uh, yeah, right. Go, Judy!"

"So lemme show you more about the site. As you can see, a web surfer can visit any of our eight locations with the click of the mouse. Even Malibu, although right now there's nothing live." Stew navigated to the icon for Malibu. "But whether we're live or taped, there's always something happening. This is Jessica. This is basically footage from yesterday being re-loaded today—only until the girls begin work in fifteen or so minutes." Stew clicked the mouse again. "So now, let's go to Atlanta. This is one of my favorite places to visit. One of my favorite homes. We've got seven acres down there. The house is huge. It's got an indoor pool, a movie theater, all that. But it's also got : . . here they are! *Girls, girls, girls.*"

Stew was taking Elliot on a roller coaster ride around the website. From the still photos that were uploaded to the screen, Stew dug deeper, tapped in his personal four-digit code, and entered the boudoir of Atlanta's Studio A. There on the screen were two women, naked, with limbs twisted around each other.

"Whoa! Is this stuff *legal*?" Elliot asked in shock. "I mean, they can *show* all this right there on the screen?" Elliot was thinking about his teenage daughter having access to the Internet, wondering if she'd ever seen . . . "Can *any-one* see this?" he asked.

"Relax, Inspector. There are rules for businesses like ours. Rules that were put in place to protect innocent eyes. Children. Old ladies. You know what I mean?"

"Yeah, but how?"

"Every visitor to Platinum Dolls has access to the home-page and the still photos you saw. But those photos are no different than what you . . ." Stew reached into a magazine rack. "Speaking of which, check it out. The June issue of *Sports Illustrated.*" Stew slapped the latest issue of the magazine on the desk.

"As I was saying. There's no difference between this and *this.*" Stew indicated the magazine cover, and then the com-puter screen where he'd clicked back to the Platinum Dolls home page. "It's only when you are a member, when you type in your four-digit code"—Stew did as he said—"that you get, well, this . . . *the raw stuff.*"

"Oh, I get it. So there *are* protective measures."

"Exactly."

"More to this business than I thought," Elliot said.

"Thanks, Suzie," Stew said, as he got up from her chair.

The two men continued through the office, and Stew explained that the locations in the other cities were set up the same way. He took Inspector Elliot from the business office into Studio B, which was set up like Studio A. There was also a larger bedroom on the floor, another master bedroom that was arranged like a stage, with a lot of overhead lighting, tripod cameras, and a director's chair. "This is where the actual porn films are shot. The professional stuff that we mass produce on videotape and sell to whoever."

"Now, I never thought I'd see the day when all of this high-tech sex stuff was set up here in Malibu," Elliot said. "You've got a beast here."

"Yup. It's a beast alright. Question is, can we keep the beast alive?"

"Let me ask you something, Stew," Elliot said, as he and Stew each took hold of a director's chair. "Do you have any hostile competition that you know of? Anybody whose money you might be cutting into as a result of your success?"

"I thought about that. A lot of my competition has fallen off, or else they offer a whole different theme than we do. Remember, we just do girl-on-girl stuff. I have a competitor in Detroit; a big outfit, too. It's run mostly by women. But I know the lady—Ashley is her name. We kick it all the time. Not a bit of animosity between us. We even share resources and information to help one another. So, no. No hate there. And really, when it comes down to it, this is a ten-billion-dollar-a-year industry. There's so much money to go around, it's ridiculous! Anybody who's anybody in this game is livin' it up big time."

"Like you," Elliot offered.

Stew shrugged. "What can I do? I work hard. I get paid. I'm happy."

"Let's wrap it up for now, Stew," Elliott said, standing up. "I've got some investigating to do, checking into Trina's background, maybe the Coast Guard, your neighbors. I'll be in touch. Oh, and thanks for the tour."

"Inspector, before you go, any idea if I'll be able to keep my flight plans for next week? We're supposed to be setting things up in Canada."

"Not just yet. Stand by, though. Give me another day on this, I'll see what I can do. Maybe after we finish speaking with the Coast Guard."

Stew masked his disappointment. *Red tape. And if he hasn't looked already, he's interested to know if I have a criminal record.*

Not a minute after Inspector Elliot left the property, Barbara rushed up to Stew with her message pad.

"Sir, the phone's been ringing off the hook." Barbara was one of the company jewels, with eyes that twinkled, a pie-shaped face, and the lips and nose of an Egyptian queen. Barbara's phone etiquette was so intoxicating that Stew found himself sucked in whenever he returned her calls.

"Twenty-nine calls in the past hour. CNN, *Access, Extra, ET,* Entertainment Television, BET, they all want to talk to you. And those are just the television calls. There were some morning radio programs that wanted to put you on the air live, and there were newspapers. A half dozen *Herald*s, syndicated columns, and *Daily* this-'n-that. Oh, and there were personal calls. All of them called back two or three times."

"Thank you, Barbara." Stew took the message slips. "Did I ever tell you that you were sweet as a Hershey's kiss?"

"Every day, boss."

"Oh." Stew smiled as he headed for his own desk. Amid the fever of ongoing office activities, Stew's eyes immediately grew alert at the sight of his personal messages. Lex and Trent, his investors in New York. Candice. And . . . *Ashley*? A rare call.

Stew's desk was in the corner with a window view, less of a view than in his bedroom three floors down, but beautiful and blue just the same. His desk was mostly clear but for two telephones, a laptop, and a desktop computer, as well as a little teddy bear complete with a fedora hat. The teddy bear, wearing a black smoking jacket and holding a pipe, was custom made to have some semblance to Hugh Hefner. Over the heart of the little jacket was yellow embroidered lettering. The words read: PIMP HARD.

"Ash, whassup," Stew said, more curious about her call than any of the others.

"What's *up*? Are you kiddin', Stew? You're like the big news around the world right now. People getting shot up at your million-dollar beach house, and you're asking *what's up?* What's up with *you*? You alright?"

Stew shook his head, quickly reminded of the tragedy that was still fresh as an open wound. "I'm good, Ash. I guess it's not the spectacular news to me that it seems to be for everyone else. They all see it like a movie. I see it as a tragedy and a damn shame."

"Well, shit, Stew, this *is* America. You know, folks can't get enough of sex, violence, and money . . . And now you gave them *all three*."

EIGHT

Almost ten years earlier, in Michigan, Stew had been only nineteen, a sex-starved high school dropout, and barely able to purchase his first car. He was a momma's boy, from a single-parent household, with no particular goal for the future. For get-by money, he worked at Chances, a dance club in downtown Detroit. He started out as a busboy, stocking beer, liquor, carrying ice to the barmaids, and picking up stray empties that had been left on windowsills and tables. He'd grown accustomed to that age-old stench of cigarette butts, spit, and beer, the odors that remained after the crowd filed out at two in the morning.

By the time Stew left the club, the after-hours crowd of weed smokers and troublemakers were still carrying on with the party; still milling about out front or along the side of Chances. For some, this was the chance for a last attempt to take a girl home. Stew was usually tired after a long night and would head straight home. The walk was at least a mile, or twenty city blocks. One night, four minutes into his journey, two unmarked police cars, black and burgundy sedans, pulled up within a few feet of him. One got straight up on the curb and the other into a driveway, blocking Stew's way. Within seconds, all the car doors swung open, and white men in blue jeans, sneakers, and leather jackets jumped out into the night to surround Stew. There had to be seven or eight of them.

Stew assumed that they were cops because of how aggressive they were; how easy it was for these men to stake a claim on the dark city streets, especially when they swooped in as a group with guns drawn.

"On the ground!" "Lay down, boy, or get sprayed down!" "Hit the floor!" "Do it! Now!" The commands were screamed at Stew like rapid fire. Before he could bring his second knee to the pavement, one of the vultures already had his hands on Stew. Then another pair of hands was at his neck. He felt a fist, a baton—or maybe it was a flashlight—to the back of his thigh. Stew crashed face first to the ground, the impact instantly knocking him unconscious.

Later, Stew was awakened by smelling salts waved under his nose. The smell stung his senses and immediately called up the pains from his body. His limbs were sore. His eyes were swollen like footballs. His head pounded as if it was the inside of a motor, the wheels cranking on and on. It was hard to tell what exactly was broken in his chest or midsection, but he knew he didn't want to budge to find out.

"Put some'a that Morton's on his knee. That'll wake his ass up," a voice said.

A second later, Stew screamed until his voice died out. Until his eyes watered again. Stew was awake now, enough to know that his hands were cuffed behind his back. He was seated in a chair with his feet bound to its legs.

"You 'wake now, boy?" The white man standing in front of him had hair combed back in a slick, wet look. His lips curled in and his puny eyes pierced through Stew. The man was crouched with his hands on his knees, his head slightly turned to mean business. "Say, whas yo' name, boy?"

Stew coughed up phlegm and blood in his attempt to answer the man.

"Shee-it, son!" The man's gloved hand came across Stew's cheek. It was so loud, an echo filled the room. "You tryin' a give me AIDS?"

Stew unconsciously let out a moan. He was too weak and numb with hurt to answer the lesser blows.

"Lemme have at 'im, Doobie," said another voice. And a moment later, hot coffee was tossed in Stew's face. Stew shuddered and pissed himself at once, the urine soaking into his jeans.

"This is how this works, boy. I ask the questions, you give the answers. You don't answer like I want, I start to tattoo yer ass with this here cigarette lighter. And trust me, son, your pain is my pleasure."

Stew couldn't imagine what these guys wanted, but he'd heard about run-ins that friends or distant relatives had had with the Detroit Police Department. But then, Stew wondered if these were even police, were they a posse?

"A girl was raped up by the club last week. You familiar?"

Stew nodded as best he could.

"Good, good. Boys, I think we're off to a running start. But just so you don't think I'm jokin', lemme let you feel the flame." The man flicked his lighter and the terrible heat singed the skin on Stew's thigh. Stew's cry was met by the men's laughter. Stew couldn't see them all, but he figured there had to be at least four of them. His lip quivered from the agony. *This* was just the beginning.

"Well now, I guess we've got ou'selves a workin' relationship, huh, boy?"

This was so insanely unjust, inhumane, and plain bizarre that Stew was almost tempted to laugh. Laugh himself into unconsciousness again. Even coma or death would do him fine right about now.

"Answer me, boy!"

Stew nodded vigorously.

"Okay. Here's the deal. The girl was raped by a nigger. The girl was, say, a friend of ours. And she was only sixteen." The man up in Stew's face was fleshy around the chin; so much so that he had jowls. He was fat, like he could have been a circus attraction. And he, too, had slicked-back hair, except it was a lighter shade of brown, whereas the other guy's was black.

"So the way we figure it, yer gonna tell us exactly what we need to know, else we're gonna wup yer ass proper." The fat man put the lighter's small flame next to Stew's eyes. Stew trembled more than ever. The fear was worse than the pain.

"An'na tell ya' the truth, we might just go 'head and wup yer ass any fuckin' way."

"Ask 'em 'bout the girl," Dobbie said. "*The girl.*"

"Yeah. The girl, nigger. Who done it? I want a name and an address."

Doobie said, "Burn 'im, Haas. *Burn* his ass! *Make* 'im tell it."

Stew screamed as the flame touched his bloody knee. The men laughed in concert over Stew's misery.

"Lemme get a have at 'im, Haas. Shee-it . . . this's better than sex."

"You know that bee-ach ain't givin' you no sex, Crout."

"The fuck you callin' a bee-ach, Asshole-Bob."

"I'm callin' Freda a bee-ach, on a count'a 'bout three of us up in hrr had a piece of 'er."

Crout and Asshole-Bob went at it. The beer pushing all of them in wayward directions. Focused and unfocused on the business at hand. Jackson-True jumped into the center of it all.

"I'm fittin' a kick both 'a yer asses if'n you don't cut the shee-it. Now, we got this boy in here to persecute 'im and get information. Now git to it. And stop"—Jackson-True popped both men across the backs of their heads—"fuckin' around!"

Whenever the pain became too unbearable, Stew fell unconscious. They'd wake him up again either with the smelling salts or cold water from the hose in the garage where he was being held. This went on for at least two hours, but Stew said nothing. He said nothing because he knew nothing. He heard them say, "We'll get somebody else." Badly burned and bruised, bloodied and broken, Stew was tossed from the back of a pick-up truck as it sped along Interstate 80 at five in the morning. Stew was left for dead, just another victim of police brutality.

NINE

At that time, Ed Lover and Dr. Dre were the funny men of WKLA Radio—"Where Hip Hop and R&B live." Their radio show was legendary in Los Angeles, and the number one program during the morning drive. "Ed and Dre in the Mornings" kicked off every day at 5:30 A.M. with old and new music, as well as contests, comments from listeners calling in, comedy skits, and live interviews with who's who and who's hot in the world of hip hop.

Radio's "dynamic duo" initially assumed that an interview with Porn King Stew Gregory (a man who was black and under thirty like they were) would stir up excitement for their audience. Talk of sex and money was, they expected, inevitable.

Once they were on the air, Stew was introduced and the website was promoted. Ed couldn't wait to jump in with his personal testimonies, exclaiming that he was a frequent visitor to the website.

"I'm especially fond of Georgette," Ed announced. "In fact, can we talk about a phone number, Stew? I mean, not to put you—the CEO, head chief, cook, and bottle washer—on the line. But, just . . . Could ya put a brother down?"

On cue, Dr. Dre blew his whistle and spun a noisemaker, the show's usual indication of a shameless plug.

"I'll have to see what can be arranged, Ed. I mean, especially for you!" Stew played along to make the host happy, and the digital applause of a hundred or so people sounded off in celebration of the moment.

"So tell us how you got started with all of this, Stew Gregory—mister porn king and entrepreneur. How'd it all kick off?"

A soundtrack of a familiar hip hop beat played low in the background. Stew told them how it had started with the late night/early morning beating at the hands of (he knew for sure) the Detroit police.

Stew kept it as diplomatic as he could. "Not all Detroit police officers are like that. Just some bad apples that snuck in the barrel," he said. "But that was somehow where my life began: When I *survived*. I wasn't *supposed* to survive, but I did," Stew said.

After he explained that, Stew was ready to leave the subject, to keep things on an upbeat theme. But following those first few minutes, and Stew's testimony of the bitter details of that long-ago violent police beating, the usual comedic angle was impossible to maintain. As it turned out, the subject caused a telephone traffic jam.

"All those who've been victims of police violence, please raise your hands, honk your horns . . . yah-mean! Damn!"

Ed was speaking directly to Stew, there in the WKLA studio, their headphones in place with microphones extended before them. But he was also in the ears of millions of Californians, devoted listeners who didn't hesitate to join in on the conversation.

Dr. Dre pressed the foghorn; his response to Ed's calling.

"So they beat you down, tossed you on the highway, *then* what?" Ed asked, well aware that the phone lines were burning up.

"Well, I took a long time to heal. . . ."

Dr. Dre activated the hospital PA system sound. That famous *Ding-dong . . . Paging Doctor Dre, paging Doctor Dre.*

Meanwhile, Ed Lover was falling out of his seat. "Excuse me . . . Oh *damn*, excuse my laughter, but you takin' this shiz-nit so calm, dog! 'I took a long time to heal,' that sounds like a punch line. I wanna know, did you get back at those key-stone, flatfoot, bend-over, ass-wipe cops? *That's* what I wanna know!"

"Well, to be painfully honest with you, no."

Dr. Dre activated the digital chorus. *Awww!* The music dramatically died off.

"No charges pressed? No spook-who-sat-by-the-door type retaliation? Yo! We already been through this here in LA, with the whole can't-we-all-just-get-along bit, and frankly, buddy, we straight ain't havin' it. Around the world, they all know how LA gets down for theirs. They go and beat a man down. Oh hell naw! I'm about tired of bad cops takin' the law in their own hands, in LA, Detroit, or *anywhere*. What about you, Los Angeles? Call us now with your comments. Eight-eight-eight-four-one-two-WKLA. What was that number, Dre?"

"Eight-eight-eight-four-one-two-WKLA."

"And we'll be back after these messages with more of 'Ed and Dre in the Mornings,' live with Stew Gregory, porn king!" Some music pumped and a commercial played.

The red-and-white ON THE AIR light blinked off in the studio and Ed slipped his headphones off his head, looking as if he'd just run the fifty-yard dash.

Stew's face twisted some, wondering how they'd gotten on that tangent. He had long since forgotten the horrors of his past. "What happened, Ed? I thought you wanted to talk about how I got started, how I built the company," Stew said suddenly.

"Sorry about that, Stew-boogie. Sometimes I lose it, ya know. I just bug out when I hear shit like that. Plus, my pro-ducer over there behind the glass was tellin' me to wrap up this segment, so I kinda went with my heart. Spur'a da moment thing, that's all."

"Whew—*man*, I didn't expect *this*." Stew could see the switchboard blazing with blinking lights. It was as if he was being sucked back into a prehistoric era of his life—a painful time that he chose to leave behind; a Stew Gregory that had been left for dead on Interstate 80 in Michigan ten years ago.

"Ed, get ready to drop the promo for Car Cash," Dr. Dre interjected.

"Don't worry, Stew," said Ed. "We'll pump a few tunes after the commercial. Dre, let's toss the Name That Rapper contest this morning." Ed turned back to Stew and continued, "Then we'll jump right into you, Stew. We'll get past the old stuff, promise. You just get ready to gimme the nitty-gritty details. I want the sex, the money—all that!"

"Thanks, Ed," Stew said, suddenly relieved, but still suspicious.

Stephanie had been waiting for the ON THE AIR signal to go off and was eventually let into the studio. Her presence set off all kinds of unseen bells and whistles in the atmosphere.

In a hushed tone, she said, "You're hot like fire, Daddy! They love you out there. I can feel it in the other room."

"But, Steph, I'm trying to move forward. That was the past. We need to progress, not digress."

Ed Lover swiveled around to check out Stephanie. "*Whoa!* What in the *heezy!* Who is *this* absolutely captivating female that just walked in the house?"

"Ed Lover, meet the one and only Stephanie Koboyashi."

"Well, may I just take my headphones off, and come around this here console, and bow down, and kiss your pretty feet!" Ed did as he said, provoking laughter in the studio.

Cathy, the producer of the show, walked in while he was in front of Stephanie.

Dr. Dre said, "*Man*, if I only had my video camera!"

Ed got back up from his knees and took Stephanie's hand and kissed the back of it. "Nice to meet you, Miss Koboyashi," Ed proclaimed.

"Ed, you're on the air in ten," said Cathy.

Ed Lover looked at Stew once he got up off the floor. He paused and waved his finger at Stew. "You . . . are a beast." And he raced around the console again to slip on his headphones. Then he seamlessly got right back into the thick of things, as the ON THE AIR sign lit up again.

Stephanie was about to hurry out, but Cathy put her hand up, indicating that she should relax and stay with Stew.

> *"And we are back to the grill again . . .*
> *the grill again!*
> *Back to the grill again . . .*
> *the grill again . . ."*

Ed Lover jumped into one of his spontaneous rhymes, something his radio audience grew accustomed to hearing.

> *"It's Ed Lover on your radio . . .*
> *not the video!*
> *And Doctor Dre is on your radio . . .*
> *and he blazin', yo'!*
> *KLA is rockin' Cali, yo' . . .*
> *and also Frisco!"*

> *"We pumpin' music thru your body, yo' . . .*
> *and in your ear hole!*
> *Don't get me twisted . . .*
> *don't be upset!*
> *We number one in the west,*
> *on your radio set!"*

> *"In your car or your livin' room . . .*
> *you can find us right hrrr!*
> *It's Doctor Dre and Ed Lover . . .*
> *And we don't crrr!"*

> *"We in here kickin' it with the man.*
> *He's the porno king.*
> *He got the Internet locked,*
> *cuz he's doin' his thing!"*

> *"So keep your dial right hrrr . . .*
> *don't move at all!*

Here's some old school by . . .
the late great Biggie Smalls!"

Ed Lover signaled his partner, and Dre began The Notorious B.I.G.'s single "One More Chance."

Stew was amazed by how smoothly everything went and at how so much went on behind the scenes in order to keep a morning radio show exciting. He immediately felt tremendous respect for the forum, and couldn't help but agree with whatever the host said. Stew didn't have a preset agenda, but he knew now that if he was going to do any more press interviews, he would have an objective. He'd have a goal to reach for and achieve so that, despite the intentions of the media—be it TV, radio, or print—he'd get his message across. He would achieve his end and make it a win-win experience.

After the Notorious B.I.G. song, Dre played Brandy, Jay-Z, and Eve.

"We're back in the house at 8:40 A.M. with Porn King Stew Gregory. And if you just missed our last segment, you missed a lot. The man is a high school dropout, tryin' to make ends meet and all the sudden, the Detroit police crash his party, beat him down and leave him for dead . . . tossed his ass out on I-eighty. So tell me, Stew, what happened next?"

"Well, Ed, I turned my tragedy into fuel for my success. I told myself I'd never ever let that happen again. Sure, I was angry . . . ready to go out and get a gun and shoot every cop I saw. But I suddenly got hit by a light. I saw that I was put here to survive. To achieve some definite purpose."

"Porn!" Ed said jokingly.

"Well, not exactly. See, I met a girl, we became friends, and it just so happened that she had her own website. The girl was a nurse at the hospital where I was recuperating. Her brother happened to be a partner in an investment firm in New York, and . . . well, the rest is history. If I never got to meet the nurse, I'd never know what could be done on the Internet."

"So, nursie had a little freak thing goin' on the side? Her own porn site?"

"Not exactly. Hers was real small. More like a homepage

where people could learn about her hobbies. When I was well enough, we, uh, got together. We made something more of it."

"So y'all was hittin' skins. Interpretation! Stew was bangin' his nurse, y'all!"

Dr. Dre turned on the applause sound effect, so that it sounded as if a big audience was commending Stew for the act.

"So you moved in with the nurse. You learned all about the Internet and one thing led to another."

"Basically," said Stew.

"What's it like to be a porn king?" asked Dre, the more sincere of the two hosts. "Paint a picture for us."

Stew took a deep, audible breath. "A lot of flesh. I mean, *a lot.* A lot of pretty faces. Personalities. It's really like a big family. The girls put on sex shows, sure, but when it comes to the bottom line, we service a large audience of men. We sell them fantasies. We stimulate their minds, their pleasure centers."

"Well, *my* pleasure center is wide open right now, since Stew introduced me to Stephanie. Say hi to L.A., Stephanie."

"Hi, L.A."

"Do you work with Stew and Platinum Dolls?"

"Sure. I keep the girls together. I keep 'em looking good, and I make sure Stew here is very, very happy."

Applause erupted over the air again.

"Oops . . . there goes *my* wet dream," Ed Lover said. "So, ahh, give us a clue up in here. How, ahh, *exactly* do you keep Stew very, very happy?"

Stephanie was quick to reply. "However and *whenever* he wants." As the applause sounded yet again, Stephanie made sensual eyes at Ed Lover, turning him all the way on.

"*Whoo-eee* . . . It must be nice, Stew. It *must be nice.*"

"We have eight locations and over two hundred girls in various parts of the country, Ed. All of them can be found on Platinum Dolls dot-com. But also, I employ a staff of one hundred and fifty men and women who work behind the scenes to make the website a winner. We're feedin' folks, Ed."

"Well, if Stephanie here is on your staff, *as fine as she looks*, you ain't gotta convince me, dog. I'm sold! How much money is in this Platinum Dolls venture of yours?"

"In the industry? There's ten billion or more dollars floatin' around every year. Us? Platinum Dolls is close to winning three or four percent of that."

Ed Lover began to whistle as he did the math on the air. "Take away seven, carry the four . . . *Whoa!* That's over two hundred or three hundred *million dollars. Dayy-um!* I think I wanna quit, Dre."

"Don't do it, Ed."

"Nah, Dre, I'm quittin.' I'm startin' my own website."

"Don't do it, Ed," Dre said again.

But Ed took off his headphones, which was heard on the air. This was dramatic radio.

"O-*kay*," said Dre. "This portion of the Doctor Dre show was brought to you by Car Cash, the *leaders* in the auto loan industry. Meanwhile, we'll be back after these messages with your phone calls at eight-eight-eight-four-one-two-WKLA. What was that number, Ed?" There was silence, so Dre answered his own question. "Okay, Dre, that's eight-eight-eight-four-one two-WKLA. The phone lines are blazin'! You're locked in to WKLA, the Doctor Dre show! Where hip hop, R&B, and Stew Gregory *live!*"

The music thumped on in the studio, the segue into the next set of commercials. Dre chuckled to himself as he pressed a few buttons and pulled down the slide bar so that the studio microphones were muted.

Stew looked at Stephanie, amazed. "Did Ed Lover really quit?"

Dre said, "Don't worry. He's probably in the bathroom kickin' himself in the ass. He'll be back after the break." Dre took a swig of coffee. "The last time he did this was when a few of the Lakers cheerleaders came by. They said Ed should be their publicist. He flipped that day, too."

When things were back to normal, Stew explained on the air that although Platinum Dolls was dealing with hundreds of millions of dollars in revenue, the profit was only a percentage of that. He explained that there were the salaries of three hundred fifty people to consider, the overhead for his homes that served as offices, as well as many other operating expenses.

"But you still a millionaire," Ed said, looking for testimony.

"Let's just say my bank account is *interesting*. I still have to answer to my investors." Stew had an urge to explain *that* thorn-in-his-ass problem. "But at the end of the day, I *do* feel like a million bucks. And that's something I almost never lived for."

"You tellin' *me*," said Ed Lover. "You hear that, you scum of Detroit police officers? You done made the man a millionaire!"

"Let's take a call, Ed." And Dre went on to introduce the caller. "This is KLA, you're on the air with the porn king, Stew Gregory."

"Yo wassup! Dude . . . I'm feelin' your whole karma, man. You ain't nothin' but an inspiration for a brotha. I mean, I dropped outta high school, too, got beat down by cops here in L.A., and yo—you got me feelin' some type' a way 'bout dat! I been boilin' inside 'bout how ta get back at them fools."

"Caller, what's your name?" asked Stew.

"Benny the Butcher!"

"*Whoa*, Benny! Whassup dog! This Ed." Ed made a face. "Peace, God. *West Siiide!*"

"Yo, Benny, tell us what the man said that inspired you. Ain't you the same Benny the Butcher who be up on Crenshaw?"

"You *know* that be me, Ed. Stop playin'. Yo, but I'm serious, dog. A nigga like me ain't got no future 'cept for slangin' and bangin'. Yah-mean? But dude done been where I been, at the *bottom*, ya heard? Ready to die 'n all that. And he *still* came up! Yo, that nigga a king!"

"That's love, God. And holla' at my dogs on Crenshaw, ya heard? *West Side!*"

Benny repeated the chant, but just as Ed was about to go on to the next caller, Stew spoke.

"Yo, Benny. One thing. This is Stew again. You said you

been wantin' to get back at the cops. So I just wanted to answer that before you go. See, I never got back at them cops that beat me down. Not literally. But every time I make anotha million dollas, I feel like I'm kickin' them back in the ass twice as hard. I feel like I'm puttin' that lighter to *their* skin. So, I say all that to say, make your own success your get-back. Laugh inside at those fools the day you reach your goals. 'Cause, trust me—and you brought up that word *karma* earlier—*karma* is gonna come back at your enemies tenfold. I believe if someone does you dirty, life is just waitin' to give dirty right back to them. Might be now, might be later. But never spit in the wind."

"Damn! That's some advice for yo ass!" said Ed.

"Next caller," said Dre. "Wassup, Charmaine from up in North Hollywood."

"Okay, Charmaine, you're on with the porn king, Stew Gregory!"

"What's up, babe?" said Stew.

"Hi, Stew. I was just wonderin' how a girl could get into the business."

"Well, well, well! Our very first contestant on *Show Yo Ass*!" Ed Lover exclamed.

"First of all, Charmaine, you gotta be of age," said Stew.

"I'm nineteen," answered Charmaine.

"Okay. Then . . . well, in our business we like our girls to come in with a clean bill of health."

"Ya hear that, Char? No crabs up in Platinum Dolls!"

"Bigger than crabs, we're most concerned about the spread of AIDS. So far, for the past five years we've been fortunate to remain AIDS-free. And our girls get tested bimonthly."

"Safe sex is next to godliness," added Dre.

"Once we see the doctor's okay, we have orientation and some training for those without talent, and we simply audition those who claim to have talent."

"Now how in the *hell* does the audition go down? Tell us about that, Stew-boogie!" Ed was as animated as ever.

"I mean, it speaks for itself, Ed. We're in the sex trade. So we need to see, and hear, *the sex*. We want girls who will excite our website visitors. It's a show. Sight and sound. We're selling a fantasy."

"Okay, Charmaine, you heard the man. So imagine that this is *your* audition. You're big shot at a job with Platinum Dolls. You're in bed waitin' for Big Ed to come in. The cameras are rollin', I walk in, tell me what's next. Paint the picture for me." Ed grinned. This little stunt was definitely going to add some excitement.

"Hmm, well, you're lookin' real healthy, Ed," Charmaine said. "I mean, is that a sausage in your shorts, or are you just glad to see me?"

"Ohhh, I think it's the sausage, baby."

"Well, I'm layin' here in nothin' but a bow tie, my long black hair is spread out under my head, my arms are stretched back. I got the phone cradled to my ear. And, Ed?"

"Yeah?"

"I'm soooo horny. I've been waitin' for you since last summer."

"Oh boy! Long time no see, Charlie!"

"Exactly. So, uhm, let's cut the chitchat, Ed. Come to bed and hover over me like the dragon you are. I'm lickin' my lips, and I can hardly wait, so my hand is already keepin' things warm for you. Ya know, gettin' the party started."

"Jeeee-*sus*! L.A., are y'all even *ready* for this so early in the morning? Damn, it's gettin' hot in hrrr!"

"Ed, it might be gettin' *too* hot. There's an accident over on the freeway," Dre said, interrupting the audition. "Dawn, why don't you fill us in with the traffic update."

"Yes indeedy. And it seems to be heating up on the roads, as well as the studio this morning, as they're rubbernecking along . . ."

While Dawn gave the traffic update, Ed addressed Stew. "What do you wanna do with Charmaine? She's still on the line. Says she wants to be down."

Stew laughed. He'd originally thought the call was a setup. He'd put nothing past Ed Lover after this morning.

"Stephanie can take her number, if you want. We can *always* use girls, Ed."

"Me too. Hey, Cathy, can you hook that up?" Ed said, trying to calm himself and still stay focused on the things he had to handle: live tags at the ends of commercials, public service announcements, keeping track of the time and the traffic and news feeds. Everything raced along, and it had to move smoothly.

Once the traffic was done, Ed went back on the air. "*Whooo-eee!* I had to get a glass of cold water for *that* call. Thanks for hollarin', Charmaine, but you done caused an accident out on the freeway. We got time for a couple more calls before Stew leaves. Busy man, ain't you, Stew?"

"Very, Ed. We have to navigate so much content between our various home studios. We're in Atlanta, Houston, D.C., Seattle, we have two spots up in New York. Of course you already know about Malibu."

"Yeah, I was about to ask you about that, on a more serious note. You had a little problem out there the other day. It was the news of the day. Porn queen slayed at porn king's lair. Whassup with that?"

"That was an unfortunate tragedy the other day, Ed. Trina was one of our best girls. Many men have requested her on the website, her videos."

"Well, what the hell happened, Stew?"

"They're still investigating, Ed. But it appears as if someone—maybe from a boat, or maybe from down the beach, nobody's sure—but somebody took a shot . . . *uh,* they shot Trina. I mean, Ed, there's no subtle way to put this. It was cold-blooded murder."

"That's a coward's work. For real," said Ed Lover.

"For real, for real," Dre added.

"So . . . What? A stalker? Angry boyfriend?"

"Nobody knows, Ed. This is a first; the first tragedy of this kind since I started this business over five years ago. We're still a little shaken up."

"I can imagine."

"But with all due respect to Trina, the show must go on. We'll treat her funeral with special attention, tie up whatever loose ends there are, and for sure, we'll be cooperating to the best of our ability with the investigation. This wasn't a drive-by, Ed. This was a hit. An execution. It's like you said, cowardly. But we're gonna move on. We love you, Trina!"

"And that goes triple for us here at KLA. Caller, you're on the air with Ed and Dre and Mr. Stew Gregory."

"Hey y'all. I just wanted to ask Stew what his take was on the morality issues behind his business."

"Whoa! Hey, now you know we likes controversy up in here, babe. Can you elaborate on that a little more for our guest, and maybe for those of us who are un-edumacated?"

"Well, the whole bit, the sex—the girl-on-girl features—I mean, it isn't exactly godly to engage in these things. I'm not hatin', I just wondered what Stew thought about that."

"Well, thank you, caller. That's a mouthful, Stew. You need me to cut to commercial?"

"Not at all, Ed. To be honest, I had to battle with the morality bit myself. Things the Bible says, and what the public conscience says. And frankly, I've just personally decided to stay on the left. You know, there are many politicians, for example, who play middle ground, tryin' to satisfy everybody. But me? I keep it real. This is a part of my life. At least now it is. I've become successful within a number of years, where some large corporations took decades. I became something from nothing, feel me? All I'm concerned about is those two hundred thousand–plus customers and my staff around the country. My goal is to make them all happy. Let the critics, the moral right, and other special interest organizations think and say what they will. In the meantime, as long as I'm not hurtin' anyone, I'mma get mine."

"That's my Dizz-og!" Ed Lover said. Dre sounded the applause effect. "A man who's 'bout it 'bout it. Yah-mean!" Ed looked at the time. "KLA is on your radio, we're here with Stew Gregory, entrepreneur, playboy, porn king extraordinaire, and it's nine twenty. Watch your time . . ."

"Watch it if ya want, cuz you're twenty minutes late if yo' ass is in bed," said Dre.

"And this is Ed Lover . . ."

"And Dr. Dre . . ."

"On your dial. Keep it here for some classic Snoop Dogg and more on your number one morning show!"

Stephanie leaned over to kiss Stew's cheek when they went to commercial break. "You did good," she said. "All the girls will be proud of you."

"Thanks, Steph."

Stephanie left Stew's side to get coffee while things came to a conclusion there at KLA radio. There were a few more calls before Stew headed home with his chin up and the feeling of a mission accomplished. He had to admit, this press stuff could actually grow on a person. There were autographs requested and photos taken on the way to the limousine. Stew called to find that his voice mail was full of positive messages, recordings from his various Los Angeles associates and friends. There were other messages left with Barbara at the Malibu home.

All of this was happening so fast, propelling Stew toward his objectives. But deep down, he knew something was wrong; that there was a cancer somewhere. He swore he'd find out what it was.

TEN

Sitting in the back of the limo, Stew called Barbara, while Stephanie, sitting across from him, was on the phone herself coordinating various business activities. Suddenly he put a hand over the mouthpiece of his cell phone and asked with urgency, "Steph, do you know anything about being able to fly?"

Stephanie, her phone still held to her ear, shrugged and shook her head in response. Stew gave her a sidelong look. He told Barbara to hold on, while he turned around and knocked on the window separating the driver's side from the rest of the car. The window was lowered. Timmy was sitting up front with the driver.

"Yeah, boss," answered Timmy.

"What's this Barbara's tellin' me 'bout us bein' able to travel now?"

"Sorry, boss. I meant to say somethin' but I guess I was too focused on security and whatnot—the autographs and photos 'n stuff—I didn't get around to it. Inspector Elliot says we've got the green light. We can fly."

"Yesss!" Stew said, pumping his fist as if he'd just scored a touchdown. "Barbara? I guess that means we're on for Canada."

"Yes, we are, boss. I'll tell you what I was thinking, since you suddenly grew to like this publicity. I spoke with the producers of *Access Hollywood* today and they've come up with a great idea. We were thinking to have a camera crew follow you from Malibu to Seattle; you know, covering your average activities for a day. They thought they'd stay with you all the way to Canada, watch you set up the new site."

"All this publicity all of a sudden and I don't have to pay? It's free? Somethin's fishy."

"Boss, with all the interest I'm getting here, all the phone calls, I think that you're America's next hottest thing. They're fascinated. They like you. So, ride the wave—what can I say?" Barbara suggested.

Stew thought about it and said nothing for a time, staring through Stephanie as if she wasn't there. He wondered if it would be right to accept all this publicity. *Would it?* After all, Trina's death was the cause.

Stephanie looked at him curiously. *What?* she mouthed, shrugging her shoulders.

"Boss? You there?"

Stew shook off the spell. "Sorry, Barbara. Just set it up. Set it *all* up. See you shortly."

Stew hung up with Barbara and called Candice. He poked in her digits from memory—her number was always fresh on his mind. The limousine navigated through traffic on Hollywood Boulevard, as Stew carried on with his conversation.

"Hey, it's me," Stew said.

Candice recognized his voice instantly. "What gives, playboy? Jesus! Four friggin' days it took you to get back to me!"

As Stew listened, Stephanie came to be by his side, embracing him with a day's worth of love and congratulations.

"I feel like I owe everybody an apology, Candice. Sorry about that."

"So what's goin' on? I've read all the press; the bad and the not so bad. I'm shocked! I'm friggin' shocked! Of all people, they had to kill *Trina*?"

"I know, I know," Stew said, as he was being warmed by Stephanie's caress.

"I sent that girl to you, Stew, Jesus! I feel like a doggone grim reaper."

"Don't sweat it, Candice. It could've been worse. The

investigator could be at *your* doorstep right now. They were asking all kinds of questions about where she came from; how'd I get to know her. All that jazz. But I kept your name out of it."

Stephanie started picking at Stew's zipper. He lightly smacked her hand away.

"Yeah, but these guys have a way of making up things, creating their *own* how's and why's."

"Trust me, I know. It's not pretty to be told you can't leave L.A."

"Wow! They told you that?"

"Well, they just changed their minds. I guess I'm off the hook. You never know what it feels like to be a suspect until you actually *are* one."

"Whooo, so is Canada still on?" Candice asked.

"Indeed. Everything is back to normal. Or, at least as normal as it can be without Trina. We'll give her the best funeral money can buy."

As Stew spoke, Stephanie persisted in tugging at his zipper. After a few seconds she succeeded, despite Stew's half-hearted protests.

"Any idea?" Candice asked.

"Uh, about what?"

"About who did it?"

"Not at all, Candice. I was just gonna ask *you* that." *Cut it out!* Stew mouthed to Stephanie. *This isn't the time or place!*

But Stephanie was in a playful mood, already with her hand inside his pants—already feeling him grow.

"Stew, honestly . . . The girl sent me some photos, I chatted with her, and I followed my vibe. She wasn't like Misty. I mean, I felt like I knew her personally. You all probably knew more about Trina than I did, ya know."

"Yeah, yeah," Stew said, no longer fighting off Stephanie. She had her head in his lap now. His erection in and out of her lips. "Uh, anyway . . . Business as usual, Candice, alright?"

"Sure. You should have fifteen girls waiting for you in Toronto on Thursday. That should give you a whole day to enjoy the atmosphere. Go sightseeing or something."

"Hmm . . . What a . . . a concept."

"What's that?"

"The sightseeing. Candice, I get more than enough of that. Trust me."

"Yeah, I hear," Candice said knowingly.

"Say good-bye, Candice."

"Good-bye. And don't come too fast, Stew."

Stew put the phone down and said, "Stephanie, you're gonna make me smack you."

Stephanie didn't answer, she just kept her momentum, pulling at Stew's foreskin, ignoring him and the rest of the world. Stew sat back, somehow still caught up in the past few hours—the fun he'd had at WKLA, and the excitement of the live radio. He considered the interest of the media and how *Access* would be following him from Malibu to Seattle to Canada. It was almost as if he were a rock star, and Stephanie was another of those rock star fringe benefits.

Back at the beach house, Stew sent Stephanie in after Timmy and asked to be left alone in the limousine. *Quiet time,* he called this. But in truth, he was recuperating. He got out about five minutes later and stretched, forcing his legs to overcome their stiff buckle. When he felt he'd recovered, he headed into the house with his usual swagger.

He knew that Stephanie was down in the master bedroom, packing a light travel bag for the Sunday-night flight, as he'd directed. While she was doing that, he went up to check on the state of affairs on the second and third floors.

It was Friday, a usually busy day for Platinum Dolls, with employees rushing about, most of them with that whole TGIF energy; that fever and motivation for spending money or maybe for some weekend R & R.

When Stew reached the second floor, where most of the girls slept, he noticed the new girls, Kim and Lisa. Lisa was a Korean girl whom he'd renamed Fabulous. The two were giggling and carrying on amid a couple of the other girls. Stew told himself that they seemed to blend in well. Rather quickly, actually. And it was in that instant when he wondered if that wasn't strange. But then he thought better of it. *It's just a girl thing,* and he kept moving toward the third floor. Barbara was there at the top of the landing. She had a sad smile on her face.

"What's wrong, my Hershey's Kiss?"

She smiled more broadly, but Stew could tell it was fabricated.

Barbara took a deep breath. "Nothing much. Just finished your itinerary for the weekend. There's the film shoot tonight and tomorrow night. Leslie wants to have a big dinner on Sunday—a little send-off. You know, the usual." Barbara handed Stew some slips of paper. "Your messages." Then she started to pivot away. "I should get back to work."

"Barbara, front and center. Now tell me what's wrong."

Stew took hold of Barbara's elbow. Girls were passing by on the stairway, preparing for the day's webcast. The business office down the hallway was buzzing with ringing phones. For privacy, Stew felt it was necessary to take Barbara aside, so they went into one of the bathrooms, and Stew locked the door.

"Alright. Spill it. What happened?"

As soon as the words left Stew's mouth, tears started rolling down Barbara's cheeks. She stammered through her sobs, a build-up from soft sorrow to hushed cry.

"Y-You're . . . y-you're leaving a-again."

"Okay. And?"

"I miss you, Stew. When you're not here, it's not the same."

Stew pulled Barbara in and embraced her. He sucked his teeth. "I thought you were hurt or in trouble or something. Silly woman! Didn't you do what I suggested? I thought you found someone. You gotta go out and *live,* Barbara."

"But, Stew. You don't understand. This *is* my life. I live to come work for you, to hear your voice every day, even if it's on the phone." Barbara's voice was muffled, but she'd managed to compose herself some. "And then you come back, and . . . and . . . I *need you, Stew Gregory.* You don't know how much I think about you. My every thought circles around your agenda, your business, and . . . I . . . Oh, *Stew!*"

Barbara collapsed against Stew's chest, distraught and desperate and missing him madly. He had been with Barbara twice in the past; the second time had been two months earlier. Since then, he'd made it clear that the sex wouldn't be frequent, that he'd be here today and gone tomorrow. After all, that was Stew's life.

His business had him bouncing around the country like a tennis ball. Stew had suggested that Barbara find somebody to love. He explained that he was a free spirit and that he couldn't be tied down or limited. Stew could only shake his head at the idea of his winning assistant, his Hershey's Kiss (the one with the spirited eyes and drop-dead-gorgeous body), was somehow stifled by his absence. *I can't be in eight places at the same time. Damn!*

"Listen to me, Barbara. And you listen good. I very much appreciate your devotion. You're my star assistant out here in Malibu, and my business affairs across the country go smoothly because of you. You do incredible phone," Stew said. It was an inside joke that the two had between them. Of course, "incredible phone" wasn't the only thing she did. "And all of my business associates say the same thing. *She's great! She's this, she's that.* But Barbara, I said this to you once, and I'm gonna say it—"

"I know, I know," she interrupted. "You're not a lover, you're a businessman."

"Thank you," Stew acknowledged.

"But, Stew, I don't need you to profess your love for me. You're a free agent, I know. I'm not askin' for you to marry me. I'm not askin' for much, just a little affection. It's been *two months,* Stew. I need you so much, I'm *trembling.*" Barbara threw her arms around his neck, her watery eyes beckoning his attention. Pleading, even.

"Barbara," Stew said, sounding exhausted, his thoughts lost.

But Barbara had already lifted up onto her toes and turned her lips to meet his. And Stew was captured, just like in the beginning. Just like he was whenever beauty called. Swallowed by it.

"Oh, Stew," she exclaimed, in between hungry kisses, her eyes closed in ecstasy.

Stew, already tapped of his urge and excitement, was numb in answering Barbara's assertiveness. He didn't have the energy for this, back to back with Stephanie's generous assault in the limousine just an hour ago. Stew couldn't help feeling withdrawn and somewhat used. Yet, still, for the sake of satisfying another one of his devotees, he hung in there.

Barbara slithered down Stew's body, unbuttoning his shirt and kissing him all the while. Stew stopped her. There was *no way* he could survive this twice over in so short a time. But when he saw the disappointment on Barbara's face, he conceded. She continued downward, until seconds later, Stew's pants were on the floor around his ankles. Barbara had him limp in her hands and in her mouth.

Is this what they all want? Just to suck my dick? Is that all I gotta give 'em to make 'em happy?

These thoughts formed even while his face twisted from the pleasure. Soon, he could feel himself getting aroused inside of Barbara's mouth. Those moist sounds that her lips, tongue, and breathing made turned him on even more. She was carrying on as if to save her own life. Unconsciously, Stew caressed her cheek and raked his fingers through her hair.

"Take it easy, Barbara. Please." Oh, how he *meant* that! And gently, her hands cuddled him, with her fingernails lovingly clawing underneath his scrotum. And that did it. Stew was alive again, standing like a stiff board. Moments later, Stew was on top of his assistant on the floor, inside of her, immersed in passion that he could never quite avoid. Consumed by emotions that he couldn't quite deny. No matter how hard he attempted to be a businessman (not a lover), he failed. And as Stew and Barbara fixed themselves, both spent in one way or another, Barbara again proclaimed her love. She thanked him, too; as if he'd provided a service.

"Well, if you *really* love me," Stew said, helping her fix her hair, "you'll straighten your bra and you'll go out there and do a good job for me. And I mean, I wanna see fireworks shootin', you hear me?"

"*Loud and clear*, boss. Maybe I'll do a backflip, too."

"What am I gonna do with you, Barbara?" It wasn't a question that required answering, since Stew was already turning away, heading back down to the kitchen.

It's been a helluva morning, but God, I need food.

Seattle, Washington

ELEVEN

For a company such as Platinum Dolls to make money, it had to have products and services to sell to its consumer base. It was not good enough to merely have a few hundred thousand visitors going to the website and then walking away without something tangible, or intangible.

Platinum Dolls' services included direct Internet access to any of the exclusive studios around the nation, most of them set up like the Malibu home, with a Studio A and a Studio B. A Web surfer could apply for any of three packages, be it the Bronze, Silver, or Gold. Bronze allowed a visitor access to any studio for an entire day, and access to other studios around the country during that same day. The Silver package allowed such access for an entire week, and the Gold, for an entire month. The package prices were three, fifteen, and twenty-five dollars.

Another service included the Platinum chat room, where individual conversations were held between web surfers and their favorite Internet babes. The chat rooms were a popular place for dialogue that involved everything from merely friendly to as raunchy as the personalities allowed. The price to use the chat room was ten dollars per hour, a service that the company offered even while the girls relaxed, exposed on a bed in Studio A or B, being watched by Internet voyeurs the world over and bringing in further revenue for the day.

Along with the services, there were the products. At midnight each day, Eastern Standard Time, an auction was held for viewers to purchase the intimate apparel, such as panties, brassieres, and other lingerie that had been worn by Platinum Dolls entertainers from any of the various locations during the course of their appearances on screen. Depending on what the performer participated in, whether it was some girl-on-girl frolic, or a masturbation scene, or even if the performer did nothing but lie on her stomach on the bed in a cut-off T-shirt and panties, painting her nails, website visitors and fans alike would log on for the midnight event to bid on the apparel. If ten to twelve performers appeared during the course of a day, and since there were eight sites—soon to be nine—there were always close to a hundred items available at auction. Panties and thongs were always the hottest items sold, earning anywhere from $450 to $25,000, depending on the popularity of the performer.

Stew always affirmed that it was personality that made money. For example, if Misty was in a great mood today and she showed it over the Internet, she'd have a large number of fans and viewers who'd want to know more about her. And how much closer could a fan get to Misty, short of being with her physically? The panties were the closest thing to her sugar walls. For that dirty old man in Wisconsin, or that blue-balled preacher from Mississippi, the panties were just as good as being there in person. What these clients did with the remnants of their website escapades was their concern. Maybe Misty's scent would linger on in their minds and fulfill their lonely, miserable lives. Or maybe, to smell her was to love her.

Platinum Dolls sold autographed photos, posters, baseball caps, T-shirts, and calendars that featured its beautiful girls. There were the porn films, the swimsuit videos, and *Platinum Magazine*, which had just been launched at the Scarsdale estate in New York in January, that included interviews and photo spreads with Platinum's top girls.

Beyond the tangible products, there was an incentive plan called the Platinum Plus program, where for a grand a year, a member had the best that Platinum Dolls had to offer. All access, all the time, videos sent once a month, and two of every hat, calendar, or T-shirt that was available. The subscriber also received a poster and a photo of every performer, autographed and sealed with a kiss, and a subscription to *Platinum Magazine*. And the greatest opportunity for a devoted customer, the chance to meet, mingle, and party with all the Platinum Dolls personalities at the big New Year's Eve bash in Atlanta, Georgia.

During that time, the website would operate on autopilot. Prerecorded footage of the various studios would be webcasted, and the auction would be shut down for the holidays. The entire Platinum Dolls staff would fly down to Atlanta for the gala event. They'd celebrate the growth and success of the company, and at the same time there'd be a significant degree of handling customer relations—those two thousand–plus members of the Platinum Plus program.

Every transaction on the Internet resulted in the immediate deposit of the funds into the L.T.S. Industries account; from the Bronze, Silver and Gold access, to the product sales and auctions, to the memberships, and right on down to the caps and T-shirts. L.T.S. stood for Lex, Trent, and Stew, who all had principle interest in Platinum Dolls. Betty was the L.T.S. accountant, handling tax filings, company ledgers, quarterly updates, and profit disbursements. She also took care of the extras, such as the time-share agreement that Stew had with AirPlus, a leader in the private airline industry.

Within an hour's notice, Stew could have a private jet fueled, staffed, and waiting for him at LAX, JFK, National in D.C., or Atlanta International, ready to take him to wherever his heart desired. The time-share could be for his exclusive use or for a shared ride with other elite passengers who also held time-shares and were bound for the same destination. But usually, Stew was alone on the jet; that is, alone with his staff.

On an early Monday morning, Stew's limo drove into L.A.X, where a Learjet was waiting to take him to Seattle. There

were cameramen and an on-location producer accompany-
ing Stew, capturing his every move along the way. The feature would inevitably be edited for showing on *Access
Hollywood* in less than a week for all of America to watch.

Stephanie was in the seat next to Stew while he spoke
with the accountant.

"Betty, I'm gonna need a check to go down to Sal for a little emergency he took care of. Trust him on the details. Also,
send Candice a commission check for forty-five hundred.
Oh, and if you would, give me an update on things. I'll be in
Seattle for breakfast. Call me there."

Betty gave an okay and Stew disconnected to speed dial
Seattle. He looked out the limousine window, anticipating
his words, thinking about a thousand different things, somehow oblivious of all the planes that were coming and going
in the sky, and unconcerned with the camera inside the limo
as it recorded his words and actions.

"MaryAnn, my sunshine. Whassup, girl?"

"Hi, *baby*. You on your way?"

Stew put a hand on Stephanie's knee. "Just getting to the
airport," Stew said. "Is everything cookies 'n cream over
there?"

"Very. Are you with them now?"

"Of course, of course."

"Well, since they're looking for a show, we're gonna give
'em one."

"Nothing too crazy." Stew smiled at Stephanie and the
curious expression on her face.

"Of course not. Just wait 'n see. You're gonna be proud of
me, baby."

"I already am," he replied casually.

"Will we have time alone?" MaryAnn asked.

"That depends on *how* proud I become." Stew smiled, not
revealing any of his personal business to those in the car.
"Now, say good-bye."

MaryAnn gave Stew an audible kiss through the phone
and he clicked it closed.

Once the limo cleared the gate and airport security, it

glided out onto the tarmac. Stew knocked at the window separating him from the front. Timmy was in the passenger's seat next to the driver, as usual.

"Yes, boss."

"How long 'till Seattle? I'm starved."

"Should be thirty minutes. Wanna stop for something? You know they'll have that good cuisine on the jet."

"Oooooh, yeah. That should be good," Stew said, and he unscrewed and downed a vial of ginseng, his quick fix for the morning, where others might have coffee. Minutes later, he was on the luxury jet with Stephanie and Timmy, and feeling free as a bird.

The moment Stew saw the Space Needle, erect in the air like most other breathtaking monuments, he could feel Seattle's energy. The dot-com millionaires infused the city with so much financial investment that one couldn't help but lose himself to the sports arenas, museums, and theaters the city had to offer. From the sky, Stew could see the tram that carried tourists around the huge metropolis. But Stew also knew that the city streets were spotted with homeless people, something that he wondered about since that day, years earlier, when he'd met Stephanie Koboyashi here.

Stephanie had been homeless on these streets, that the dot-com millionaires never quite cleaned up all the way. Back then he had come to be part of a big Internet expo, doing some of the grunt work that made Platinum Dolls what it was today. This was a three-day event, and Stew had leased space to further promote his company's growing website. It was grueling for sure, to try and maximize on all the valuable associations, business contracts, and opportunities that flooded the convention hall.

But at the end of the day, Stew would find relief meandering through the downtown area. He took in the sights, amused himself with the newest gadgets in the Sharper Image store, and purchased sweaters from Eddie Bauer, which were thick enough to handle the winter chill. All the while, Stew observed the heavy concentration of Native American residents who proudly expressed their culture through music, dance, and storytelling. He wondered how far their reservations were from downtown. He was even interested in seeing how and where they lived, except he never had that kind of time.

One evening, as he maneuvered through the throngs of pedestrians who were also navigating their way along Main Street, Stew nearly collided with a wandering girl.

"Sir? Can you help girl down on luck?"

"I . . . uh . . . excuse me," Stew said.

Not that he'd bumped into her, because he didn't, they only *nearly* made contact. But then there was something that told Stew she had targeted him. That the near miss was intentional. That she was desperate. And then those thoughts were banished from his mind as he took another look at the young woman. She couldn't have been more than seventeen years old. Her face was hauntingly bony. Her eyes were withdrawn in their sockets. Her clothing was dark, heavy, and tattered. Her hair was long and black, but dusty with lint and matted. Looking at her, Stew saw that she was of mixed race. And if she wasn't, she had to be the darkest Asian woman he'd ever met.

"Sure. I can give you something," Stew said, feeling his pockets for something manageable. "You look real hungry, Miss," he said, studying her.

She nodded, but her eyes were interested only in what might come out of his pockets.

"Would *this* help you?" Stew asked, as he handed her a twenty. Again, the girl managed a nod. And Stew shook his head in response. *Damn!*

"You want sucky-sucky?" she asked.

But sex was the furthest thing from Stew's mind. He was too caught up in how devastated this young girl—this young *woman*—appeared.

"Miss, the money is yours. You don't need to do any of that for me. It's from my heart, really."

She looked at him a little guiltily, before putting the money in her pocket.

Stew felt the urge to do something more. "Listen, I was

just going to have something to eat. Would you like to join me?" He pointed to a restaurant.

"Sorry. I cannot afford. I eat from back of pizza store. In back of restaurant."

Stew winced. "In back? No, listen. *I'm* paying. Do you understand me? I pay." Stew showed the young woman more cash. "You come with me." Stew patted her back as they headed toward the closest restaurant, Salmon King. The place was large inside, with a lobster tank, the lobsters crawling all over one another.

"Excuse me, but *that* is not permitted in here, sir." A man in a suit greeted them at the door.

"What are you talking about, '*that*'? She's eating with me. How dare you refer to her like that."

"I'm sorry, sir," said the man. "But we don't permit thieves in here, and I shall call the police if—"

"'Thieves'?" Stew looked toward his new acquaintance in time to see her turning back to go out the door.

"No, no, no, come back here, you." Stew grabbed her arm tightly, suddenly aware of how thin she was underneath the coat. "Sir, excuse me. But are you sure you're talking about the right girl?"

The distinguished gentleman said, "I'd stake my business on it."

"*Your* business? What did she take, sir?" Stew asked, his tight grip still on the woman's arm.

"This . . . this *thing* . . . reached in here and stole a lobster." He made a face. "The *audacity*."

"Can I ask you what that cost, sir?"

"It isn't a matter of cost. It's the *principle*. We don't want *it* in *here*," the gentleman said, reaching for the phone.

"Sir, wait. If you would. Please. I'd like to cover the cost of the lobster."

"You *would*? Is *that* so?" The man put his hands on his hips and said, "What if I told you *it* took *twenty* lobsters? Would you pay *then*?" The sarcasm in his tone and his raised eyebrow were becoming difficult to take, but Stew remained calm.

"Then . . . then I'd say you're being unreasonable, sir. I *know* she didn't take twenty lobsters. And I doubt she took even *two*. Look, I'm willing to pay for your most expensive dishes for me and the lady here. Plus, I'll cover what she took and promise you such a thing will never happen again. Would you work with me here? A little win-win, for a new visitor to your town?" Stew saw that the man's attitude was giving in. "I'm with the Internet convention, sir. I'm sure many of my comrades have been in your dining room this evening." Stew's name tag with the show's title was still pinned to his blazer.

"Well, would that be cash, sir?"

"If I must; if my credit card isn't good enough, cash. No problem."

Stew and his new friend were escorted to the farthest area of the restaurant. It was a booth and round table in a corner, suitable for a party of at least six, but Stew made no bones about it. He just sat down, taking a closer look at his dinner guest.

"A thief, huh?"

"I no thief. I hungry."

Stew could've cried at the sight of her, but he didn't. *Of course she took the lobster. She was starved.*

He thought back to when *he* was beaten and left for dead on I-80. He thought about Iris, the nurse who gave him special care and healed his wounds with ointment and his heart with her love. It was just a little bit of faith that helped him then. Eventually, once he and Iris became involved, he moved into her apartment, and it was her brother who had that little bit of faith that helped him further along, to the point that he could get his foot in the door of the Internet business world. It was all due to that first bit of assistance in his time of great need that he could then help himself. And because of that experience, Stew always gave of himself.

The food came and Stew's new friend ate like a starved castaway. He was almost embarrassed to watch. At the meal's end, after an obscene belch from the girl whose name he had just learned, Stew said, "Stephanie . . . I wanna change your life."

They left Salmon King and crossed the street to go inside the mall. Stew noticed that the mall security was paying quite a bit of attention to Stephanie. He wondered if she'd ever stolen from here, or if the security guards were merely suspicious. Stew took her into a half dozen clothing stores, spending hundreds of dollars at each stop. He asked the sales ladies on the sly what would look good on Stephanie. He asked them to suggest makeup. And he humbly purchased a bag full of feminine hygiene products.

"What can I do about her hair?" Stew asked a hairdresser.

The hairdresser wrinkled her nose and suggested a home visit. Stew knew that Stephanie smelled offensive and that he'd have to get her cleaned up first.

"I'm at the Four Seasons Hotel. Can you come by after work?" Stew left the hairdresser a hundred dollars to secure the deal.

Back at the Four Seasons, the hotel staff twisted their noses as Stew and Stephanie walked by. Stew had been with her so long that he didn't seem to notice her homeless vapors any more. If he hadn't been so interested in helping her, he'd have run away in the other direction. As they were about to step into the elevator, Stephanie pulled away.

"No. I no go. You rape me!" Stephanie said, her eyes skirting around wildly.

"Me? I don't wanna rape you. I wanna *help* you."

Stephanie was unconvinced. She turned to get away, but Stew grabbed her.

"Wait," Stew said, ignoring the nosy bystanders. "You want money, right?"

Stephanie looked at him warily but then nodded vigorously.

Stew dropped the shopping bags he held and reached into his pocket. He took out what money he had left. He felt this was the only thing she understood. Stew approached Stephanie and stuffed the money in her pocket. "Here. Take it all. Take the clothes, too. Enjoy, and good-bye." Stew got on the elevator and the doors closed behind him.

Ten minutes later, the phone rang in Stew's room. It was the reception desk downstairs. They wanted to know if the horrendous-smelling woman standing before them was a friend of his, and whether she was welcome to come up.

Stew didn't even hesitate. "It's okay. Yes."

Less than five minutes later, there was a knock at his hotel room door. Stew took his time answering it. He opened the door and stepped aside. The bellhop walked in with the shopping bags, put them down, and left after Stew tipped him.

"I sorry," Stephanie said.

With that first measure of trust, the programming had begun. There was the long shower, then the long bath. The hairdresser came to tend to Stephanie's ragged hair. When she was done, Stephanie had incredibly lustrous black hair. The only problem after that was that she was as thin as a pencil and malnourished.

Over the next few days Stew had Stephanie help him through the remainder of the convention. She slept in his bedroom at night, while he slept on the couch. When his stay in Seattle was over, Stew gave Stephanie the option of coming with him, or staying in Seattle. But as far as she was concerned, there was no option. She went with him back to Atlanta, the headquarters for Stew, Iris, and the challenging beginnings of Platinum Dolls.

Those memories were five years old; profound memories, indeed. And yet now as the Learjet cut down through the atmosphere heading for Seattle International Airport, Stew couldn't help but see how far Stephanie had come, thanks to his little bit of faith.

"Why you starin'?" Stephanie asked.

"Eight million reasons," Stew said.

"Well, dammit, gimme one."

Stew took a deep breath. "This is where it all began for you and me. Whaddya want me to say? I get the chills every time we come back this way."

"Remember Salmon King? And that man's face?" Stephanie asked.

"*Do I?* How about the people in the hotel elevator, when I stuffed the money in your pocket and left you?"

"You embarrassed me so bad."

"You? What about me? You were cryin' rape!"

"And I'm *still* cryin' rape. How about tonight?" Stephanie asked, eyeing him devilishly.

And as the jet descended into Seattle, the video camera caught this all on tape, further detailing the wild lifestyle of Stew Gregory, porn king.

Before Stew and company left the airplane, the on-location producer for *Access Hollywood* asked if he could have a few minutes to set up.

"This scene outside is *killer*," said the producer. "And I want to catch it all as you're getting off the jet."

Stew shrugged. If that was what floated their boat, then whatever.

The 8:00 A.M. scene out on the tarmac was fit for a sultan's welcome. There were close to two dozen girls out there in black fitted dresses, hinting at varying cleavage and reaching just below the hips. Each woman wore stilettos, and their hair was pulled back into slick ponytails. Some ponytails were longer than others—some reaching down to the lower back—yet all of these women, at first glance, appeared to be cut from the same mold.

Once the stairs were rolled over to the jet's exit, a red carpet was laid out, and the Seattle staff of the Platinum Dolls empire arranged themselves at the edges of the carpet and awaited their boss, their provider. Standing at the end of the carpet, close to the four limousines with their chauffeurs, was MaryAnn.

MaryAnn was to the Seattle site what Leslie was to the Malibu site. She kept things in motion. She held down the fort and made sure that business and pleasure mixed in a practical manner and according to the overall objectives of the company. In short, MaryAnn was the head bitch in charge.

Born and raised in Seattle, MaryAnn was one of the first few to show up when Stew decided to set up shop there. She had a work ethic that overwhelmed even Stew, offering to work for free to help launch the fourth location on the Platinum Dolls site. MaryAnn had a squeaky clean image, with dirty-blond hair and ivory-tan skin, and she could easily pass for the Swedish girl next door. She liked to wear her makeup conservatively and her hair in trendy styles. This morning, however, MaryAnn, like all the girls, had her hair pulled back into a shoulder-length ponytail. Her mascara-accented eyes seemed to draw Stew forward, as he left the jet and descended the steps in front of Stephanie and Timmy. Next to MaryAnn stood Hank, part of the new security that Timmy had instituted only days earlier.

Stew stopped to kiss the hand of each woman along the carpet, remembering their names—first names, at least—before approaching MaryAnn, his Seattle ace.

"And here we are," said Stew.

"Welcome home, Mister," MaryAnn said, as she met Stew's body with her own, her hands smooth against his chest and making a trail up and behind his neck. Not caring who was watching, she turned her head to kiss Stew sensually.

"Great show," Stew said.

"Just tell me you're proud enough to play house," she said.

Stephanie was but a few feet away, within earshot of both Stew and MaryAnn, but her face showed not a hint of concern.

"Hi, Mary," chirped Stephanie, and she stepped up to kiss MaryAnn's cheek. The two women exchanged a hug.

"What's it been? Three months?" asked MaryAnn.

"Too long, baby. Let's eat," Stephanie suggested.

The Seattle branch of Platinum Dolls was set up two blocks away from the Space Needle and the four-acre park surrounding it. The block where the business was situated, Chambers Street, was a street rich with two- and three-story manufacturing plants, warehouses, and office buildings. Most façades were red brick and glass. Platinum Dolls occupied the top floor of a four-story building at 247 Chambers Street. The entire floor was lofty enough to be set up as a duplex—with catwalks, open staircases, and ceiling fans—and it had the depth of a pro-basketball court. One could shout from one end of the facility to the other, and depending on what was going on at the time, that shout might not be heard.

The loft had once been used by a large printing press—complete with forklifts, partitioned offices, and room enough for stacks upon stacks of paper and giant rolls of paper. It was said that over one hundred workers had been there at one time, working various parts of the printing business. But when Stew walked in years later, the place was barren. The machines had been sold off, the paper auctioned off, and the building abandoned. Stew offered to lease the space for a grand a month, on a twenty-year lease. The owner took the deal once Stew mentioned the renovations he was going to make. Stew also agreed to rent increases in accordance with inevitable inflation.

For a landlord with an empty building—too huge for any one business at that time—there was nothing to lose. Within a month, Stew had the place steam-cleaned and painted, and wood flooring was installed. The upper rooms that had been offices were renovated into bedrooms and lounges (sixteen in all), the majority of which formed a U-shape and had terraces that were high up over the great opening in the center hall.

The centermost area of the warehouse had the feel of an atrium, with offices and studios set up right in the open, and an artificial indoor park designed to imitate an outdoor look. To complete the illusion, Stew even approved picnic tables, park benches, a waterfall (with rocks and a pond), as well as grassy areas, some of which were often used for miniature golf. The park was landscaped with rocks, artificial grass, real trees, and winding paths of cobblestone. Finally, there was accent lighting set into the small dirt hills alongside the plants and flowers.

Just as Malibu had its beachfront setting, the Seattle

location was set up with the indoor park for the same reason. Sure, it was a magnificent atmosphere to work in, but Stew wasn't in it just to make his staff comfortable. No, this indoor paradise served as a convenient setting for videos.

Day or night, a web surfer could visit the Seattle location on the Platinum Dolls site and see one of a number of beautiful girls stretched out on a park bench or a patch of lawn. The same park setting was also used as the stage for the ever-popular Platinum Dolls girl-on-girl videos. Where Malibu shoots resulted in *Platinum Dolls Presents: Sex in the Sand* and *The Ocean Between My Legs*, Seattle video shoots gave the public *Doin' It in the Park*, *It's Raw Outdoors*, and *It's Raw Outdoors II*. These videos were sold as fast as they were produced.

And just as the other sites, Seattle had its Studio A and Studio B, its business offices, home theater, and all the amenities of home.

MaryAnn, Stephanie, and Stew were joined by three other Internet babes for the drive to Chambers Street. The *Access Hollywood* team was in Stew's limo as well, as it and the other three cars, assembled in a motorcade, made their way toward downtown Seattle.

"I don't know about you guys, but I'm starved," said Stew, striking up some conversation in the name of entertainment. There was agreement from all, and MaryAnn followed up with a phone call to check on the catering for Stew's arrival.

"So how's work, Andrea?" asked Stew.

Andrea sat in the middle of the three performers. She had a distinct heart-shaped face, smart almond eyes, and full lips. Stew remembered Andrea's name because of her cheeks. Hers profoundly flattered her face and gave her a sweet smile. So whenever he thought of her, he recalled the first three letters of her name—*A N D*—which stood for extra . . . more . . . additional. *The woman had extra cheeks*! As silly as that may have sounded, this was Stew's way of associating faces and names, which was key in any leadership position.

"Work is good," replied Andrea. "I get a kick out of the Web surfers I meet over the Internet. Interesting conversationalists. A lot of them are predictable—"

"*Predictable* is *right*," said Sparkle, the platinum blonde to the left of Andrea. They made eyes at each other, as if they knew a secret.

Stew could *never* forget Sparkle's name, because that's what her eyes did. They sparkled. Sparkle had the face of a cookie-cut pop singer, with those all-American-girl features. The cute nose that wriggled, and the clever eyes that somehow knew their way through life. Stew was stuck on Sparkle's lips. Of all the things to think about, he suddenly knew where he wanted those lips to be. He hadn't had her yet, so it would be something new for Stew. And something new was always something nice.

"I like the end of the day," said Sandy, just as shapely and alluring as her coworkers.

Sandy: *the Cleopatra of Seattle*, Stew recalled. Camay complexion. Her mouth always formed in a pretty pout.

"The auction keeps things competitive," Sandy went on. "Keeps things exciting. We're always saying things like, whose underwear will make the most tonight?"

There were giggles in response.

"We're always like, hey, she did such-and-such with so-and-so, and her stuff is nasty. . . . But those are the panties that always sell the best."

The giggles again.

Stew and MaryAnn locked eyes for a moment, aware that the camera was capturing all of this raw dialogue. *Access* was certainly going to get what they bargained for. By the looks of things so far, it was gonna be an exciting three days in Seattle.

"I want to make a toast before we dig into all of this delicious-looking food," said Stew.

A banquet table was set up on the patio, in the center of the indoor park. The entire Seattle staff, including the thirty performers and the twenty-two behind-the-scenes personnel, were there with the caterers, who were busy making thick French waffles and standing over bowls of fruit, skillets of warm omelets, and cartons and pots of breakfast drinks—tomato juice, orange juice, apple juice, and coffee. The aroma of it all filled the air, mixing with everyone's fresh morning fragrance.

"Here's to three of our Seattle branch's most important years, and to all of the staff and the performers who have worked tirelessly to make my dream . . . *our* dream—Platinum Dolls—a major success. I know it's early, but I gotta do this: *hip-hip!*"

"*Hooraay!*"

"*Hip-hip!*"

"*Hooraay!*"

"*Hip-hip!*"

"*Hooraay!*"

"Good, good. Now that *everybody* is awake, I'd like to commend two very important people. As they say, these people deserve their props!"

There was brief laughter among some sixty early risers.

"This woman inspired the Seattle site. She was the reason I came back here. She's one of the sharpest women I know, and her roll in Platinum Dolls is indispensable. If I haven't made myself clear, then let me do that now. I'm saying we'd be *nowhere* without this woman. She's struggled through a history of family tragedies, her ancestors were once banished from ports northwest of here, due to the war and the bombing of Pearl Harbor. Now, I know, for most of us, the mention of such a long-ago occurrence is very distant from who we are and what we do day-to-day. But for her, the past means *everything*. The past had her struggling as a child, picking strawberries as a field worker at ages four, five, and six. The past had this woman run away from the circumstances that essentially imprisoned her as a teenager. The past found her homeless here in the streets of Seattle. So, I'd like to take this very special moment to give props where props are due. Here's to a survivor. Here's to a woman of the world. And here's to one of the sexiest executive assistants I know. Miss *Stephanie Koboyashi*!"

Applause and whistles filled the facility, probably the most ruckus the place had experienced since the printing presses. Stephanie cupped her hands beneath her watery eyes, covering her mouth in complete shock. Stephanie shivered in acknowledgment of his kind words, as MaryAnn helped her to where Stew was standing. The applause continued.

"Speech! Speech! Speech! Speech!" the crowd shouted.

Stew hugged Stephanie, kissing her lips and forehead. "Be strong, baby. This is for you. You're a leader. Now tighten up and say a few words." Stew tapped her lightly on the ass with his palm. Encouragement.

"Speech! Speech! Speech! Speech!"

Stew raised his hand and the room quickly hushed.

"You know . . . This man . . . This . . . *man* . . ." Stephanie was shaking her finger at Stew, tears trailing down her cheeks. MaryAnn patted her face dry with a napkin. "He just doesn't know. He has no *fucking* idea—excuse my Japanese—what he's working with. Every day I see it." Stephanie took the tissues from MaryAnn and blew her nose. "Thank you, MaryAnn. Every day I see how much love and devotion surrounds this man. He's a freakin' magnet and he pulls at people's hearts because of who he is. He's frank and he's honest, and *damn*—you can't get that anywhere today. So, thank *you*, Stew. Thank you for making me a part of your dream."

The applause built up.

"Steph-y! Steph-y! Steph-y!"

Stephanie hugged Stew again. "I love your fuckin' ass," she said quietly, for his ears only. He stroked her hair then raised his hand again.

"Okay, okay. Now we need to wind up the congratulations. It's time to get back to work, so I'mma keep this simple. This woman is a *beast*. She's one of the sharpest women

I know in the Internet business. She's also the captain of the Battleship Seattle. If there's a problem here, she can solve it. If there's no problem, then the woman is just *not happy!*"

Laughter filled the room.

"In fact, if half the men who visit our site knew what I know about MaryAnn, they'd probably crash our doors down to meet her. But we got her first! So thank God for small favors!"

More laughter and applause.

"But seriously, I couldn't run this leg of the business without your leader, your boss, your friend and mine. MaryAnn Russo!"

The applause tore through the air. And now MaryAnn's eyes watered some. She wasn't as emotional as Stephanie, yet she was humble and appreciative. She came over to hug and kiss Stew. And now MaryAnn was in his ear. "I'm hungry, Stew," she said. But she wasn't talking about food, and Stew knew it.

"Speech! Speech! Speech! Speech!"

"So let's eat," Stew said, looking at her but not committing to anything in particular.

MaryAnn made mock-evil eyes at him, then turned toward the crowd to speak. "Listen, you guys see me every day. You know I love you all. And we all love this man, and Stephanie, too. Platinum Dolls is as much of a dream come true for me as it is a business. It puts food on our tables. We're all provided for and living lives of financial freedom. We go on trips. We meet exciting people, and we keep growing. So I raise my glass and I encourage you all to do the same.

"Long live Platinum Dolls!"

"Long live Platinum Dolls!"

"Now, beautiful, voluptuous felines, you be sure and make our guests feel at home. And, uh, here's my very first order of the day—me being the captain of this battleship and all—let's *eat!*"

Applause and whistles followed. Music began to play and everyone started talking among themselves. The chefs performed their magic, dishing up plates and smiling, while many tried to capture Stew's attention with short conversation. Stew tried to speak with everyone he could, being as charismatic as possible, infusing a fresh energy into his workers. They didn't get to see him often. And if he didn't have time to make another quarterly visit, such as this one, it might be six months before the next one. Blame the Internet, and how things became universal over the years.

No matter how broad or vast his empire, it all boiled down to one entity: the website. Everything else was mere duplication. One branch of the business—be it Malibu, Seattle, or New York—was no different than any other branch. Sure, the people and their personalities were different, but the way business was done was the same. One set of rules, one set of instructions, all overseen by a business/office manager. The rest, as they say, was gravy. Money was being made. Betty cut the checks, and Stew's bank account continued to grow.

If there was a problem, it was Stew's to resolve. But he was just one man. One man who was spread out, sometimes too thin for his own good.

"Steph, I'm gonna go over some figures with MaryAnn," Stew said, as Stephanie took his empty plate.

"Adding or subtracting?" asked Stephanie. "Or will you be multiplying?" Stephanie looked at him knowingly, eyebrows raised.

But Stew didn't take the bait. He couldn't tell if Stephanie was serious or kidding, if she was showing jealousy.

"Umm, a little of everything?" He winced playfully.

Stephanie was coy about it. She stepped up and whispered into his ear, "You do all the math you want. Just know that I'll be waiting for you later . . . to do some multiplication of my own." Stephanie looked over Stew's shoulder as she spoke. MaryAnn was in the distance, apparently patient, waiting, with her eyes fixed elsewhere. But Stephanie was a woman who had grown aware; aware enough to see through charades. Aware enough not to be stupid.

"And you make sure you fuck her for me, too." Stephanie pivoted away, all smiles and not an ounce of scorn about her. She had grown accustomed to this.

Stew shrugged. There were figures to get to. And MaryAnn was waiting. Patiently.

TWELVE

"I can't wait to show you my new place, Stew," MaryAnn said. The two were being chauffeured away from the rear entrance of the Chambers Street loft. It was a little getaway they managed in order to avoid the *Access* crew. This liaison was definitely none of their business.

"I can't wait to see it," Stew replied. "Update me about Seattle. How's the staff? Anything new and exciting?" Stew always referred to the Chambers Street location as Seattle, just as his other sites were named for their location.

"Just like it's always been, Stew. Business as usual. I've had a couple girls leave—one was using drugs, and she's in a drug program now, the other suddenly left the state. I think it was a fan of hers, and the two may have built something bigger than a business relationship."

"That's something we've gotta be careful about, Mary. If all our girls fell in love with customers, we'd have no talent left. The business would be nothing short of prostitution."

"I know. I've gotta say though, that most of the girls are dedicated. They never cross the line. I've banged it into their heads over and over, that *once they give it away, there's no more fantasy*. There's nothing left to buy."

"I guess we'll always get a weak one here and there," Stew said. "So how far is this penthouse of yours?"

"Actually, just a block or so."

"Oh, close!"

"I *am* dedicated. I *must* be close to the loft."

"Good."

"And as far as excitement, you know the business, Stew. Every day's exciting. I'll tell you one thing. A lot of our girls— I'd say twenty of them, at least—have become bisexual. There's a few that call themselves *strictly dickly,* but those that *really* get into the sex on camera, those that are *really* making us the most money? It's the girls who have relationships with other girls. They've learned to love the lifestyle. And it's all your fault!"

"Hey, listen. I'm just providing a service, entertainment. I can't help it if they can't separate business and pleasure."

"Mmm-hmm. And turning girls out in the process. Hey, I'm kidding. You know I'm with you till the end, Stew. And look at it this way, you're not hurting anybody. And whatever these girls are is harmless. A lot of 'em do it for safe companionship, ya know?"

Stew said nothing. Maybe that was the only moral sacrifice here, this accepted practice that he perpetuated. But then if he wasn't making money from it, someone else definitely would.

"Is this it?" Stew asked, looking out of the car window at a doorman posted in front of a limestone high-rise. An oval drive-through led up to it, and from outside, an all-glass lobby brilliantly lit up by chandeliers was visible.

"Yup. We're here," Mary Ann said.

The doorman came to stand by, as Timmy opened the rear door. MaryAnn stepped out, then Stew.

"Hi, Jerkins."

"Ms. Russo."

Stew approached Timmy and said, "We'll be a while, Timmy."

Timmy concealed a smile and nodded, not saying a word.

In the building's elevator, the two of them alone, MaryAnn kept a respectable distance in her black dress and pumps. The business manager and her boss.

"So who stays here with you?"

"Are you asking me if I have a man?"

Stew looked over at her without an answer.

"I *don't* have a man, Stew. And *that's* crazy. I'm twenty-five. I'm making fabulous money. I'm in control of an arm of a big business, and I'm without a man. Now, how do you suppose that feels?"

Stew didn't answer. After all, what could he possibly say to that?

The elevator doors opened and the two headed down a hallway. MaryAnn took out her key and pushed it in the lock, but before she entered, she turned toward her boss, her back to the door.

"What you're gonna see might surprise you, Stew. I hope you'll still respect me."

"What are you talkin' about?"

"Kiss me?" MaryAnn seemed to need some confirmation.

"You're buggin'," he said, and he stepped in to kiss her. It was a longer kiss than any that morning.

MaryAnn pushed her back and ass into the door and the two walked in. Brilliant light embraced them from a wall of floor-to-ceiling windows. The sheer curtains made downtown Seattle a mere silhouette beyond the windows.

Sucked into this inviting atmosphere, Stew stepped down from the entryway into a sunken living room, furnished with cosmopolitan flair. His eyes danced around the residence, taking in the marble floors, the plush carpet beyond that, the decorative lighting, the potted plants, and the art on the walls.

"Oh shit!" Stew exclaimed, as he caught sight of a poster-sized portrait. MaryAnn was quick to join Stew, waiting for his response.

"That's—"

"Yes, Stew. That's me."

"And—

"Sparkle," MaryAnn said. She had her hands clasped behind her back as she walked away, knowing he'd want an explanation. Knowing he'd follow her.

Stew was bewitched by the image he saw. It was a black-and-white photograph. MaryAnn was sitting on the floor, and Sparkle was right behind her, also seated. The two were intimately close. MaryAnn sat with her back to Sparkle's breasts. Both women were absolutely nude.

Stew turned to say something to MaryAnn, but she had walked away. *A lot of our girls have become bisexual.* And *now* Stew read between the lines.

"Mary—MaryAnn!" Stew went to look for her.

MaryAnn was in her bedroom, standing still a few feet past the doorway and near her queen-sized bed. She had her back to Stew, as he came in after her.

"Okay, so you took a picture," Stew said, already assuming that there was more to it than met the eye.

MaryAnn had her head and face in one hand.

"Turn around," Stew said. "Turn *around*." Stew helped her. She hadn't yet shown Stew this face. Not ever. It was a defeated face. Nothing like the business-minded woman he'd come to know. Nothing daring like the woman he'd slept with maybe five times over the years.

"Are you *kidding,* Mary? You're *ashamed* of that photo? That photo is some dope shit."

"Stew. Sparkle and I *live* together. We're lovers."

"And?"

"And I got tired of being lonely. *And* I got tired of men who had nothing to offer, who still lived with mommy, or who couldn't compete with my intelligence. And even if *all that* didn't matter, they'd be intimidated by my . . . Well, my power."

"Okay. So you found a friend. I still can't see the big deal."

"A lover, Stew. Not just a friend."

"So, are you happy?"

"She makes me happy, yes. But it's not the same, Stew. She's my fucking *employee*! She does what I *tell* her. It's not like having a man with whom you can give and take."

"I'm surprised at you, Mary. What about your ivory tower upbringing? All these dot-com men up here with interest in this company and that, and you can't find—"

"Stew, it's not as easy as it sounds. I'm a homebody, and

Platinum Dolls is my home. I have very little time for bull-shit. Very little time for little boys, who only want to show off their little toys. I went out with a Microsoft guy once. Harvard grad. Porsche. Nice bank account. Trust fund. Good family. All the bells and whistles. But guess what? He wasn't for me. He was the type of guy who was afraid to kiss on the first date. *Huh?* With *me*? Miss Seattle-porn-site-manager? In a way I'm jaded, Stew. I'm a demanding woman. No time for red tape and la-di-dah. When I want it, I want it *now.* I can't tiptoe into relationships anymore. Those days are over and done."

MaryAnn had begun to pace back and forth, like she was speaking at a board meeting. And Stew liked that. It was the reason he hired her: for the dominance she projected. It also turned him on.

"So if Sparkle—who, by the way, looks just like that *I Dream of Jeannie* broad—is making you happy, then what's the problem?"

"Stew, wake up! I can't *marry* her. I can't make babies with her. She can't *fulfill* me!"

Stew put his hand to MaryAnn's cheek and encircled her waist with his other arm. She felt warm and her skin was a little flushed. "You sound a little frustrated, Mary."

Mary let out an exhausted sigh. "*Yes*," she murmured.

Stew stood behind her. He massaged her shoulders and she rolled her head around, getting the most of this. Stew eventually freed her hair out of the ponytail.

"Sounds like maybe the big battleship captain needs special attention. . . ."

"*Yesss,*" she murmured.

"The boss—the lady with all the power—callin' the shots . . . hiring and firing. And she see something she wants, huh? Something just within reach."

"Mmm-hmm . . ."

"Could that be me?"

"Yes. Yes, Stew. It *is* you. I want *you!*"

"How bad?" Stew said over her shoulder into her ear.

"Very! Why are you teasing me?"

"I'm not. Really. I just wondered, could it be you're . . . a little . . . desperate?"

"A little."

"A lot, huh?"

She sighed heavily. "Okay. I'm a lot desperate."

"And, uhh . . . what about *I Dream of Jeannie*?"

"What *about* her?"

"Won't she be jealous?"

"What she doesn't know won't hurt her. And besides, this isn't about her. It's about you and me."

"Oooh . . . a vicious bitch, aren't you."

"I've been called worse."

Stew came around and stood in front of her. He backed up and inspected MaryAnn from head to foot. "You know, I sometimes find myself in the same predicament as you."

"How's that?" MaryAnn asked, crossing her arms, feeling naked in front of Stew's peering eyes.

"Well, sometimes women don't totally satisfy me."

"You're not even going to tell me what I think—"

"*Fuck no*," Stew said, then sucked on his teeth. "Men are the *last* thing on my mind. I can't even believe you would go there."

"Sorry."

"Over three hundred women working for me, many of them begging for me to be their man, and you have the nerve to even suggest—"

"I'm sorry. I'm *sorry!*"

Stew took in an angry breath. "As I was saying, one woman doesn't do it for me. I'm a man who came back from his deathbed, baby. And now that I'm living again, I want it all."

MaryAnn knew the story as well as everyone else.

"And why *shouldn't* I have it all?"

"You should. I agree."

"So now, back to you. You're a woman of means. You've got your nice place to live, your secure job, I'm payin' you an asshole full of money. Don't gripe, baby. Go out and get yours. You're twenty-five and alive. How many women can claim what you have? Your intelligence? Your wit? Your looks?"

MaryAnn seemed to lose some of the tension.

"Pick your goddamn chin up off the floor. *You hear me?*"

MaryAnn nodded. It was the response Stew was looking for. He wanted her inspired, but submissive to him. Let her use her so-called power where it counted.

"Now, I didn't come here to give a speech, and I've seen enough penthouses to throw up. I came here for one thing and one thing only."

"Damn you, Stew! You turn me *right on.*"

"Prove it. Come up out of that dress. And I don't have all day."

MaryAnn wiped a happy tear away and rushed to peel the dress from her shoulders. Then she worked it down over her ivory breasts, wiggling it down past her hips. Stew tucked his thumbs into his waist and stood cavalier before her. He took in her sense of urgency, her hunger, and her nervousness. She just wanted to please him, just as they *all* did. Just because of who he was, because of *his* power.

MaryAnn stood before him, expectantly, in her bra and panties.

Stew frowned, and she immediately understood. In seconds, she peeled off her undergarments and stood there naked.

Stew made MaryAnn stand there, as he took in the sight of her breasts, jutting out like those of a healthy farm girl. And she was shaved down between her legs, which he always remembered about her. As MaryAnn stood at the mercy of Stew's will, waiting for his next breath, he approached her. He didn't touch, only circled around her, continuing to look her over.

"Why should you be any different than any other girl?" he asked, snatching a handful of her hair, and yanking her toward him. "You're just another piece of ass to me, girl." He kissed her and then quickly pulled away. MaryAnn was suspended there, humiliated and yet captivated, wanting more. "A piece of *white* ass at that," Stew complained. He was back in front of her now. "Can you do *tricks*?"

"You know I can, Stew. What do you want?"

Stew snatched MaryAnn's panties up off the floor, and seconds later had her wearing them on her head. He adjusted them so that the crotch was right over her nose, and she'd be inhaling her own scent. "Now that's a trick." He laughed aloud.

"Stew?" MaryAnn had her hands on her hips.

"Take your hands down. You're not in charge here. I am!" MaryAnn did as she was told.

"Now how about laying on the bed? Feet up near the pillow. I got another trick for you."

Through the openings in her underwear, MaryAnn looked curiously at Stew. He could see her crooked smile as she got on the bed, still willing . . . still cooperative.

"On your back," he said. And Stew began to pull down his trousers and take off his shirt. Eventually, all he had on were his socks and boxers.

"Scoot down some so that your head's hanging off the bed. Come on!" Stew ordered MaryAnn like an irate drill sergeant. And she obeyed like a humble recruit.

"Yes, baby." MaryAnn's naked body was stretched out across the length of her bed, her faced masked by her panties, as her head hung down over the edge near where Stew stood.

"Now find the dragon," Stew said. "Put it where it belongs!"

MaryAnn instinctively reached back behind her and slid her hands inside of his boxers. Stew was partially erect when she exposed him.

Stew moved in closer so that MaryAnn had only one option: to take him in her mouth. He quickly grew between her lips, as she massaged him with both hands, breathing as best she could. Stew reached down and caressed her neck, anticipating his muscle working its way down her throat. Her throat muscles opened under his touch. "That's right, girl. Take it slow. I wanna see it all disappear. Every inch." And he leaned in more, molding his hands over her breasts, pinching her nipples. MaryAnn still had the panties over her face, still the circus act doing tricks.

Stew was enjoying this, his thrills met by her cooperation. Her dominance subdued by his directives, controlled
by his will. No matter *what* went on while Stew was away,
MaryAnn didn't belong to Sparkle. She belonged to *him*.

"Keep it there. Right there." He bent over and grabbed
MaryAnn's waist. He lifted her up so that her hairless pussy
was close to his face, while holding her upside down, still
with Stew full in her mouth, her legs clasped around his neck.

MaryAnn gasped in surprise, but once they were steady—
Stew standing upright and holding her tight against his
body—she continued to engross herself with pleasuring him,
her sounds alone filling the room.

Stew deliberated as he blew his warm breath onto her.
Whenever he breathed on her she moaned. She wanted his
mouth on her, and he knew it. He was sending chills down
her spine; a sensation that caused her to shudder, and she
sucked on him ever more senselessly as her only means of
returning the pleasure. But Stew didn't put his mouth on her.
He merely kept her wanting.

Suddenly Stew said, "You want my tongue, don't you?"

A muffled "mmm-hmm" was all that MaryAnn could
manage. Stew let her down until she was back laying on the
bed. The panties had worked their way off her head.

"Make love to me, Stew." MaryAnn was facing him now.
"Make me your woman."

Stew chuckled some and said, "You're *already* my woman."

"Then make me *more* woman," she countered.

"Show me where you want me. Lemme see it," Stew said.

MaryAnn turned her body around so that she was on her
back, her legs opened, exposing everything.

"Play with it," Stew said, his fingers stroking his chin.
"Make believe the world is watching."

"Oh, Stew." MaryAnn gasped, her head turned sideways
on the bed and her hands toying with herself. "*Ohhh . . .*" She
sighed.

"That's right, Mary. I wanna hear you. Loud and proud,
Miss Captain-of-battleship-Seattle. Beg for it," he said.

Then Stew turned away and went to the sheer curtains of

the bedroom. He opened them and looked down at the streets and the rooftops. He gazed at the buildings below the penthouse and in the direction of Chambers Street. He did this casually, as though there wasn't a woman behind him begging for him to stick it to her. And as high as MaryAnn's penthouse was, nobody could see Stew standing there naked, unless of course they had a telescope. *So what*, he thought.

"Oooh, baby. Come and put your big black dick in my pussy. . . ."

Seattle was out there in the distance, while behind him, with her fingers pushing in and out of her walls, was one of Seattle's daughters. A pretty white girl, too. Somebody's dot-com fantasy answering to his every whim.

Stew had been against this once upon a time. Never had he considered fucking a white girl. But then came his struggle of life and death, and he was born again. He'd met Iris, who was also white and who'd nursed him back to health, and then some.

Thoughts of Iris caused Stew to look down at his knee. The scars—even many of the mental ones—had faded some. It didn't hurt that he had everything to live for these days.

MaryAnn's pleas filled the room again. "Baby, make me come. Take my love. Take *all of me*. I want all of your dick in me! Please, please, please, Stew. Come and fuck your piece of white ass!"

MaryAnn sounded strung out, and Stew was getting an absolute kick out of her trying to talk dirty. Proper speech from his Seattle business manager on the one hand, and then just like that she makes a complete three sixty turn into a superslut. Too funny.

Stew turned back to MaryAnn and propped his foot on the bed, resting his elbow on his knee so that he could take an exclusive look at this show—MaryAnn carrying on like an amateur porn chick. It was times like these that Stew realized the truth about women; that they were freaks, just like men. Every last one of 'em. It was just a matter of the right person to bring it out. And, of course, the timing had to be right.

Look at this fool. A smart fool; but a damn fool. Stew

considered this, but then he remembered how even he had the wildest thoughts right before he was sexually satisfied. Something that he was now ready for, as he mounted MaryAnn.

"Who's your daddy?"

"You are. Ooh, ooh!"

"Whose pussy is it? *Whose*?"

"Yours, daddy! Y-Y-*Yours*, da—*ddy*!" MaryAnn went on shrieking in the name of pleasure; sounds that moved Stew to thrust harder and wilder. He bent her legs back so that her knees were by her ears. He knew she couldn't take all of him, and if she did it would be painful. But if he hit it just right, there was that *good* pain. And that's what Stew hammered her with, again and again, until MaryAnn was screaming and shaking and grabbing Stew's body just to have him stay inside of her.

She wanted to have him close to her for the finish. But Stew didn't want it to end there. He didn't want to make babies yet, didn't want anything tying him down. Tense and ready to burst, Stew rolled over on his back and with MaryAnn's hair clutched in his hand, he directed her head immediately to his throbbing dick so that he was wet in her mouth once again. And as he lay there with her pulling at his foreskin, working frantically to reciprocate the thorough joy he'd given her, he thought about Sparkle and MaryAnn. He thought about what MaryAnn had said. *She's my fucking employee. She does what I tell her.* And at that instant his mind and his loins reached a definite conclusion. It was the irony of MaryAnn switching roles that caused his body to suddenly flush with that familiar release, all of it pushing into her mouth. And she seemed helpless down there before him. Seattle's daughter trying to take on more than she could swallow. Stew snickered under his breath, her words still fresh in his mind. *She's my fucking employee. She does what I tell her.* Exactly!

Both Stew and MaryAnn laid spent on her bed. He was trying to catch a quick nap. For him, it was the previous night's dinner party in Malibu that wore him out. For MaryAnn, however, this was bliss, to be laying against Stew's bare chest, cooing and rambling and praising his existence and all that he meant to her.

"I'm gonna spend all day today with Stephanie. Tomorrow too," Stew said. "We'll be at the site most of Tuesday."

"Can you come back here Tuesday night?"

"I don't know, MaryAnn. Stephanie is true to me, ya know. And I don't want to keep ducking in and out, if you know what I mean."

"Yeah. She sure looked funny this morning when you told her—"

"She knows about us, MaryAnn."

"I figured as much."

"How?"

"It's a woman thing. Trust me. Just when you think we don't know? We know."

"We've gotta look at things logically, baby. I don't think I'd have a problem with seeing you once when I come here. But time just doesn't permit us to be at this all day. Number one, I'm only one man—"

"Wish I could have a clone of you," MaryAnn interrupted.

Stew ignored her comment. "And number two, there are only twenty-four hours in a day."

"If I could be your executive assistant—"

"Shut your mouth! Don't say another word! Stephanie is my assistant, and you *know* that!"

"Stew, I was just—"

"You were *just* going too far. Sometimes you have to accept things the way they are, MaryAnn."

"I know," she said when Stew simmered down. "I know. Can I ask you something else?"

"What's that?"

"Do you think you could ever use *two* assistants?"

"When I do, you'll be the first to know," Stew lied.

MaryAnn smiled and snuggled to Stew's chest again.

"You make me so happy, Stew."

"I know, MaryAnn," he answered boldly. "Oh, Mary?"

"Yes?"

"It's been like thirty minutes since I came. This could be your last shot for a few months."

"Say no more," MaryAnn said. And she went back down to take him in her mouth.

THIRTEEN

At 11:00 A.M., Stew left MaryAnn alone and headed back to Chambers Street. Business was in full swing by now. He stopped into each area of the loft and stood inside the doorways of the studios, watching the performers as they pretended to be casual; pretending that this was their actual bedroom being exposed to the world. In Studio A, Andrea was in a chair with a flimsy nightgown on. Her foot was propped up on a hassock so that she could paint her toenails. In the same studio, Jackie was on the bed beside Tina, both of them wearing see-through teddys. Jackie was laying on her stomach, looking at a fashion magazine, while Tina sat with her legs crossed, operating a laptop computer. Stew knew these to be warm-up activities before the forthcoming main events in which the girls became physically involved. Andrea was pretending to be the third leg and she would sit and watch the two until she eventually joined in.

In Studio B, Stew immediately focused on Sparkle. She was laying on the bed having a conversation with Wendy. Both of them had only bikini bottoms on and laid topless on their sides. Stew could imagine the internet viewers, their eyes glued to their computer screens and their hands between their legs. He also knew that many of Platinum's clients were executives, logging on from their smug offices.

Very little work getting done, thanks to us.

Stew smiled to himself as he watched Sparkle, thinking about how his dick and her mouth had been in the same place. But he soon shook off the spell.

There were three other girls on the floor in Studio B; Olivia was in a lavender brassiere and panties, and Tammy was applying body lotion to Pamela, who was totally nude and laying on her stomach.

Stew could easily calculate in his mind the build-up of internet viewers. He'd seen it plenty of times in his tracking and the weekly reports that he was given. It was almost always inevitable, with all of this flesh showing, that the numbers would remain at a certain average. And to think, it wasn't even noon yet.

The business offices were abuzz and the makeup and powder rooms were busy with performers preparing to take the next shift at one o'clock.

"Stew, Betty on line four," said Stephanie, who was busy at the phone in MaryAnn's office. They hadn't seen each other since earlier, when he'd left for the penthouse.

"You okay?" Stew asked before he took the phone.

"Great. You *relaxed*?" asked Stephanie, flashing a knowing smile. Stew could see some forgiveness in that smile. Or maybe it was compassion for some kind of sickness that he had.

"This is Stew. Talk to me."

"Hey. You wanted figures."

"Okay. Ready." Stew put a pen to pad.

"L.T.S., seventeen million on account. Six million four hundred thousand in debentures that come due by Friday. The leaves eleven-point-six as a net."

"*Man!* And my personal?"

"Four million seven hundred thousand. You have sixteen thousand in debentures that also should clear by Friday. Your balance, four million six hundred thousand eighty-four."

"And on L.T.S., did that include Sal's payment?"

"Yes. I cut him a check already. Two hundred and seventeen thousand. FedEx."

"Good. Any idea where the increases came from on L.T.S.?"

"Malibu. New York. Malibu had over four thousand transactions in the last week. New York, half as much."

"Wow."

"But overall, there's been a forty percent increase since . . . well, the incident."

"Crazy, huh? It's like the public craves the hype and misfortune. And I bet the hits we got, the increase was mostly new visitors, wasn't it?"

"Yes, it was."

"Okay, Betty. That's all. Talk to you in a few."

"Everything alright?" Stephanie asked, once he'd hung up.

"Yes and no, Steph. The money is better than it's ever been, but only because of Trina's death. I don't know if I should smile or frown."

Stephanie's expression was sedate, as she put her hand on Stew's chest in an attempt to soothe him. "Like you say, *we must move forward*."

"True."

"We doin' lunch like we planned?"

"Salmon King. Just like we said."

Stephanie lit up. "Yeah!"

On Monday evening, Stew had MaryAnn and Sparkle join him and Stephanie for dinner at the top of the Space Needle. Until now, Stephanie hadn't said a word about Stew's disappearance earlier. Nor did Stew disclose MaryAnn's special circumstances regarding Sparkle being her lover. It was only now, as the four sat in conversation at The CitySky Restaurant, that the subject came up.

"Actually, Stew, I was considering my own personal assistant. . . ." MaryAnn looked at Sparkle as she spoke. "And Sparkle has expressed an interest in the, umm, job."

Stew traded glances with Stephanie, wondering if she could read between the lines, but he kept his response professional. "MaryAnn, that sounds like a good idea. But do we have anyone as talented as Sparkle to put in her place for the website? I watched her today . . . with Wendy . . . topless."

Sparkle blushed.

"And I don't know if she's replaceable, as pretty as she is. Something tells me that she's drawing a lot of attention to the Seattle branch of the Platinum site."

"I don't know. I mean, Wendy and Andrea are pretty hot," MaryAnn said.

"Yeah, but a thousand dollars says that if I check the charts, Sparkle is doin' better than all of them."

"Okay, okay. You've got a point, Stew. Sparkle *can't* be replaced. That's a fact."

"But," Stephanie interjected, "Stew, if Sparkle is making life a lot easier for MaryAnn . . . If MaryAnn's work efforts improve as a result of a, umm, personal assistant, then—"

"MaryAnn, I know what you're doing. You want me to foot the bill for you and her to have more time together. That's what it boils down to."

Stephanie bowed her head, feeling the intensity of Stew's admonishment. She didn't think that she was supposed to hear this. She stood to excuse herself.

"No, Stephanie. Stay here. Let's keep this all-the-way real, shall we, MaryAnn?" Stew gave MaryAnn a no-nonsense look.

"Why not," she answered, and wiped the corners of her mouth with a napkin. Sparkle had her head bowed as well. Then MaryAnn asked, "Don't you think I deserve it, Stew? We're profitable. I run a tight ship. And as I've told you . . . on another occasion, I *live* for Platinum Dolls. Can't you see that, Stew?"

"I just don't wanna leave here approving such a promotion only to find that the battleship Seattle has capsized because my business manager and her, ahem, assistant are, if you'll excuse the expression, playing house."

"Excuse me, but is it possible that I can have a say in all of this?"

"Oh? Why sure, Sparkle. Speak." Stew propped his chin on his fist and gave Saprkle his undivided attention.

"Well, first of all, Mr. Gregory, I *highly* respect you and the business you've built. And, really, if it wasn't for Platinum

Dolls, I wouldn't have met so many interesting people. People like MaryAnn. As long as I've know her, she has never been one to squander money or just let the responsibilities of the day slip away. She's sharp. But from what I've seen, she *is* heavily burdened. There are a lot of tasks I can handle. And, as Stephanie says, I can help make life a *lot* easier for her. We get along great. I know how she wants things done, and so far, there's been no task too great for me. And one other thing . . . She *does* deserve it."

MaryAnn's eyes now lost that challenge and aggression. Instead, they now pulled at Stew for some consideration. If he could only see that Sparkle was right. If he could only take into account all that MaryAnn had done for him, both in and out of the bedroom.

Stew gave the issue some thought. He was aware that such a decision was financial. What they were really asking for was more money—another fifty grand or so a year. It meant less of a net profit as the bottom line; money out of his pocket.

"I'll tell you what, MaryAnn. If you can guarantee me that the Seattle branch generates at least five percent more than the average revenue—in other words, cover at least twenty-five thousand dollars more than the site does for the year—I'll agree."

"You've got a deal."

"But wait a minute. If you *don't* meet my quota, then this pretty girl here will be your, uh, personal assistant for free. In other words, she'll be out of a job."

"Hey, that's not fair," Sparkle said.

"Stew, you're unreasonable," MaryAnn said.

"Stew!" Stephanie exclaimed.

Everyone's comments came all at once, in a chorus.

"Ah, ah, ah, that's my deal. If this luxury is gonna help improve you, and the *improved you* is gonna help my company, then as they say, *show me the money.*"

"Is that the best you can do, Stew?"

"That's my final offer."

MaryAnn gave him the evil eye.

Stew gave her the look right back.

"It's a deal," she said, after looking at Sparkle. And she put a hand out to shake on the gamble.

"I hope she's worth it, MaryAnn."

"Oh, *yes* I am," Sparkle announced.

Tuesday was busy with plans for the evening video shoot. *Access* could record this, but only so much. They'd have to use censors to blur and beep out what was too explicit or vulgar, but there would be *some* skin shown, indeed.

Stew looked forward to these video shoots because they were filled with spontaneity. He wasn't anticipating becoming a great movie producer. He didn't need to, he was already selling. So what if a million people didn't buy his videos. If a few thousand bought them, he was content. And so far, he was always content.

"Action!"

Twenty Platinum Dolls performers stood nude in the center of the indoor park, their hair and makeup done to perfection. Each of them wore heels and held a white cardboard sign. The signs were painted with bold black numbers, one through twenty.

"Okay, ladies," Stephanie said from behind the cameras, "I want you to make four rows—five girls in each row. Hold those numbers up high so we can see them *and* so our *clients* can see all of you, as well. Hurry now!" Stephanie clapped her hands to urge a quick response.

Stew sat next to her in the director's chair, deliberating, pointing, and selecting who they wanted from the group.

"Turn around, ladies." Stephanie clapped again. "Let's see those pretty asses."

At Stephanie's call, all the girls made slow turns, their naked bodies illuminated under the stage lights.

"Good. Now in runway fashion, I want each row to follow its leader down the winding path, past where I'm standing, and hold your numbers up high. When I call out your number, you'll head straight for the soundstage upstairs. The rest of you are finished for the night, and we'll see you at work as usual, tomorrow. Am I understood?"

"Yes," the girls all answered in unison.

"Row one. Number two, you're going to the soundstage. Number four, you're going to the soundstage. . . ."

The girls strutted along the cobblestone path, past Stephanie and the live video cameras.

"Row two. Number six, you're going to the soundstage."

When the selections were done, there were seven women in all who went up to the soundstage to be featured in the forthcoming Platinum Dolls video. Meanwhile, those who weren't chosen went back to the dressing room and packed up for the night.

"I can't believe I didn't get picked, Vickie," said Jasper, a sexy Latina. "Damn, and I was looking forward to gettin' my freak on tonight, too."

"You? What about *me*? I haven't had sex in, like, a couple months, at least," said Tina, still naked.

"I've got an idea," said Vickie. "Maybe we can just have our *own* fun. You know, just the three of us."

Jasper said, "I'm game if you all are." She already had on a T-shirt.

"Maybe one of the studios is empty," said Tina.

"A 'n B are busy. You know that's an all-night thing."

"Well, what about the boss's office? Soft bearskin rug. Soft leather couch," said Jasper.

"And privacy while the boss is away," added Tina.

"Come on. Let's get in there," Vickie said excitedly.

The three crept toward MaryAnn's office, careful not to attract the attention of their coworkers still in the building.

"Close the curtain," said Tina in the darkness. "We don't need unwanted attention."

A few seconds later, a dimmed light was turned on. Jasper looked uncomfortable, as she sat down on the couch. She had her arms stretched out in front of her, and her hands on her knees. She watched as Tina and Vickie closed in for a deep tongue kiss, their arms around each other, and their heads slanted into the kiss as if this was the most natural position. Jasper's lips parted in shock. She was surprised at how much Tina and Vickie were into each other. On camera was one thing, but this was different. Jasper continued to stare. The kissing suddenly stopped.

"What's up with you?" asked Vickie, addressing Jasper abruptly.

Jasper looked away quickly, then stared down into her lap.

"Don't tell us that you never did this," Tina said.

Jasper didn't answer, but her eyes betrayed the truth.

"Oh my God! Get *out!*"

"You're shittin' me!"

Both Vickie and Tina reacted jubilantly, as though this revelation was the most exciting news. When they stopped carrying on, Vickie whispered into Tina's ear, and both their expressions suddenly changed. The two of them strutted over to Jasper, a condescending way about them.

"So all this time you've been faking it with us, haven't you?"

"Son of a bitch! As much shit as she talked! As much as I've . . ." Vickie grabbed Jasper's chin. "What the *fuck* are you pullin' here, bitch?"

"I . . . I'm just an aspiring actress. I never meant to trick you or anything." Jasper's eyes darted fearfully between the two women standing over her.

"Move, Vickie." Tina pushed her to the side and came up and slapped Jasper across the face. "I had mad love with you, bitch!" Tina turned to Vickie. "Can you believe I even put my tongue in this girl's ass? And *she played me!*"

Tina jumped on Jasper and the two of them struggled on the couch. Jasper fought to escape, but Vickie joined in until they both had the girl pinned. Jasper screamed, and Tina smacked her again.

"Move this heffa to the floor," said Tina. "We'll make her a lesbian right here. Right now."

They pulled Jasper onto the bearskin rug and stretched her out spread-eagle. Vickie ripped off Jasper's shirt and

Tina covered her mouth so that no one could hear Jasper scream.

"You scream again and this'll get worse. I promise you."

"Maybe we should tie her up . . . handcuff her," Vickie suggested.

"Do we need to do that, Jasper? Huh?" Tina asked, staring down at Jasper.

Jasper's eyes widened with fear. She shook her head vigorously.

"You'd better keep quiet then, girl, or else I'll twist you like a pretzel!"

Jasper could only stare up at Tina, who was sitting straddled over her.

"You go first, Vickie. Make this slut pay! The *actress*." Tina laughed.

Vickie straddled Jasper. She braced herself with her hands on the floor, and lowered her exposed privates over Jasper's face. She stopped abruptly and made eye contact with Jasper.

"If you bite me, I swear . . ." She let her threat hang in the air, and then continued down until her wet pussy was rubbing over Jasper's face. Vickie shifted back and forth so that she covered the helpless girl's forehead, nose, and eventually her lips with her natural juices. Vickie just let her pussy sit over Jasper's lips, and she settled there.

"Eat it, bitch," commanded Tina. "Eat that pussy and eat it good."

Lapping and sucking sounds filled the air, and Vickie soon got caught up in the lust. Before long, both of them were moaning with pleasure, as Vickie worked her way toward climax. Tina watched the two of them, her fingers massaging her clit.

"Oh, shit!" Vickie exploded, leaving Jasper's face slick and glistening with her juices. She lifted her body off Jasper's face and switched places with Tina. But Tina had a different agenda.

"Surprise, bitch! This ain't gonna be the same. I'm going

straight for the nasty stuff. You're gonna eat this ass, now!"
Tina looked down at Jasper's watery eyes, and then lowered
her ass onto the girl's face. She rubbed it across Jasper's nose.
"You like that smell, bitch? Huh?" Tina pinched Jasper's nipples lightly to get a response.

"Um-hmm, um-hmm," came Jasper's muffled reply.

Tina laughed. "Rub your nose in it, you fake-ass actress.
Rub your nose in my ass."

Jasper did as she was ordered. On top of her, Tina and
Vickie began to kiss. Vickie began grinding her clit against
Jasper's, while Tina squeezed her breasts. Tina climaxed,
letting her fluids spill all over Jasper's face, into her mouth,
and down her chin.

When Tina felt that their victim had had enough, she got
off her and sat down on the rug next to her. Jasper sat up. She
was a mess! It was an awkward moment and nobody spoke.
Both Tina and Vickie looked remorseful.

"Sorry we had to do that to you, Jasper," Vickie said.

"Yeah, you really ticked us off," Tina said.

Jasper sat quietly for a while. Finally she spoke. "I'm sorry,
too. You guys really know how to punish a girl." She got quiet
again. Then she wiped some of the wetness off her chin with
her forefinger and put the finger in her mouth, licking it like
a lollipop. She grinned guiltily. "Can we do it again?"

"Cut!"

Applause followed the director's call on the set. The camera crew, staff, and others began complimenting Vickie,
Tina, and Jasper for their superb performance.

"Bravo!" shouted Stephanie.

"Whoo-eee!" yelled MaryAnn. "Yay, Tina!"

"Tina! Tina! Tina! Tina!" the chorus of spectators
cheered.

"Okay, ladies, take a half hour break. We'll begin shooting the second film in forty minutes," Stew said.

"Wow," said Stephanie. Stew and MaryAnn were next to
her. "I like doing these in one take. If I hadn't been behind
the camera, I'd swear that was the real thing going down."

"Yup," said Stew. "That's the idea."

Stew produced two more videos that night. By Wednesday morning, he, Stephanie, and Timmy were back in the air heading for Canada.

Toronto, Canada

FOURTEEN

The cost of living in Canada is much more attractive than in the United States. A traveler can get more for their money when they visit, although that wasn't Stew's concern. Stew's intentions in Canada were to capitalize on the country's untapped sexuality. The women of Canada were like young flowers waiting to blossom. The country of the red leaf was very conservative, but like most things that come of age, Canada would come to recognize the sign of the times. The inherent sexual desires of human beings, the experimental and the taboo, would inevitably reach daylight. Stew and Platinum Dolls were intent on making that happen sooner rather than later.

Though this was Stew's first visit, he didn't expect Toronto to be any different than any other town or city he'd visited over the years. But Canada *was* different from what he'd expected. Everywhere else he'd been, skin color was an issue. Even though his money was just as good, he still ran into problems. In Canada, however, people were extremely polite. The average citizen showed unconditional kindness, or at least had an open attitude that seemed to welcome any kind of living creature.

The streets of Toronto were immaculate, as in a utopian world. They appeared to be wider, with more room to breathe, and they seemed to match their colorful, carefree names—like

Mayfair, Sunnydale, and Brightridge. From the signs that named the streets, to the great gardens and flower beds that bordered the sidewalks and parks, flowers seemed to be everywhere. And where they didn't grow, artificial ones were placed.

This all hit Stew as being very lighthearted and merry; far from the hard times that he had survived with police brutality and racism. Here in Canada, it seemed like the worst thing a person could be was sad, and happiness was no more than a sunrise away.

In downtown Toronto, day-to-day commerce was no different from what it was on a Main Street or a Broadway in the United States. The central artery in the downtown area, Bay Street, was where clothing boutiques, jewelers, florists, and bookstores conducted business. This was where eateries and cafés such as Starbucks, Veggie Man, and Bruegger's had their outdoor seating, the customers shaded under huge umbrellas. The beautiful sunlit sky seemed to stretch for miles, flooding Bay Street Square. At the center of it all, towering over a fountain surrounded by flower beds, stood the landmark statue of a Canadian soldier.

One of the cross streets that branched off Bay Street was King Street, a narrow, one-lane street with townhouses, brownstones, and two- or three-story commercial dwellings.

"This must be it," said Stew. The three of them were standing in front of a brick colonial, a short flight of steps leading to an entrance and then down toward a cellar. The building had a pair of pane glass windows on each side of its entrance and a bronze antique sign that read, 6 KING STREET.

"Barbara said to ring the folks next door," Timmy said. "I'll go."

"Steph, the first thing we're gonna do here, if we go ahead on this deal, is buy curtains."

"I know. It's like the folks across the street can see right in."

"Exactly. And we don't get paid by peeping Toms."

Timmy returned with an extremely pale, short woman, her hair wrapped into a bun on top of her head. Her prairie dress was printed with flowers and hid whatever shape she may have had underneath. What stood out the most were her fingernails, which were almost two inches long. They looked like claws.

"How do?" the woman said, her gigantic smile stretching across most of her face.

"This is Mrs. Greetree, Stew. Mrs. Greetree, meet Stew Gregory and Stephanie Koboyashi. Stew is the president of L.T.S. Industries, and Steph here is his assistant—sharp as ever." Timmy, with the flattery.

"How are you, ma'am?" Stew asked, his hand politely extended.

Stephanie greeted the woman, as well.

"So, you're the friends that my niece spoke about. The ones with the Innernet website 'n all."

Stew recalled the conversation he'd had with Candice about opening a branch here; about the low-cost setup, and the low purchase price of the colonial. But Candice never mentioned anything about family.

"Ahh, yes," Stew said. "Candice is your niece?"

"Indeed. Her poppa is my brother. I *do* miss him so," she said.

Stew looked at Stephanie and raised his eyebrows. *Is she for real?*

"Shall we take a look-see? I sure don't know anything about that innernet stuff, but I hear yer doin' well."

The trio watched as Mrs. Greetree took a key from the planter on the stoop. Stew threw a look in Timmy's direction. The super-relaxed security here in Toronto indicated more changes that would need to be made.

"It was just coincidence that I mentioned this li'l place to Candice so long ago. Who'd have thought . . ."

Stew wondered how Mrs. Greetree was going to open the door with those eagle talons on her hand, but she worked it out with no problem. She swung the door open and stepped aside so the others could walk in.

Inside was a single hall with support pillars, a shiny wood floor, and brick walls. The lighting was provided by cone-shaped fixtures that were dimmer controlled.

"Used to be a gallery in here until the owner died some

ten months ago. He had little family, 'cept them in England, and the Andes Mountains and such. They asked me to look after this place for 'em, and if I come across a buyer to make arrangements. And here ya have it"

"Roomier than I first thought," said Stew. "Any idea how many square feet?"

"Each floor, I understand, has two thousand five hundred. There's three floors, including the basement, so—"

"A little over seven thousand," Timmy said.

"I s'pose as much."

"You mind if we take a run of the place?" Stew asked, wanting to be left alone.

"Not t'all. If yer innerested, come on by next door. I'll have biscuits and hot tea waitin'."

"Thank you. We sure will be there," Stephanie said for the others.

As soon as she was gone, Stew, Stephanie, and Timmy climbed the staircase to the side of the main gallery and found the top floor to be entirely carpeted and sectioned off into a series of huge rooms. There were four bathrooms, six bedrooms, and two additional rooms that looked as though they could have been the maids' quarters at one time. Everything was connected by a long, wide hallway, the floor was of wood—like downstairs—and here, too, the lights along the walls were dimmer controlled.

"I already see it," said Stew. "This is perfect. And we haven't even seen the basement yet."

"Let's," suggested Stephanie, doing her immitation of Mrs. Greetree's homey personality.

"Lots of windows, Timmy," said Stew, walking around the spacious basement.

"I know. If you do this, I wanna install electronic sensors. Anytime a window is opened, broken, or touched, an alarm will go off."

"Can you imagine us leaving the key in the planter with so many girls working in here?" mused Stephanie. "Guys would be stalking them, and they'd grab the key and come right in." She shook her head in amusement.

The three stepped down into the main gallery and found a short hallway leading to a country kitchen, a bathroom, and several closets. There was also a large room that, by the looks of it, would make a good office.

They moved along and reached the top of a stairway with a lower landing and a door to the cellar. There were coat hooks along the wall and a mirror on the cellar door.

"Let's do it," said Stew, as if there might be bigger surprises behind the door. He pushed inside and then stopped. "Whoa! Cages?"

The cellar was roomy and dark even after someone turned on the lights. They continued to explore the room, even though a flashlight would have been a big help. Stew moved over to the cages he'd spotted when he opened the door. They were huge, made of mesh wire, and had floor-to-ceiling gates. A few easels had been left inside. Apparently artwork used to be displayed in them.

"Probably from the gallery," said Timmy, advancing ahead of Stew and Stephanie, and strolling through the rest of the cellar.

Stew studied the space and wondered what it could be used for. They didn't have equipment that needed storage. Then it came to him. "Hey! I have an idea. Timmy!"

Stephanie whirled around to look at Stew, wondering what he was thinking.

"What's up?" Timmy called, hurrying back.

"This is great. This is *grrreat!*" Stew stood behind Stephanie and wrapped his arms around her. He looked over her shoulder at the cages. "We can make a dungeon out of this. I mean, make it even more ancient than it is. Dark. Put in some chains, shackles, and one of those old-ass torture machines. I'm talkin' the stuff they might've used in the medieval days."

FIFTEEN

Back in high school they'd called him Lexington the Great. But the only thing he was great at was being cunning, deceitful, and dastardly. Born into Boston's elite Roland family, Lexington was the only son, and just a year older than his sister, Iris. His father was a bank president, and his mother was a happy homemaker.

Traditional was how Lexington's life was expected to be. After all, as a banker's son, he had all the right stuff—the education, the connections, and the easy access to resources. Yet his life was anything but traditional. Growing up he was a scoundrel, and as he got older, he simply became a con artist. That Boston, Kennedy-like accent of his, the arrogant demeanor, and those pretty-boy looks had people falling for his schemes—hook, line, and sinker. Besides that, he had the gift of gab like any great car salesman or politician. This kid was born to win.

But that wasn't always enough for Lexington. He liked to have the advantage. If there was a test in school and he wasn't prepared, he made sure he got hold of the answers. In high school, he tapped into the school's computer system, broke the easy code, and made adjustments to his grade point average. Not that he needed to, if he'd only done his class work, study, and be the A-student he had it in him to be. But no, Lexington liked the easy ride. He liked to be able to put one over on somebody. It didn't matter who, anybody would do.

In college, Lexington lived fast and on the edge. He continued to hack into the school's computers, more for the sake of creating confusion than anything else. He spent time at raves, picking up women, sometimes juggling four at a time. He always swore them to secrecy, feeding them the line that one day he might be president, and he didn't want to subject them to media scrutiny later in life. Lexington also scouted the raves for business partners and suckers, which sometimes were one and the same.

By the time he was nineteen, Lexington was working as a sales rep at Morgan Stanley, the brokerage house that managed billions of dollars of other people's money. It was a job that came as a direct result of rubbing elbows at the raves he'd attended, and this position gave Lexington incredible access to big money. It was easiest here for Lexington to be sly and cunning. It was easy for him to talk *this* CEO or *that* business owner into placing their money into *whatever* investment, or buying and selling this or that stock. It was all in the talk-game. A talk-game he knew well.

Lexington's talk-game turned risky when he began to manipulate funds so that they'd be transferred or deposited into a business account that he'd set up. It was an account that he dipped into for day-trading and ventures that he considered profitable, far and away from the objectives of Morgan Stanley, the company he was *supposed* to be representing. It was not beyond Lexington's ability to shift four hundred thousand dollars into his side account, then buy a quarter mil worth of stock. By eight the following morning he would have turned a twenty-five-hundred-dollar profit. Lexington's game was foolproof, and he was winning.

On September eleventh, tragedy struck. Extremists, who lived and died for jihad, commandeered several commercial airliners and used them as guided missiles. The rest, as they say, is history. For months, Americans were bombarded with daily news reports on television and radio, and bad news spread like a killer virus. It wasn't just that there were suicidal extremists, or that so many people had died; what stood out just as much was that airport security was a joke. Since those who launched the attack died in the act, someone or something else had to bear the burden and the blame. That someone was the airline industry. Saturn Airlines was the hardest hit.

Once recognized as the leader in low airfares, Saturn Airlines almost overnight became the scourge of the airline industry. Every news report began with something derogatory about the airline. There were extended news features and investigations about how relaxed security was. And, inevitably, even as the worldview shifted from placing blame on the airlines to placing it on the allies of various terrorist groups, Saturn's stock plummeted.

"*Who knew*," was Lexington's favorite response.

Soon after the numbers began to dip, Lexington went into hiding. It had been only the day before, on September tenth, that he'd sworn by Saturn. Its stock performance had experienced a consistent growth since day one and never dropped below 20 percent earnings each year it was in business. Lexington's sales pitch had been sharp as nails. It was no-lose for anyone who wanted in. But as it turned out, the hype-man at Morgan Stanley became the biggest sucker of them all. Lexington had purchased 1.2 million dollars' worth of Saturn Airlines stock with money from his biggest accounts; money that he didn't have approval to spend. Money that, in all actuality, he'd stolen.

The manhunt didn't last long. As slick as he thought he was, Lexington was no career criminal. He had no idea where or how to hide. The idiot who they'd once called Lexington the Great—the one who never lost at chess, and who played to win—was indeed the fool who'd used his own credit card to retrieve cash out of his account.

The FBI swooped in on his motel room. Lexington's father disowned him. His mother was powerless and had no choice but to follow Mr. Roland's rules. Only his sister, Iris, kept in touch. She'd been in the courtroom when the federal judge sentenced her brother to three years. The judge further ordered that Lexington was never to work at a brokerage or bank during his five years of probation.

Back on the streets of New York City, he was simply Lex. That had been his nickname in prison, and he figured he'd keep it while he made a fresh start.

"Lex, did you see the news?" Trent asked, barging into the office like he had no sense. Lex held up his hand so Trent would be quiet while he finished his phone call.

"Yeah. Why don't we, ahh, just finish discussing this in the afternoon. I'll be able to, ahh, give you more information." Lex hung up and he and Trent gazed at the two TV monitors on the wall. One was tuned to MSNBC and the other to NY-1. Trent grabbed the remote from Lex's desk and turned up the muted television.

"Investigators say that the fire was a possible arson. However, officials couldn't give exact details at this hour. NYPD and the fire department are still investigating, and, of course, New York One will bring you updates as they are received. Once again, fire has swept through the upper floors of a Grand Concourse penthouse, claiming five lives so far. A sixth young woman is currently in intensive care at St. Barnabas Hospital in the Bronx. More on this story as it develops . . ."

Trent flipped the channels until he came to another station telling the same story.

". . . Citizens of downtown Seattle are outraged at the idea of foul play where a young woman's life is now hanging in the balance at the Bill Gates Burn Center. . . ."

On the TV, a person was talking. *"I hear she was a pretty girl. It's too bad there are people—monsters—out in the world today who advocate this kind of violence. They should be put away forever."*

An older woman then came on and testified for the camera. *"I knew the young lady in passing. . . . Sparkle, I believe her name was. It's a pity, too. I heard there was an attacker or a forced entry or something. The first thing I'll do tonight is bolt my doors good."*

The reporter came on and said, "Mr. Jerkins, the door man at the high-rise, had this to say: *'This is senseless and cruel and nobody deserves this kind of punishment. No matter who it is. I'm sad. I knew the young lady, and I'm sad. My prayers go out to her.'* And the investigation moves forward as officials try to find a motive and a suspect. Back to you, Brad."

Trent watched Lex for a reaction. "You're not surprised about all of this, Lex? That's our *investment!* I mean, it's just a matter of time before they find out the fires are related to Platinum Dolls."

"Exactly," Lex said coolly. "And that's what we're counting on, *isn't* it?"

"We? *'Counting'* on?"

"Come on, Trent. Don't pretend here. This is a matter of dollars and cents. Publicity brings us attention, and attention makes us money. Look at what happened last time."

"*'Last'* time?"

"Well, the last tragedy," Lex began. "Trent, the girl got hurt. . . ."

Trent looked at him strangely. "Killed. She was *killed,* Lex!"

"Okay, well, that happened, and look at the numbers. They speak for themselves. The hits went up over forty percent. The L.T.S. account is boiling hot right now. And now, with this? *Wow!* We couldn't have asked for—"

"Lex, if I didn't know any better, I'd swear you *planned* this stuff. You're money hungry and you just might go to any extent to chase the dollar."

"Come on, Trent. How can li'l ole me plan such incredible tragedies? It's ludicrous for you to even *think* something like that. I just like to squeeze the good out of a bad situation, that's all. I'm as harmless as a fly."

Lex's voice was velvety smooth; one of his conniving talents. He could relax a person with the tone of his voice, and in the same breath deliver devastating news.

"You *better* be, Lex. 'Cause I ain't goin' back to prison for you or anybody else. I don't care how much money's at stake."

"And it's perfectly fine to think that way, buddy. Come on, Trent, loosen up! You don't trust me after all we've been through together? We built this investment company from nothing, you and I. Of course, you know we've taken risks, but *never* lives."

"Alright, alright. It's just . . . sometimes your mind works a little backwards, Lex."

"You know me, Trent." Lex flashed his politician's smile. His eyes glistened. "Go with the flow," he said, spreading his hands apart.

"So, do we call Stew?"

"Nah. Not now. Too much heat, for lack of a better word. Let him handle the emergencies, we'll watch the numbers, as usual. As long as Stew's out of harm's way things are fine. As long as he's alive, we're gonna be makin' money. The way it's always been. When it dies down we'll give 'im a ring. Make sure everything's alright."

"I need a coffee break," said Trent. "Wanna get some Starbucks?"

Lex waved Trent on. "Nah, you go on." Lex winked. "I'm gonna crunch some numbers."

"Somebody's gotta do it," Trent said apologetically.

"Right."

Trent closed the door behind him and Lex swiveled around in his chair to look down Wall Street. He saw it differently than many others. It was a type of Vegas strip, with all the fools in suits and ties; all of them answering to one boss or another; all of them kissing ass in some kind of way.

Lex picked up his phone and pressed the speed-dial. Janice answered.

"Helloooo, Janice. How's my girl?"

"Just fine, Lex. You'll be home in time for dinner?"

"Better than that. We're goin' out to Tavern on the Green for dinner."

"Oh? Did my baby close another merger?"

"Bigger than that. I probably made another million dollars today."

"Kisses and hugs to you, darling."

"I want you to take the credit card and buy the sexiest, most expensive dress you can buy. And make sure there's easy access, something that I can pull a zipper to undress you."

"Oooh, sounds like a big night ahead."

"The biggest." Lex hung up then dialed another number.

"Steele here," answered the voice on the other end.

"Hey. Me again. So where were we?"

"The money," he answered.

"Of course," Lex said. "You were saying?"

"I'll tell you what, slick," Steele said icily. "You go ahead and run that Mister Wall-Street lingo if you want, but you heard my demands."

"But, Steele, dude, we go back what, seven, eight years, don't we? Since when did we start to go back on our word?"

"Since we started droppin' bodies, and the total's almost eight now."

"So I got more than I bargained for. . . ."

"No, that's not how it works. More bodies means more risk for us. Each one of those bodies has a letter to go with it; the letter L, which stands for *life*. Are you with me?"

"Dude, you'll never get caught. You're a professional. You only *deal* with professionals. The investigations are going nowhere. You did your job well."

"I don't think you're hearin' me, Lex. We're done talkin'. I want one million per body. That's gonna add up to eight within a few hours. But for now, I want half, and I want it now!"

"Naaaah, dude, you . . . Steele? *Steele*?" The line had been disconnected. *"Shit!"* Lex redialed quickly. The phone rang more than ten times before Steele picked up.

"Dude, listen," Lex began, but before he could continue the line went dead again. It was enough to make Lex worried. Steele was the *last* person he wanted to piss off. The two had met when they were both doing time, and he knew Steele was nobody to play around with. Lex redialed.

"Steele, it's a deal. Whatever you say. Let's just work this out. You said half, will you take two now?"

"Now you're talkin', dude," Steele said, using Lex's own lingo on him.

Stew and his friends were discussing the recent events. Timmy determined that someone was advocating this violence. Someone, maybe a group of individuals, was out to hurt Stew's business. Timmy hadn't thought it necessary before now, but he felt it was time to call in the troops. He was sure that someone had an intricate plan in motion.

But just as important as finding the cause of these travesties was the need to keep the business going. Could Stew maintain his drive and fortitude as a leader? Could he even think straight with so much pain and death swirling around his empire? What about the plans for Transylvania? All the wheels that were now spinning hinged on Stew's word. The disruption brought about by these tragedies could possibly ruin Stew's credibility.

"Stew, if you want, I can stay here and see your plan through. Your vision will still be followed, and we can stay in touch by phone," Stephanie said, sensing the weight on Stew's mind. She had been beside Stew for years and knew what he wanted for Platinum Dolls. She flew where he flew and sat in on meetings. She'd adopted much of his strong will, so much that his vision became her own. The sex and raunchy activity between the two of them was one thing. That was tension-relieving entertainment. But when it came to business, there was only one way to do things: Stew's way. His way was the successful way, and Stephanie understood that.

"I don't know, Stephanie. I'm just not inspired like I was a few minutes ago. It's like I've been knocked down, and I'm on my back."

"Timmy? Can you give us a moment alone?"

Timmy nodded—he had things to do anyway, security issues to handle—as he whipped out his cell phone and exited; he hoped to reach his father at the office. He closed the door behind him.

"Stew, take a sip of this," Stephanie said, handing him a Styrofoam cup. "It's cappuccino, it won't hurt you," she said when he hesitated. She pressed the cup into his hand.

Stew was in a daze. He took the cup and sipped. Stephanie could've offered him poison and he might've drunk it. He was completely bewildered. The cappuccino was strong and offered a quick pick-me-up, as well as soothing his mind and body. If that was even possible.

Stephanie looked at him, and knew she had to do something to snap him out of his shock. She had to get him back on track.

"Stew, listen, you're always telling me to snap out of things when I'm down or when I'm feeling miserable. So now I'm gonna give you a dose of your own medicine. Practice what you preach, mister! What was it you said about business *as usual?* We've always gotta bounce back from challenges. Isn't that what you said? Did you mean it, or was that some bullshit you were feedin' us? Was it the real thing, or just some more of your Les Brown tapes? *Look, I know it'll be hard, but life is hard!*"

Stew didn't say anything. He was caught in Stephanie's spell, but at the same time he wasn't. He heard her, but he couldn't quite believe what he was hearing. She never spoke to him this way. Never!

"Oh, now you wanna look at the little Jap girl like she's crazy," she pressed. "I'm awake now, playboy! Sure you turned me out. Okay, you freak me. And yes . . . yes, Stew, I'm your goddamn bitch! Is that what you wanna hear? But guess what, Mister Multimillionaire. You also taught me a lot of things. I *watched* you, I learned, and I—grew—up! And guess what? Now I'm smarter. I'm wiser." She paused for just a second, not sure if she was reaching him, but knowing she had to keep trying. "A lot of you is in me, and I'm not just talkin' about your dick! So now this is the third or fourth inning, we've had some problems in the game, but *so what*? There's still more game to play, so you have to play it. Are you a quitter, Missa Gregory? Is that it?"

Stew looked at her and raised his hand. "Enough, Steph." He could tell how high-strung she was. Her language was wavering.

"Or maybe you want me to call the coroner to pick up your dead body?" Stephanie added.

"I said *enough*, you crazy bitch!" Stew pulled Stephanie to him and hugged her. "I know what you're trying to do. So cut it out before I turn soft." He kissed her, able to feel the intensity of her heartbeat. It matched his. When he pulled away, his concern returned. "Are you sure you can handle things here?"

Stephanie nodded. "What I can't handle I'll call you for, okay? But don't hold your breath."

Stew felt revived. Stephanie had been right. It was time to get his head back in the game. He reached for his cell phone.

Stephanie smiled and then grabbed his hand. "Oh, and Stew? When I do this to your expectations, I want a present from you."

"Really?" Stew replied, already dialing Barbara.

"Oh yeah, really. Deal?"

"Barbara? Yeah, this is—" Stew couldn't get another word in. Stephanie had pulled the phone away.

"Deal?"

"Alright, deal. Jeeze!" he said, giving Stephanie the answer she wanted. When she let go, he continued his call. "Barbara, have the jet ready at Toronto. See if you can arrange for car service from LaGuardia. Hold on." Stew pulled the phone away to hear Timmy.

"No need for the service, boss. We're gonna have company in New York," Timmy said.

Stew nodded. "Barbara? Scratch the car service. And listen, put Leslie on, would you? Conference is okay." Stew turned to Timmy again while he waited for Barbara to get Leslie. "Who's in New York?"

"Pop," Timmy said matter-of-factly.

"Oh," mouthed Stew. His attention returned to his phone call. He told Leslie to fly to Seattle to stand in for MaryAnn at the office. Even though he was getting back to business, Stew had a bad feeling—a pain in his stomach. But something told him that this was merely the beginning of something very ugly.

SIXTEEN

Timothy Andrews Sr. had been a weapons specialist with the FBI for almost fifteen years when his partner was killed. They had gone on a stakeout with absolutely no intentions of trading gunfire, much less being caught in the middle of a battle. But that's exactly what happened.

The stakeout was in Astoria, Queens, where the Shower Posse, the Jamaican version of L.A.'s Crips or Bloods, had a string of houses along Ninety-fifth Street. Forty-two FBI agents were posted at each end of the suburban block of one- and two-story buildings, and confirmed that at least fourteen members of the posse were inside, with enough weapons and ammunition to start a war.

It was discovered that one of the places was a safe house where many hundreds of weapons were kept, which was why Agent Andrews and his partner, Agent Perry, were called to the scene. But just when agents swore they had the operation under control, Shower Posse members preyed on all posts from the outside. The forty-two-member FBI force was ambushed by almost three times the number of men and weapons. And although all the agents wore Kevlar vests, and some also wore headgear, twenty-seven agents were seriously injured. Fourteen of them were killed in cold blood. It was a massacre that the Agency would never forget, and one that caused Agent Andrews to turn in his badge.

Since the tragedy in Astoria more than twelve years earlier, Timothy Andrews Sr. had started his own business as a private investigator and bodyguard. He was still in his late forties, and as fit as an ESPN aerobics instructor, so he figured he'd live life on the edge. Only this was an edge that he'd have more control over. If there was any ambushing to be done, it'd be he who'd have the upper hand.

Timothy Sr. was known as Pop, not because of his age but because of his marksmanship. He had been very active since the days in the Agency. He took on a few of those suspicious wives as clients in the beginning, but those turned out to be too easy. No challenge. Men were such morons when it came to cheating. They could do nothing right while doing wrong. In the end, Pop Andrews would tell his clients that they could do this themselves. All they needed was a zoom lens on their cameras. Most of these men were idiots enough to do things right out in the open.

"Just rent a car," Pop would tell them.

So, Pop, with his Chuck Norris looks and a legal right to kill assailants, began to protect celebrities, sports stars, and diplomats. He used his credit to lease fleets of vehicles when the Los Angeles Lakers came to New York, and he had plenty of manpower to join him when the democratic convention called. This was the classier work; less risky. And he made good connections and associations enough so that his name would get around.

On occasion, when Pop was short a man, and if he deemed it safe, he'd bring Timmy Jr. along. He had been training his son all the while. He took him to gun shows, taught him about weapons, and they went to the shooting range constantly. There were hunting competitions, conventions, and of course, meeting many other gung ho types who endeavored in the profession of personal security.

Eventually, Timmy Jr. was off on his own, establishing his own clients. And through word of mouth, Stew Gregory came to meet the twenty-seven-year-old Timmy. As Stew's business grew, so, too, did his need for protection. He was determined *never* to fall into a situation like he did in Detroit. And Timmy made a promise that that would never happen again once Stew took him on as his around-the-clock bodyguard.

"Pop, meet Stew Gregory, my boss. Boss, the one and only Pop." Timmy introduced the two men as they walked through the arrival gate at LaGuardia Airport.

"Heard a lot about you, young man. Congratulations on your success," Pop said.

Stew had heard so much about Pop from Timmy that he was in awe of the man. "Thank you, sir. If I could just keep my employees alive I'd at least *feel* successful."

"So my son tells me." Pop patted Stew's shoulder. "Some jokers are gettin' at you, are they?"

"That's an understatement."

"Well, relax. You're in good hands now," Pop assured. "I don't know if Timmy told you, but this is my kinda work. Tracking 'em down. Smoking 'em out."

Stew was immediately impressed. He was in the best company. If anybody could get to the bottom of what was going on, he felt certain that it was the two men beside him.

"Hop in, fellas. Timmy, you already know Porter," Pop said, as they got into a big Chevy Suburban.

"Hey, Porter, long time," Timmy said.

"Yup," answered Porter. "Still wup ya out on the huntin' grounds though."

Timmy chuckled. "Maybe if I had that fifteen-thousand-dollar rifle you got, I'd beat you out," challenged Timmy.

"Tough chance. You know when it comes to huntin', I don't miss. We gotta go out again sometime. See how far you've come along."

Timmy laughed again and beamed proudly. These were his favorite people in the world. He gave Stew a look that said not to worry.

The Suburban carried the quartet across the Van Wyck Parkway and over the Whitestone Bridge into Pelham Bay and then Pelham Manor, a gated community where Pop owned a ranch-style split-level home. The professional bodyguard trade paid him well. Porter pulled down the visor overhead to press the electronic garage door opener. He eased the Suburban into the garage alongside a blue Chevy sedan. Pop was a Chevy kinda man.

"You all sit tight. I'm goin' in to get us some vests," Pop said.

The other three men sat in the Suburban in the garage. Stew and Timmy filled Porter in on the details of all that had happened. But Porter was only half listening to them. He already knew many of the things they were telling him, some of which he probably shouldn't have.

They say that there are merely six degrees of separation that stand between one person and another, whether that next person is a blood relative, or a close friend, or even an acquaintance. You know somebody that he knows; or you know somebody that knows somebody else, and so on. Charles Porter was somebody who knew a lot of somebodies. Just like Timothy Andrews Sr., Charles Porter was a former agent, although his exodus was a very different story.

"It was a setup," Porter had tried to explain to his superiors.

Over a million dollars in cold cash had somehow gone missing from a bust in a Mafia don's Minnesota mansion. It was such a well-planned takedown, too. Months of maneuvers had been executed in order to plant receivers and taps in the home just to catch the don slipping. Some people just couldn't keep their mouths shut. And that was something Agent Charles Porter was counting on. So they crashed the don's party. The primaries went in through the front and rear doors with battering rams, and others leaped directly through the windows. They were aware that the don had an escape route, a tunnel under the home, and they were quick enough to catch him still in his underwear before he made his move.

Porter had been with the secondary squad. They generally backed up the primaries, handling loose ends that might be overlooked. One of those loose ends happened to be the don's twenty-seven-year-old son, who'd tried to get away with a duffel bag full of cash—the million plus.

Porter was the agent that made the tackle. Two other agents rushed in to assist, and the son was taken in as part of the organized criminal activity. Reports were filed, arrests were completed, and the district attorney commended the agents. It was only later that night when Charles Porter received his very own surprise invasion. FBI agents came and bashed in *his* door and took *him* in. It all happened in such a whirlwind that it blew his mind. The next thing he knew, he was in the interrogation room, handcuffed, wanting a lawyer.

Charles Porter, immediately terminated from the agency, was tried and convicted of interfering with a federal investigation as well as the theft of the money.

After a three-year term of imprisonment, a bid he did with bitterness and the want for revenge in his heart, Charles Porter—now considered an ex-con—emerged from prison to join his old colleague Timothy Andrews in a venture to provide personal security. But Porter also had a side job going. He considered himself one of the best when it came to hunting game, a sport that both he and Pop enjoyed. His love for killing, however, was not limited to fowl and deer. Porter, aka Steele, killed people as well.

Pop had four Kevlar vests, two on each arm, when he came back to the garage.

"One size fits all," he said.

Stew had been wondering why they'd come here from the airport instead of stopping by St. Barnabus Hospital, or even the Grand Concourse, where the fire had been set. But now he understood, since Pop was in charge.

"You *always* have to be prepared," Pop said. "You never can tell who will be the target when you walk into the danger zone."

Stew nodded absently, recalling the story Timmy had told him in great detail about the Shower Posse ambush and how, even though Pop had never expected to be the target of gunfire, he wore a vest. The vest had saved Pop's life, but unfortunately not his partner's. Stew quickly put on his vest, along with everyone else, and then a thin, black windbreaker over the vest.

Once everybody was ready, the truck sped back onto I-95, along Pelham Parkway and Fordham Road. They arrived at the hospital in minutes. Stew was impressed when Pop showed his credentials to the hospital's administration in order to allow them easy access. The administrator escorted them straight to the emergency room waiting area.

Sharon was sitting there with a handful of other women in matching red velour robes, their names embroidered over the heart, their hair in scarves, curlers or simply pulled back into hasty buns. Stew's eyes immediately locked with Sharon's, and they ran into each other's arms. Sharon's cries were muffled into his shoulder.

"Come on, baby, get a grip. It's gonna be alright," Stew said, patting Sharon's back, while his other hand petted her hair. The other girls gathered around the two of them, each one waiting her turn to speak to Stew.

"What's the status on Cathy?" Stew asked, after greeting the girls with a concerned nod.

"We're still waiting for word," one of the girls said. She wore her long hair pinned up in a swirl. Her cheeks, just like the others', were tear stained.

"You're Jordan, right?"

"Yes," she answered, somewhat glad that Stew remembered.

"Okay. And Bobby, and—"

"Monica," another answered.

"That's right. I remember. But who are these two? I don't think we've met."

"I'm Cheryl," said one girl, with a humble smile and sad eyes.

"And I'm Octavia," answered the fifth girl.

"Well, since I'm paying you, I guess it's just as well we meet. How are you all holding up?"

"I'm really scared, Mr. Gregory. People are saying that Platinum Dolls are targets. Is it true that another girl died today? In Seattle?"

Stew's mind blanked out for a moment. He remembered

his talk with MaryAnn earlier; about Sparkle's life hanging in the balance. Had she died?

"I don't know," Stew said honestly. "The last word I got on the way here was that she was hanging on."

The girls exchanged uneasy glances. "Mr. Gregory, what's going on?" asked Bobby. "Everything was great just a week ago. . . . Then Trina, now Cathy, and—"

"We have professionals on the job now, ladies. Men who are trained to protect you." Stew nodded over in Timmy's direction, hoping to assure the girls.

Sharon seemed to gain some composure. "Stew . . . the penthouse . . . it's . . . it's all gone. We're lucky we got out alive, but all of our stuff . . . our clothes . . ."

"Forget that stuff, Sharon. I'm just glad you're okay. All that other stuff, the clothes and equipment, we can get that again. That's nothin' but money."

"What about Platinum? What about—"

Stew cut her off. "I'm gonna try to work something out, Sharon. But we will *not* fold because of a fire. We *can't*. We've come too far. Where are your other girls?"

"I have nineteen girls staying at a neighbor's place. Mr. Perkins owns a building across the street from us."

"Perkins?"

"Yes. Remember? Perk's? Where we had your birthday party?"

"Right."

"He had a couple of vacancies in his building and let the girls stay there. Lance, the guy that Timmy sent to us this morning . . . he brought us sleeping bags and food. But, Stew, we don't have clothes."

"Don't worry about that, Sharon. I'm telling you, by tomorrow we'll correct everything. New clothes, a place to stay, everything will be straight. Whatever."

"Oh, Stew." Sharon sighed and fell against his chest. It was sad that it took this, a tragedy, to draw Stew back into her arms, but she was content to hold him just the same. This time it wasn't just Stew's voice; she actually had him there *physically*.

"You guys look tired."

All five girls replied in the affirmative.

"Have you even eaten?"

"Not breakfast," said Monica. "A snack. Coffee."

"My babies are hungry and tired, Stew. It's been a long day and—"

"Excuse me. Are you all here for—"

"Ohmigod! She didn't make it!" Cheryl assumed.

Octavia screamed. Jordan began to slump to the floor, but Timmy caught her. Two of the girls broke out into sobs. Sharon just wailed against Stew's chest. Just like that, Cathy was gone.

"Pop?"

"Yeah, Porter."

"I think I can get these guys. I know the type. Well-financed hits—that's all it comes down to."

"Corporate espionage is what I see. Something high-level. Someone don't want this guy in business," Pop said.

"Maybe. It's always jealousy or revenge," Porter suggested.

"Or greed," added Pop.

"Yeah," Porter acknowledged. The wheels of thought were spinning wildly in his head. "Or greed."

Stew had already assumed the worst. It was as if he'd had an instinct about what was to come on the flight from Toronto. Eight girls had been killed; Trina, the six girls in New York, and Sparkle, MaryAnn's lover. When Stew closed his eyes, it was like a fog filled his mind, and in that fog he'd seen eight faceless figures. Not six, or seven, but eight. Something of a daze he was experiencing. It was confirmation from a higher power that these people were taken away. Their lives were sacrifices, like innocent lambs.

It was also on the flight that Stew found the nerve to face this monster, whatever and whoever it was. He would stand up to it, just as if he was David and the adversary was Goliath. His first concern now was the safety of all of his employees at all of his locations. Timmy had been right all along. He'd wanted to add another man to each location. It was now clear to Stew that the extra manpower was a must. The security for the girls must be as special, as reinforced, as it was for Stew himself. The girls were the personalities who attracted the money that paid Stew. *They were the Platinum* in the company.

Timmy immediately called in the forces. By noon that day, it wasn't just Malibu and Seattle that had an extra man. New York's Bronx and Scarsdale locations, even though there was the fire, had Lance and Boom looking over the girls. In Washington, D.C., North Carolina, Atlanta, and Houston, a man was added at each location. And Canada was next to get a man.

". . . And now that we have trained professionals on duty, not only will our staff and talent be protected, but they're also going after whoever did this. It's a coward, for sure." Stew looked at each of the women as he spoke, trying to reassure them.

"We know this because whoever it was chose to torch the penthouse early in the morning, when people were sleeping. Women. You all were harmless. There's just no sane person who would do such a thing. This was wicked. . . ." Stew felt his cell phone vibrate on his hip while he was midsentence. He reached down and switched it off so that he wouldn't be bothered.

"So I'm saying all of that to say this: We are a profitable company. We're worth millions of dollars, but we're also doing hundreds of millions of dollars in commerce. For those of you who don't care how large it all is, I'll put it like this: We're not going anywhere. I see your faces. I see the uncertain expressions, your worries, and your concerns. I know how you feel. I'm right there with you.

"But I didn't come all this way, with branches of my company all over the country, to close up shop. I came here to recognize our challenge and forge on toward the success and prosperity we deserve. They say a chain is only as strong as its weakest link. Well, if there *is* a weak link in Platinum Dolls, then we've fixed it. We are stronger because of our loss. And what purpose would the deaths of our friends be if we didn't push on? Their deaths would be in vain. Instead of being able to live as they might've lived in prosperity, if we didn't move on, their passing would be a mere memory. And we want their names to live on, don't we? Well? Don't we?"

The small audience warmed into nods. Many of the girls were still sad and frightened. But most of them were pushing tears away, looking for strength.

"So I need your help. I have to make a decision now that requires your input. As you know, we have a Scarsdale estate not far from here. I know a lot of you have seen their activity on the website, and you know there are thirty-some-odd girls there who are much like you. They perform for the same audience and they do a lot of the same things every day, like you all do."

The girls were clearly not comfortable with what Stew was saying, and they started voicing their opposition.

"They're not like us," said Egypt. "A lot of us are from the streets. . . . The city. Those are suburban girls."

"See that? That's exactly why I'm in need of your help here. I have two options. Since the Scarsdale site is already set up with all the luxuries of home—the pool, the fireplaces, the great lawns and gardens, and all the accommodations you can imagine—I was wondering how you all felt if we put you all together as one big family."

"Oh *hell* no!" exclaimed Tempest. "Pool or no pool, I ain't no uppity bitch." Tempest looked to the others for support. "I mean, excuse me for gettin' all loud with you, Mr. Gregory, but I don't see it. We'll be fightin' to use the bathroom."

"And wouldn't the house be overcrowded? That'd be like fifty girls in one house. I'd go out of my mind."

"What's the other option, Mr. Gregory?"

"Yeah! Give us somethin' we can work with."

"Do we have a choice?" asked a girl.

Stew gestured to Sharon and she came over to him. She turned so that she faced everyone.

"Okay, okay, let's get a little attention in here," Stew said in a loud voice. Then he whispered in Sharon's ear, as he wrapped an arm around her waist. "Sharon, I like their spirit. It's family. But there's too much hate. Talk to them. Go 'head."

"This is real hard to do, to preach to you all at this time— but you gotta hear us out," Sharon said. Stew squeezed her some for encouragement. "Those girls up in Scarsdale, just like the others in Malibu, Houston, all of 'em are our friends. They're just like you and me. They work for the same boss." Sharon turned her upper body slightly to look at Stew. She put her palm flat against his cheek and continued. "They all love and live just like us. So don't hate. Now I happen to agree with the girls, Stew, that we have our own clique, our own little family within the family . . ." Sharon was turned toward Stew now, the representative.

"So then let me make a proposal here. I'm prepared to get us into another penthouse, but it's gonna take a while to set up. I've spoken with the owner of the building you're in right now, and we should be able to close a deal. But, as you see, this isn't the same as you had across the street, before the fire. It's gonna have to be renovated."

A girl named Jackie raised her hand. "Mr. Gregory, boss, if you ain't mind me saying, whas' wrong with this place the way it is? I mean, the rooms is big enough."

"Well, I was just thinking you might want some luxury," Stew began.

"Sir, I ain't never had no luxury in my life and I'm still Egypt, ya know. Like, that was a big thing with us cuz of who we *is,* not cuz of the atmosphere."

"Yeah, the customers, they like that attitude, and even how we talk to them—ghetto 'n all."

Some of the girls smiled slightly, as if in agreement.

"So, okay. There's still a little work that has to be done on these floors—"

"Why can't *we* do it?" asked Bobby. "I don't know about the others, but I'm angry, I'm frustrated, I'm sad about my girl dyin'! I kinda need to work, before I lose my mind!"

"I'm down to help," said Jackie.

"Me too," added Tempest. "Can't be more than some paintin', washin', and what not."

"One thing I know is if we movin' in here, there's gonna have to be some checkin' for mice and roaches," exclaimed Octavia. "I get crazy at little things crawlin' around."

"True," the others chimed in.

"Okay," said Stew, hugging Sharon tightly. "This is good energy. Lemme have a show of hands for those in agreement. How many wanna stay here in Mr. Perkins's building? Two big floors, with maybe some connecting stairways . . . open up some walls, and in the meantime, get back to work."

Everyone, including Sharon, raised their hands. Sharon kissed Stew on the lips. "When do we start?" she asked.

"*Jeeze* . . . lemme *make* the deal first," Stew said in mock outrage.

"Excuse me! Aren't we forgetting something here?" Cheryl stood and raised her hand, then she folded her arms in response to all the attention brought on. "Don't we need to say something about Brenda? About my *girl?*"

"Cheryl, you're right. You're absolutely right. In fact, we should have a few words about everyone. Cathy, too," said Stew.

"And J.J.," added Sinclaire.

"And Ann, LaToya, and Julie, too," said Sharon.

Stew thought quickly. "So how about this: We'll observe a moment of silence for our friends for now, and once we've finished the work in the building, we'll have a nice reception . . . a dedication. We'll dedicate the new home to the memory of our friends that have left us."

Many of the girls hugged one another or held hands. Sharon was wedged between Stew and Egypt. Everyone bowed his or her head during the silence. The only sounds that could be heard came from outside—car horns, an airplane overhead, and an air conditioner.

"Now, before we do another thing, those of you who *were* able to get clothes out of the fire, raise your hands." Stew looked over the raised hands. "Okay, you five are going with Sharon here on a little shopping spree. That means you need to jot down the sizes of everyone else. You guys are gonna pick up pants, shirts, and undies."

"I don't need undies!" called out Octavia.

"Me either," said Sinclaire, giving a sly smile.

"Anybody else?" asked Stew, trying to inject some humor to uplift their spirits. "Alright. You girls start chattin', get all the info together. Just simple stuff, okay? Tomorrow I'll have you *all* on a shopping spree to correct your wardrobes."

Stew took Sharon for a walk out of one apartment and into another. Every door on the floor was unlocked for them to view the premises. There were six residences that filled the sixth floor, and just as many on the fifth floor. Some apartments had two bedrooms, some three, and there were two studio apartments on each floor. The building had only one elevator, which moved as slow as molasses, and there was a wide stairway that stretched from the top floor down to the basement. Timmy was close by all along as Stew and Sharon walked through the building.

"I think this can work, Sharon. Here's my idea, just picture it. We open up walls to make the rooms bigger, we clean up, but we keep it ghetto. I mean, just Studio A and B. I mean, hook things up so the room only *looks* like a slum. Instead of thousand-dollar beds and furnishings, we put a grimy mattress on the floor. Maybe we fix it so it looks like there's cracks in the walls and the plumbing is exposed. Maybe some empty beer cans and cigarette butts, raggedy sneakers on the floor. A rickety wood floor . . ."

Sharon had a salty taste about her. "And you think that my girls are goin' for that, Stew?"

"Based on what I just heard, I *know* they will. Keep in mind, it's only pretend in the studios. Outside of the studio, it'll be same ole-same ole; makeup table, a prop table, business office; just like all the other locations. Everything I have in Malibu, Atlanta, or like I'm setting up in Canada— oh shit! I almost forgot!" Stew reached for his cell phone and switched it on. It began ringing immediately.

"Yes. Stew here."

"Hey, babe, Steph. I got the carpenter here, can you talk to him?"

"For a minute, put him on." Stew held a finger up to

Sharon. She snuggled up to him, the two of them sitting on a radiator against a wall.

"*Yellow*," greeted the carpenter.

"Yellow to you, too," Stew said, making a face for Timmy to see. "I want to give you an idea of what I want done. Did you see *The Hunchback of Notre Dame*?"

"Eh?"

"The movie, sir, did you see it? Or did you ever see *Robin Hood*, or *The Three Musketeers*?"

"Now yer' talkin'."

"Good. In all of those films, there was a scene where someone was held captive. You might have to see the films again to catch my drift, but I want to create those prisoner experiences in the basement of Pearsall Road."

"Okay."

"I hope this doesn't sound too crazy, but it's what we need. If you could just—"

"A bit crazy indeed. But that 'tis not my concern. You say it; I build it. 'Tis my job."

"Marvelous. Would you mind taking a look at those films today to see what I'm taking about? Once you do, we can talk again."

"When are you looking to—"

"I need this done as soon as possible. I can get you a deposit and everything, but I need to know you can build me what I need."

"Tell ya what. I'll stop by the Blockbuster store over in Sunshine Square, 'n I'll get the movies today. Call ya in the mornin'."

"Sounds great," said Stew. "Can you put Stephanie back on the line?"

"Sure."

"Stew?"

"Beautiful, Steph. What's up with the girls? Will you be meetin' them at Bruegger's?"

"As we planned, babe. Everything's going smoothly. I'm with the phone company now, talking about installations."

"Good. What's up with Sal?"

"S'pose to be here in the morning. First thing. How're things there? How's Sharon holdin' up?"

"Good. It's not pretty, but you know how we do. We just keep on truckin'."

"Of course, I miss you already, babe. This is the first time we've been apart in awhile."

"Mmm-hmm . . . Keep up the good work," Stew said.

"Love you," Stephanie blurted

But Stew was already gone. When he hung up, he noticed Timmy had left the apartment. He and Sharon were alone.

"Baby, I know that this isn't the best of times, but I need to be with you," said Sharon.

"You mean . . . like, lay down *be* with me?"

"We don't even need a mattress. The hard floor is good enough for me." Sharon dug into Stew with a determined look.

"Damn, Sharon. It's like that?"

"It's like *that*," she replied. Sharon got closer and their lips met and their tongues entangled.

Just like there was only one Stephanie, one MaryAnn, and one Barbara, there was only one Sharon. But interestingly enough, there was only one Stew. Except Stew felt like a different man whenever he was with any one of these women. He had it all, and that included the women.

Sharon Griffin was five feet seven inches, with curves, soft black hair twisted into braids, and a fragrance that was infectious. That was one of the most alluring things about Sharon. Besides her penetrating brown eyes and full luscious lips, it was Sharon's scent that pulled at Stew's senses. It made kissing her and holding her a rich, rewarding experience.

She was also a bit demanding, which he liked, too. Nobody he had lain with had her audacity or her dirty mouth when it came to sex. And the thing was that Stew *allowed* it. It was like a little role reversal. Something he wasn't accustomed to, but at the same time looked forward to.

Timmy came to the door, but Stew gave him a look. "Timmy, tell the girls we're gonna be a few minutes. Give 'em a good excuse. And shut the front door. Make sure we get some privacy."

"Right, boss," Timmy said, expressionless, and left.

Stew went back into the small bedroom with its dusty wood floor and chipped wallpaint. The look in his eyes was a confirmation for Sharon—the answer was yes.

"We don't have too much time, Sharon."

"Oh, *trust* me. There's enough time for what *I* need."

"Okay," Stew said, his arms out of the way as Sharon snatched his shirt flaps up from inside of his waistband. Then she tugged at the belt and buckle aggressively. "Damn, baby, you dry or something?" Stew questioned, feeling the urgency in Sharon's words.

"Not anymore," she said. She pulled her shorts off, and then her T-shirt. She wore nothing underneath, and was naked in seconds, except for her Nike sneakers.

"Come here," Sharon instructed. She reached behind Stew's head and pulled him toward her. Both of them fell backwards against the wall. Chipped white paint fell onto Sharon's shoulder and stayed there as she lifted a leg and hooked it around Stew's ass, pulling him closer.

Generally, Stew would have protection with him so that he wouldn't impregnate Sharon, except during these few moments of spontaneity. With all that had taken place in the past week or so—in the past twenty-four hours—that precaution seemed to be less important than the union between friends, or the ultimate affirmation of the living: sex.

Sharon welcomed Stew in, begging for it as hard and as rambunctious as he could give it. Eventually, both of her legs were up, hooked around Stew's back, and he leaned into Sharon, his back empowering his entry, the wall behind her serving as her force, her assistance, and her support. Against that wall she had no choice but to take as much as Stew could give her. He was a muscle inside of her, big, fearless, and hungry for every fiber of her being.

As the two worked their way to the floor, all of the tension came out—Stew's from the weight of so much responsibility, and Sharon's from the loss of a friend and a near-death experience. Now that the two had one another to give and take and share the tension and the anxiety, nothing else mattered.

"More! Come on, nigga! More! Hit it hard, *baby*, fuck that shit!" Sharon groaned her commands and the whole of it turned Stew on as he slammed into her again and again. He couldn't get this kind of loving anywhere else on earth. It was so primitive and rough. It was just ghetto.

"Yeah, nigga . . . Yeah, mothafucka, gimme that dick! Fuck me! Harder! Again! Again!"

Sharon wailed as her body withstood his impact. His power. In no time, she was speechless, merely a mass of shuddering meat that Stew shot off into, and collapsed onto.

Moments later, Sharon Griffin, the newly energized business manager of the Bronx branch of Platinum Dolls, left with her five helpers as if she were Santa and they were her elves. She was charged. In her hand she had Stew's corporate American Express Platinum, with permission to make her girls as comfortable as possible. Stew had kissed her and told her to buy until her heart's content. Then he'd smacked her on her ass, and Sharon scooted off to pick up clothes, music, cleaning supplies, personal hygiene items, and whatever else they might need.

Charles Porter *had* to close the deal. It was a matter of eight million dollars. It was the biggest contract he'd ever fulfilled. But now he also had to fulfill another obligation. He couldn't just take the money and skip town like he'd originally planned. He needed to help Pop and his son with their objective. He was being asked to help them catch a killer, and the crazy thing was that *he* was the killer!

Porter recalled the events of the first shooting. There'd been a quarter moon's glow. Actually, there'd been less light than that. His Yamaha Jet Ski had been camouflaged by the darkness, as he sat wedged between rocks close to the sand. He'd adjusted the scope on his rifle and watched the events on the beach outside of the beach house. He remembered thinking that this was the worst kind of job, to take a shot at a woman. Especially when there was a guy over there on the beach who seemed to be filled with ego, all those women shaking their asses, some even naked, performing before him like he was some king. He considered making him the target, but no. The client wanted Porter, aka Steele, to hit a girl.

Hit her in the shoulder, the twerp had requested. He'd even paid two hundred and fifty grand up front. Once the job was complete he'd promised another installment of the same amount.

Why not? Porter wondered. If he didn't do it, someone else would, so why not go for it? The girl catches one in the shoulder, she's traumatized, hospitalized, and sent home with a bottle of painkillers in a couple of weeks. In the meantime, he'd pocket half a million dollars, tax free.

But the thing went wrong. The girl had missed a step on her way up to the beach house. The shot he'd taken for the shoulder hit her square in the temple. There was no recovering from that. As soon as she'd fallen, Porter was gone. The escape was easy. To sleep with the mistake was not. When his contact had called to have more work done, Porter subcontracted the arson work. What a mess that was!

And now here he was. His old friend needed him. Who knew? I mean, what were the odds that he'd have gotten called into this? Or that Pop's son would happen to be on the beach that day alongside King Ego. Small world.

But even though everything seemed a mess, Porter had a plan. It was a grimy one, but such is life. Porter would fulfill both objectives. He'd get paid, and he'd solve Pop's problem, too.

First, the money.

Bronx, New York

SEVENTEEN

Stew cut the deal for the fifth and sixth floors of Mr. Perkins's Grand Concourse property, including permission to do renovations such as knock out walls and add a connecting staircase. The top floor would be where the studios and business offices were located. There'd be the large soundstage as well, just as in Seattle and Malibu, to accommodate Stew's video productions. Porter accompanied Stew when he sat with Mr. Perkins, and as he was making calls to his accountant regarding this and that payment, Porter overheard something about L.T.S. Industries, and he drew his own conclusions.

Since Timmy and Pop were elsewhere, discussing further security measures for the Concourse branch, as well as for the other locations throughout the country, Porter took the opportunity to find out more about the connection between Stew and L.T.S.

"I take it you have partners," Porter began. He felt he'd built enough of a rapport, that he and Stew had that association bit happening (maybe because of their brown skin), and the endorsement of the father-son team that was now the porno king's avengers. All of those ties, real or imagined, gave Porter carte blanche to ask just about anything, and Stew felt obliged to answer.

"Yeah. They're a pain in the ass, too. I hope to buy them out soon."

"No shit." Porter perked up.

"Maybe next year," Stew guessed. "Big money, you know. But it's the price you pay when you make early compromises."

"How's that?" Porter continued to pry.

"Well, they started me off with a million dollars. But it wasn't like it was cash. It wasn't like they came to my place with an attaché case and said, *Bam!* Here's the cash. They used their resources. Credit, leveraging. They helped me lease equipment and property. They took the responsibilities when it came to billing. So it was a million dollars in *resources*. . . ."

"And now that you blew up—"

"Shit! My company did over two hundred million in business last year. We kept about twenty-five percent of that as profit."

"Fifty million?" Porter almost couldn't get the words out.

"Yeah, but split three ways," Stew said, slightly disgusted.

"Your partners?"

Stew nodded. "L.T.S. stands for Lex, Trent, and Stew. They get a third like me. That's, like, seventeen million each. But when you take off my living expenses . . . I have an ownership share in a Cessna, I have a yacht that I lease but hardly use, I have a ton of cars, trucks, and other little toys. I give the finest gifts to my girls—diamonds, trips, clothes, whatever. Then my mortgages." Stew sighed. "Man! Sometimes, I swear I wanna be poor and hungry again."

"Wanna trade?" Porter asked in jest.

While Stew went back to making his phone calls, Porter put it all together. Lex was Lexington Roland. The twerp who'd hired him was Stew's partner, and for some reason he was paying big money to sabotage things. *But why?* Porter wondered. He wanted to know, but then again, he didn't. What he did know now was that there was more money here than met the eye. *Fifty million last year!* And the twerp had the nerve to haggle about the eight million for the job. It was due time for a visit.

Meanwhile, in L.A. . . . **ON THE AIR**

It's K-L-A on your radio,
It's Ed Lover–Doctor Dre on your radio,
We're kickin' booty from L.A. to Frisco,
Hip-hop and R&B in your ear hole . . .

We're back again . . . doin' the do,
Mad early in the mornin' time just for you.
If you're a teacher, a nurse, or you drive a bus,
You betta not front, keep it tuned to us . . .

We be news, weather, and traffic, too,
We got contests, prizes, and interviews.
So don't touch that dial, don't be upset,
Just jam to the beat and don't forget . . .

It's Ed Lover–Doctor Dre, we holdin' it down,
So stay tuned to our flavor and our funky sounds.
Damn! Look at the time, it's eight twenty-two,
Time for all of our friends that's in the news . . .

Dr. Dre activated the applause and let the hip-hop beat continue, as Ed Lover took a sip of coffee and prepared to get into current events. He looked over his notes.

"Yo, Dre, did you see *Access* last night?"

"Nah, troop. You know me. Lakers to the day I die!" Dre followed his testimony with the applause again.

"Yeah, yeah, right. They need to make you the new team mascot. You could come out dressed like a water buffalo and put on the yellow-and-purple jersey. Your number could be, like, triple zero." Ed broke out in a Snagglepuss laugh. He was cracking himself up.

"I see you got jokes this morning, pencil neck. How about makin' like an antenna and broadcastin' the current events?" Dre said. More applause erupted.

Ed immediately stopped laughing and cleared his throat, sounding like he could dish it out but he couldn't take it.

"An-y-way . . . Our man was all over *Access* last night. Matter of fact, Dre, he was all over the *news*."

"Who's our man now, Ed?"

"I'm talkin' about the biggest of the big. I'm talkin' about the man who wakes up in the mornin' with Porsha, JoAnne, Susan, Gwen, Laura, LaTonya. . . ."

"Oh! You mean the freak-master!"

"Exactly! He's the black Hugh Hefner, the big-dog pimp, Porn King Stew Gregory. Yo, Dre, this dude is like the grim reaper or some ish."

"How so, Ed?" Dre bounced the convo back into Ed's court so seamlessly.

"You know how King Midas . . . how he touches something and it turns to gold?"

"Now, King Midas *is* big-big-*big* dog," added Dre.

"Well, our buddy-ole-pal Stew-boogie has had quite a few problems lately."

"Didn't a girl get shot, like, two weeks ago at his crib?"

"Sure did," answered Ed matter-of-factly, doing a Barney Fife imitation. "And just this week, there were two, count 'em, *two* fires that destroyed penthouses in both Seattle and New York. And, Dre, a total of seven women were killed in the fires. On the news they're calling it arson and foul play and even downright mass murder!"

"Day-amn!"

"Dude got body bags all over the place. And, what I was sayin' about *Access* was, they did a whole segment about Stew-boogie. They showed this dude out like the king he is. I'm talkin' the private jet, the girls, the limos . . . the girls. The Malibu spread—"

"And the girls," Dre cut in.

"Right. And they followed the dude to Seattle, where he got like dozens of—"

"Girls," Dre cut in again.

"Right, right . . . But the spiz-zot up in Seattle is *ba-nanas*! He got a master loft with studios, bedrooms, offices, and a park, yo! Dude got an *indoor* park. Somewhere you

would take a babe and camp out on a bench with the grass
and trees, kick your whole mack-vibe and be like, *what*!"

"Now, *that's* bananas! Maybe we should hang out with
the big dog sometime."

"Oh *hellllll no!* I'm keepin' my distance from *that* dude!
It's a good thing he got that website."

"Platinum Dolls, right?"

"Yeah. This way I can see all this stuff, whenever I want,
and, get this . . ."

"Get what?"

"I don't have to be caught in the line of fire."

"Now that's foul, Ed."

"And my ass won't be the next one with their picture up
on *CNN, Entertainment Tonight, MSNBC.* I'll be alive and
kickin' right here. Mmm-mmm-mmm! Ed Lover's gonna be
alive and kickin' right here on the Ed Lover and Dr. Dre
morning show, KLA style at eight thirty A.M. . . ."

"And ya got thirty minutes left before ya get fired, so
wake up! And we'll be back with more current events."

"On WKLA."

"Keep it here!"

The commercials kicked in. It was just another day with Ed
and Dre. Just another part of the media virus that took hold and
spread like fire. Some shows made light of the tragedies. Kept
it all sensational, including images or reports that were all
about the sex, money, and violence. It was the American way,
to blow up the pain to be fascinating and even entertaining.
Other major media outlets, the traditional radio news broad-
casts, like the AP wire and Bloomberg, as well as the nightly
news, world news, and cable entities, were more to the point.
Women were being killed by wickedly violent means, and all
of it was related to Stew Gregory's Platinum Dolls companies.

"I set the funeral date for Sunday, Stew. That gives you a
week to . . ." Barbara's voice waned while she was updating
Stew from Malibu.

"Funeral . . . jeeze! We're already at that stage."

Barbara took a deep breath. This was only the beginning. "Unfortunately. And Sparkle's will be a few days later."

"Wow!" There was dead air. Then Stew asked, "Have you heard from Leslie? What's happening with MaryAnn?"

"Leslie has things in control over there. MaryAnn is mourning, of course. I understand a few of the girls are staying with her. She's living on Chambers Street; Leslie's there, too." Silence. "Do you want the rest of your calls?"

"What, more press?"

"There's a lot of that, Stew. But Inspector Elliot has left a few messages. And Betty."

"Betty?"

"Yes. She says it's important."

"I'd better call."

"Is everything gonna be alright, Stew? I mean I've got this bad feeling—"

"We're gonna stay strong, Barbara. And we're gonna win."

"Are you gonna be here before Sunday?"

"Hard to tell," Stew said, meandering along the hallway on the fifth floor on the Concourse. "I should be. Say a prayer for me, babe. Lemme call Betty. I'll holler at you in a few." Stew disconnected the call, and made the next one.

"Betty, hi, you were trying to reach me?"

"Yes. Ahh"—she hesitated—"I have a bit of a problem here."

What else is new? Stew thought, unfazed so far by her words. "My life is full of 'em all of a sudden. Let 'er rip."

"Okay. There's been a block placed on L.T.S."

"A *what!*" Stew's voice thundered into the phone.

"A-A-A block," Betty stammered. "It's Mr. Roland. He's directed me to cease with any debits that exceed maintenance of the website. In other words, no checks are to be written over or above ten thousand. . . . Stew? *Stew*?"

The line had been disconnected. Stew was on fire. He dialed Lex's office at once, but reached only a voice mail. Stew hung up and dialed again. The voice mail came on *again*.

"Shit!" Stew shouted. Then he calmed himself, waiting

for the message to finish and his turn to speak. There had to be a reason for this, like there usually was for everything.

"Lex, this is Stew. Your *partner*. I know how busy you must be, but you need to give me a call at your earliest convenience. Your *very* earliest convenience." Stew hung up. He dialed once more just to be sure. No dice.

As he sat there with the phone in his hand, all Stew could think about were the bills and expenditures that were tied to L.T.S. The homes were earning equity with each mortgage payment, but they still had a long way to go until they were paid off. His car payments, at least a dozen of them, were due on the first of every month. And for more than five years now, he'd never missed a payment.

The past few days in New York had been extremely expensive. He'd taken the girls on a shopping spree that cost him close to seventy-five thousand, all billed to his Platinum AmEx. A bill that was likely to arrive in the mail, if not on the tenth of July, then definitely on the tenth of August. Stew was thankful for the breathing room that credit afforded.

But what about Transylvania? Stew had things in motion up there, and money was being spent on the new project. At this moment, the carpenters, interior designers, and others were following Stew's instructions. There had been a deposit, but the overall job would easily cost three hundred grand.

On top of that there was at least another two hundred thousand he'd promised to close two separate deals. And then of course there were the salaries of over five hundred employees. That bill alone was in excess of three hundred thousand a week. Stew thought about all of this, and he dialed Lex again. No answer.

He called Betty back. "Sorry, Betty. I lost my head," he apologized.

"No problem, I understand."

Stew thought for a moment. "Is my personal account okay, Betty?"

"Naturally."

"Is there any way Lex or Trent can gain access or block *that* money?"

"Nope. You've still got the same balance from last we spoke."

"And what was that again?"

"Lemme see," said Betty, tapping into her computer. "Oh . . . I'm sorry. I was wrong. . . . It's not the same balance. You have four hundred and seventeen thousand!"

"Oh my God, Betty! Just the other day there was, like, four or five million. How could . . ." Stew exhaled loudly, trying to think of an answer. "Betty, I need to withdraw those funds now!"

"Everything?"

"Every penny."

"How do you want it?"

"Certified. No. As a matter of fact, cash. All cash."

"How do you—"

"You hold it for me. I trust you."

"No problem. I, uh, I can have it here at my office waiting for you by morning."

"Thank you, Betty." Stew closed his cell phone. He was burning inside!

"Stew? I heard you yellin'. Is everything okay?"

Timmy had rushed in from the hallway. There were all sorts of noises surrounding them, from buzz saws to hammers, to drills to voiced instructions between coworkers. All of this was taking place up on the sixth floor of the Concourse, where the studios and business offices would be located.

"Not the peaches and cream it was weeks ago," said Stew.

"Wanna talk about it, Stew?"

Stew sat on the windowsill and put his face in his hands. He squeezed his eyes closed until he saw only an abyss of dark, gloomy colors. He wanted suddenly to be there, away from reality, immersed far away into the great beyond.

It wasn't the same. The shooting had drawn a swell of attention to Platinum Dolls. There'd been a 40 percent increase in revenues and profits after the news media picked up the story and ran with it. There was even a little help from Lex, who called one or two people he knew to spread the news. Why shouldn't CNN know about a porn king and a dead girl?

Okay, so the plan wasn't perfect and the girl died! Sometimes things happen. You eat, you shit, and then you die. But a 40 percent increase was intoxicating! It was a matter of dollars and cents. Lex just knew he could push this a little more, maybe cause legions of untapped web surfers to start visiting the website and start paying.

So he'd asked for more. Steele had somebody, a *couple* of *somebodies*, who were arsonists. They were good at what they did. A fire on both the east and west coast, both tied to the Platinum Doll empire, would certainly draw massive attention. Lex guessed that it might earn the company another 40 percent at least. After all, his method had proven that his madness was right the first time around.

But it wasn't the same. The increased viewership barely hit 20 percent, and those who *did* visit the site were only return visitors who didn't spend nearly as much money. And to think, Lex was paying so much money because of the dead women! It didn't make a lot of sense. Eight million dollars spent, and for what? Eight bodies?

"Stop the disbursements over ten grand," Lex had ordered Betty. "Just pay what is necessary to keep the website afloat." Meanwhile, he'd wait for, maybe, some hits to accumulate. Maybe the revenue stream would increase. Somehow.

And then Lex went over the line. He withdrew five million from the L.T.S. account, all of the money delivered to him in cash at his Wall Street office by armed security guards. He also withdrew over three million dollars, by fraudulent wire transfer, from Stew Gregory's personal account. *What the hell,* Lex figured. He'd helped Stew make all this money in the first place, so he'd take now and explain later. What could Stew do, argue? Call the police? In either case he'd be compromising his financial backing. He'd be threatening the very lifeblood of his company. Let him poke a few of his girls, lie back, and play porn king. That was Stew's job. Let the big boys handle the money. Maybe Lex wouldn't even have to pay the eight million. That is, if everything went as planned with his meeting. Already he'd won by getting Porter to take all the money at once.

The meeting was set for 8:00 A.M. on Thursday in a wide-open parking area at the far west end of Greenwich Village. Bobby and Tony Forman, brothers who operated garbage trucks for Forman Ltd., their uncle's trash-hauling company, were as knowledgeable as they had to be. The car would be the only vehicle out there that early, close to the northernmost corner of the lot. Behind the car would be the railing, and beyond that, a thirty-foot drop into the Hudson River.

The brothers also expected that there'd be one individual in the vehicle. A coffee-complexioned black man of medium built who might be wearing a Yankees baseball cap. If there was anyone with the black man, that would be okay, too. Lex made the meeting seem real simple. It was a job, he'd said. No biggie. He'd said the guy was extorting him, and he just wanted to get it over with. The Forman brothers wanted the same thing. They were getting a million cold for the job, with half being paid up front.

As the trucks lumbered down the West Side Highway toward Greenwich Village, towing at least twenty tons of iron and steel, they stopped at a red light just before reaching Leroy Street—the last light before the location where the rendezvous was set to go down. It was 8:05. Both brothers had their windows lowered so that they could coordinate. They had to yell over the loud, rumbling motors.

"Aye, yo! You ready?"

"Ready as I'll ever be. You see 'em?"

"Must be the blue Chevy. That's the south end!"

"Right! The only car out there!"

"Damn fool!" Tony smiled at his brother and pulled on his RayBan shades then adjusted his cap.

Bobby did the same, and then yelled, "Let's do it!"

The light changed to green and the two trucks continued in their side-by-side positions as they pushed on, accelerating toward the right-hand lane and the parking lot entrance.

Porter didn't like this already. The twerp was late, but there was little he could do except wait. He knew Lex had the money, that wasn't an issue. He knew Lex was afraid of him. He could hear Lex trembling over the phone. And there was no question Porter was in the right spot. He couldn't be missed. He was the only goddamn car in the lot!

It had been a long past couple of days, with all the assistance he'd provided along with Timmy and Pop, escorting the small army of girls for their shopping spree and assuring Stew that all was kosher, as the contractors began their work on the Concourse building.

Porter took a deep breath; eight million in cash was coming his way. What did he care? Almost instantly he dozed off.

He'd gone over this again and again, while he was awake. In his sleep, his eye was up in the scope of that rifle. The scope was scanning the beach with all of the dancing and carrying on, looking for a match on the laser-printed photo of a girl named Trina. *I never miss,* he told himself. Just like snagging a turkey. Simple.

But these days his dreams were of the twerp, Lex. He had to do something to expose Lex's culpability, and at the same time protect his own ass. He had to maintain his secrecy for the sake of his friendship with Pop. *And* for the sake of staying out of prison!

Porter was having a recurring dream about Lex nailed to a post at a hunting ground. In the dream, he'd told Pop, Timmy, and Stew that he'd found Lex and tied the saboteur to a post, but somehow he'd loosened the ropes and escaped. Now the twerp was somewhere out in the woods, and the three of them—Pop, Timmy, and Porter—had a bet going. The prize was eight million bucks. Stew had put up the money and was standing by to award the victor. The hunt was on. The three hunters took up their rifles and were heading into the woods. This was Porter's chance. If he could catch Lex first, he'd shoot him dead, just so he wouldn't be able to expose the truth about Porter.

As the men in Porter's dream set out, there was suddenly a rumbling vibration underneath them. It felt like an earthquake, like the earth was breaking into pieces. Porter could see the others—Pop to his left and Timmy to his right—rattling around like they were jack-in-the-boxes held up on springs.

Porter was suddenly alert. His eyes opened. He wasn't in the woods anymore. No trees or grass or rocks. There was a lot of pavement now, a railing in front of him, and water out in the distance. Seagulls overhead. No . . . pigeons. He eyed the clock. It was 8:07. *Shit! Where is this twerp?* Porter looked left and then right. Where was this rumbling coming from? He looked up into the rearview mirror.

"Jee—sus—H—*Christ!*"

Porter saw them coming; two big, dark-green monster trucks surging toward the back of his vehicle. *Pop's* vehicle! Oh shit!

The rumbling grew stronger. It felt like a jackhammer. Porter tried to start the car. He turned the keys too fast in the ignition. He tried again. Oh no . . . no way would he be able to start the car and move out of the way in enough time. Porter reached for the car door handle.

Tony had taken the left side, guiding the heavy truck at an angle toward the Chevy. Bobby did the same, from the right side. The two iron dinosaurs charged the blue sedan as if it were a solo bowling pin. The trucks quickly straightened out, buddy-buddy again, just a few feet apart. In seconds, the Chevy was bulldozed through the railing, kicking up sparks and burnt rubber, partly crushed and eventually forced over the side, down thirty-some-odd feet into the Hudson River. And just as quickly, the garbage trucks, unbranded by any obvious advertisement and wearing stolen license plates, swerved away from the edge and over the toppled, mangled railing, picking up speed to negotiate their way into the morning rush-hour traffic.

Just two blocks away, Tony and Bobby Forman pulled the trucks over onto a curb and hopped out onto a sidewalk. They trotted toward the nearest underground subway station, and on the way down, shed their jackets and gloves and Ray-Ban sunglasses. Their disguises were tossed into a trash can, and five minutes later they were on the train to

Coney Island. Nobody on the subway—not the members of the working class, or the homeless, or the bag ladies—would ever understand the kind of adrenaline that was there in that subway car at that moment; a million dollars' worth of adrenaline.

"No, no, Stew, it's nothing like that. You shouldn't think that way. I just needed to make a quick move. I—" Lex was interrupted by his secretary.

"A call for you on three, sir. They say it's . . . it's *super* important they speak with you."

"Hold on, Stew. Just . . . just, easy. Hold on." Lex put Stew on hold and took a breath before the next call. *They?* "Lex here."

"Done! It's fucking done!" Tony was still pumped with adrenaline.

"Oh yeah? How'd it go? Smooth?"

"Smooth as fuckin' Italian pussy! When do we get da rest of the dough, huh?"

For a moment, Lex got caught up trying to imagine what Italian pussy was like. "Easy. *Man* . . . why is everybody so desperate?"

"Desperate? Who the fuck you callin' desperate? We did your dirt, white bread, now we want what we got comin'."

"Where do I meet you? I have the cash right here with me." Lex jotted down the address given to him and promised to meet the brothers within the hour, traffic considering.

"Hey, Stew. Good news. I'm gonna lift the block now. I'm also gonna redeposit the three million in your account. I really appreciate you understanding. Okay? Everything's back to normal. Spend what you need to. Transylvania? I love it. Love you, too, dude. Gotta go."

Lex hung up and clasped his hands behind his head, kicking his loafers up on the desk. *I'm a goddamm genius,* he told himself. Then he called his girlfriend, Janice.

"Hey, my little creampuff."

"Hi!" Janice said excitedly.

"I was thinkin' of you comin' up to the office for lunch. Just you and me."

"Oooh! In the office, what, like a picnic?"

"Well, something like that. Thing is, I'm not really that hungry, dahlin'."

"Oh? Tummy ache?" she asked naively.

"Nothin' like that. I was just thinkin' of feedin' you . . . under my desk, if you know what I mean."

"Oh, Lexington. You are so *heavy*!"

"Noon, baby. I'll have the limo pick ya up."

Lex hung up and then summoned a car to meet him downstairs. He reached under his desk and pulled up two sports bags full of money. He'd refill the accounts, pay off the Italians, and come back to the office for another session of what his mentor, Bill Clinton, said was *not considered sex*.

Scarsdale, New York

EIGHTEEN

Stew sat there staring at the receiver. He couldn't believe what he'd just heard. *Why did he even put me through that after all I been through? Damn!*

In the turbulent storm, Stew's emotions had been so twisted that it seemed like his spine had been separated from his body. The money was suddenly gone, millions disappeared. It felt as if he was back in Detroit—on the throughway, lying in his own blood, in the emergency room. He was a glob of Jell-O. No direction. No sense of belonging. No women. No sex. He was nothing. Dead.

Then Lex just changes all of that. *Good news. I'm gonna lift the block now.* As if he was God.

Stew had wanted to offer a buyout of his partners next year. But now he realized he couldn't wait until then. This had to be done now. If not, he'd leave. He'd liquidate his part in the corporation. He'd take what was his and he'd move on. There was no way Stew would be put through that again. *Never* again!

As for now, there was business to take care of; loose ends to tie. At least now Stew could think straight. He could feel secure with the father-and-son team as his security consultants, and his company's bodyguards.

Serving as an ultimate workforce, Sharon's twenty-four girls and the twelve other women who helped to run the business end got the fifth floor in shipshape within record time.

Beds, couches, and chairs were delivered; carpeting was put down; walls were washed and painted; new lighting fixtures, vanities, and curtains were installed. Every bit of labor was someone's contribution to the overall effort. The only things that could be salvaged from the fire across the street were pots, pans, and silverware from the kitchen. Items that were accustomed to intense heat, or that never came close to the fire itself. All else was lost, destroyed, or sold off in a brief fire sale. What remained of three floors would long be a reminder to the staff of Platinum Dolls. *Nothing should be taken for granted.*

While Stew was in New York, he stopped by to see Betty and pick up the money he'd instructed her to take out. Next, he went to the bank, where he put in a request to withdraw all of his money, some four million dollars. It would take a day to prepare and would be ready at the Wall Street branch in the next two days, on Friday.

Stew also took a thirty-minute drive up to Westchester County, where the Scarsdale branch was operating in a business-as-usual fashion. Brianna was in charge of things at the Scarsdale estate. She was five feet ten inches, without heels—a dead ringer for supermodel Naomi Campbell, with her wheat-brown complexion, high cheekbones, and radiant smile.

Brianna Thompson was one of the few women who Stew *wasn't* fucking, but who still softened to his magnetism. She was a suburban girl, born and raised in Mamaroneck, New York, and had always aspired to be a strong, black business-woman. She was someone whom people had no choice but to respect, despite the trade she managed. And some men would flock to her for attention, for conversation, or even for a flash of her bright smile.

At twenty-three, Brianna was deep into her objective. Always photogenic, with her face in the *Daily News, The Post, Ebony* magazine, *Honey*, and *Vibe*, Brianna held that mystique of a madam, yet she was as regal as Lena Horne or Dorothy Dandridge. She had that air about her that said she'd been a spoiled brat, that she'd been through etiquette classes and that she had been someone's prom queen. But deep within her eyes lived some daring, wise soul, and maybe she'd never submit to any cunning, deceitful force looking to get over on her, or she'd never take her good-girl heart for granted.

Stew found Brianna intriguing. He was curious about the pleasures she harbored. But not to the extent that he had to have it. She wasn't someone that he had to prove anything to. Stew knew that NBA players were calling, and that she had been photographed with at least one Oscar-winning white actor. But still, he didn't feel challenged. He didn't feel as though anyone foreign was invading what might otherwise be his to have and hold.

And Brianna made it clear to him, too, when she once said, "Even if I get married, Stew, I don't think I'd love my husband as much as I love you." Those were words that gave Stew confidence in her. It told him that she was devoted to his objectives, even if they weren't tied together by physical love. And that was a love that Stew could feel, that he could carry with him anywhere around the country, and yet didn't need to have her in his company, or in his arms.

"Stewart," Brianna said in her breathy voice, when he arrived at her place. The sound was like an exhale from her sensual lips, a soft wind that just happened to carry his name with it. "So nice to have you back." And she took Stew in her arms, both of them almost equal in height, thanks to her heels, pulling him into her endearing embrace, her arms around his neck so as to give him as much of her as possible. The two of them stood this way for a long moment; Brianna knowing the trials that he'd been through, and Stew appreciating her welcome, as always.

"Nice to be back. How are the girls?"

"Actually, not too bad. And I've informed them of your coming, so they can't wait to see you. I'm *sorry,* how are you, Timmy?" She had just noticed him, standing quietly aside.

"I'm good, Brianna. Is Kevin around?"

"Oh, I'm sure he is. A really fine man you've sent us, Timmy. He holds exercise sessions and nutrition talks with everybody. He's a hunk of a man, indeed! And the girls love him to death. We really feel that much more secure with him staying here. And, what, you intend to add a second man now, I understand?"

"Yes, Brianna. We're taking no shortcuts, in terms of security."

"In light of all that's happened, I suppose it makes good sense, Timmy." Brianna turned back to Stew. "But how are you getting along, Stewart? I mean, all of this must be devastating."

"Trust me, it's been a challenge. But, like I've been tellin' all our employees, we've gotta keep living. We've gotta keep moving on, despite our losses."

"I agree," replied Brianna. "Oh . . . Stewart, you need to meet one of our newest additions. Oh, Geneva?" Brianna nearly sang out the girl's name.

Geneva was already descending the winding staircase, wearing a strapless black dress that matched her mane of shimmering hair that curved alongside her face down to her shoulders. Her skin was the color of oatmeal, and on her left cheekbone there was an attractive beauty mark. Her descent down the steps seemed so sexy, almost *too* sexy. It seemed almost calculated, except that her eyes were innocent and glassy. There appeared to be a degree of wonder there. Promise. Enchantment.

As Geneva approached, Stew made her out to be about five feet seven inches, and that was barefoot. Despite all the women Stew had working for him, he hadn't seen one more beautiful than the one who was standing before him.

"Geneva, I'd like you to meet your boss. He's the founder and CEO of Platinum Dolls. Stewart Gregory, meet Geneva Daniels."

"Geneva Daniels," Stew repeated.

"Nice to meet you, Mr. Gregory."

Stew had to catch himself. He was staring. Staring at a first meeting exhibited too much of a man's weakness. It told of a man's satisfaction, or that he was in need. It told of his confidence, or it revealed if he was shallow or intimidated.

"You too, Geneva." Saying her name felt good on his

lips. Stew glanced over at Brianna. "How long has she been with us?"

"A month now. We have her in Studio A from three to eight on weekdays. You should read the e-mails she gets. The men absolutely adore her."

"Hmmm, maybe she's ready for a calendar and poster."

Brianna smiled at Geneva, the pride showing on her face. There was a lingering silence before Brianna broke it up and said, "Well, will you be staying long, Stew?"

"I'd like to have a word with the girls, all of them at once, if we can. Just a little talk to affirm the company's goals."

"Mmm, we can't wait," said Brianna. "How about some lunch? I had a few of the girls put something together for you."

"Sounds delicious already," said Stew.

Brianna and the girls laid out a handsome buffet to welcome their boss. Ten giant hoagies were stretched out on the table alongside nachos and cheese, raw shrimp with cocktail sauce, tossed salad with four different dressings, and French onion dip with raw carrots, celery, cucumbers, and crackers. Delores and Pricilla prepared fruit salad with peaches, pineapples, sliced banana, apricots, raisins, pears, strawberries, and apples. The fruit was set in freshly squeezed orange juice inside of scooped-out watermelons.

For hot edibles, Elizabeth and Francine prepared turkey sausage cuts wrapped in bread dough with cheddar cheese, chicken wings with hot honey sauce, and steamed broccoli with sharp cheese.

The food was arranged on the patio tables near the in-ground pool, along with a variety of drinks, including juices, soda, white wine, and bottles of spring water.

By noontime, both the talent and those who worked behind the scenes at the Scarsdale estate gathered around the patio to hear what Stew had to say, anticipating the delicious food before them. Stew had just been taken through the home—inspection style—and shown the various studios and living quarters, meeting and greeting everyone who was helping build the Platinum Dolls empire.

Stew appreciated this type of gathering, how all these beautiful women went out of their way to look good and smell good for him, their leader. Everyone had on black dresses, just as MaryAnn's girls had worn in Seattle, yet something about each woman stood out in some way, whether it was their eyes, hair, skin tone, or even their cleavage.

"Thank you! Thank you! Ladies . . ." Brianna tapped her glass with a fork to get everyone's attention. The crowd of close to fifty simmered down quickly. "Now you know that these occasions are special. So please, let us observe silence. We are blessed to have a surprise houseguest today. He's a busy man, so we shouldn't take his presence for granted. Let's make him feel at home, shall we? Give a Platinum Dolls welcome to your boss and mine, Mr. Stewart Gregory!"

Applause erupted all around as Stew looked out at the many pretty faces, with their excited expressions, their eyes and smiles sparkling like diamonds.

"Thanks, ladies. It really feels good to be acknowledged by such an army of beauties. You all are like one big pool of sensation, and a man just can't help but wanna dive in. Ya know?"

Stew flashed a closed-mouth smile, as he shook his head in an attempt to show guilt. They loved him with their smiles and giggles. Their eyes dug into him, pulling at his next words.

"Well, now that I've loosened up my audience, let me mention something a little more serious. You all have no doubt heard about the recent tragedies that have come our way. Devastating tragedies, in fact. And frankly, these were monstrous acts . . . something we are not taking lightly. So we have added security to our homes and offices all over the country—and I hear that you all are pleased with the new friend we've hired for you. . . ." Stew paused, as a few giggles sounded throughout the room.

"I just wanted to take this time to stop by and say how I appreciate the work you've been putting in. This was all once a vision. That's all, just a thought in my mind. And today we not only have a successful website that attracts millions of viewers, but we have an association of employees, talented, beautiful women like you all—who are well paid and fed because of our efforts. Every one of you should have goals, if you don't already. And I hope that by working for Platinum Dolls you are moving closer to those goals every day. Another thing I want to mention specifically to you all . . . I don't know how many of you know this, but Brianna is the one who came up with the name Platinum Dolls. I originally wanted to name the company Platinum Porn. But thanks to Brianna for giving us a touch of class, let's give her a round of applause."

Stew waited until the applause died down and then continued. "You ladies are indeed the cream of the organization. Sometimes you catch flak about being stuck up, but *you* provide the suburban fantasies that drive those customers wild. You should be proud of yourselves. I mean, you should hear how others talk about you. They're *jealous!*" Stew didn't want to mention what the girls in the Bronx had said. "But that's *great!*" Stew hollered over the voices and they instantly died down. "That just means a competitive spirit. You must maintain your individuality. Both as a Platinum Doll, and as you! Keep on being you. I don't care if you've been spoiled all your life, if you were always considered the pretty girl in school, or maybe you just like to look good and feel spectacular about yourself, and some folks just don't get it. I'm telling you here and now to keep being *you*. You shouldn't care what others think about your lifestyle. They can take it or leave it. Me? I'm glad you're with us. So despite the problems we've had as a company, we must *march forward!* We must keep moving on. Every one of you is Platinum in your own special way. Give yourself a round of applause."

Stew marveled at all the happy faces and the new energy in the air. *I wish it could always be this way.* "So listen, I don't know about you all, but all of this food is making me crazy. *Bon appetit!*"

With that being said, someone turned on George Benson's *Masquerade*, and everyone converged on the good food. Stew mixed through the crowd before ending up at Brianna's side.

"They love you, Stewart."

"I work hard, Brianna. I guess I've gotta get something for it."

"Something like . . . Geneva?" Brianna gave him a crooked smile.

"*Wow!* Brianna, that woman is"—Stew took a deep breath and then continued—"she's a dime-piece. She's *breathtaking*. And it's crazy, really, because I see beautiful women all day every day. It's like a joyride."

"Oh I *bet* you do more than *see* them, Stewart."

"But I can't get enough, Brianna. I swear, I feel like a gambling addict or a dope fiend. How's the expression go? I love this shit!" The two grabbed a bite to eat and strolled off.

"Hopeless! Such a profound heart and energy you have, and you're probably spread as thin as one-ply tissue. Are you ever going to settle down? Will you ever get to a point when you can say, *Now I'm satisfied*?"

"It's hard, Brianna. No kidding. I see women like Geneva and I just lose it. It's not even a challenge anymore."

"And at twenty-eight years old . . ."

"Soon to be twenty-nine," he added.

"You should have someone to love, someone who loves you. Not just have sex because it's convenient. Did you see those girls? Any of them would be overjoyed to know you want them. Even Geneva. They'd jump at the chance."

Brianna stopped in front of a fountain adorned by a stone sculpture. She faced Stew. "But Stewart Gregory, you want to know where I believe the true power of a man is? Besides knowing what you want? Or besides being able to accomplish what you want?" She paused, making sure she had Stew's complete attention. "I believe the true power of a man lies in his ability to exercise discipline. Just because an abundance of something, especially sex, is available to you, that doesn't mean you should continue to suck it up until you can't stand it anymore. Someone who likes to eat would make themselves sick. Someone who likes to gamble would lose all their money. And someone who likes to get high would kill themselves. But, Stewart, someone who likes sex, someone like you, would miss out on one of the most incredible experiences in life. You'd miss out on love." Brianna said nothing else. She gave Stew one of those head-to-toe appraisals and pivoted away, back through the garden toward her Platinum Dolls. Brianna had spoken.

Stew checked his cell phone and noticed a call had come in while he was busy. He dialed Stephanie. "Me."

"Hi! Oh I miss you so much, Stew! The carpenter's work is coming together marvelously. The girls are hyped up. They look *so* good, Stew! Especially one named Anita. You'll like her. . . . *Any*way." Stephanie's smile could be detected in her words. "Sal has a lot going on up here. He expects to have Canada . . . oh, I'm sorry . . . he expects to have Tran-syl-vania on line by Sunday."

"Sunday . . . *oh*, you know Trina's funeral is Sunday."

"So Barbara tells me. I can take a commercial flight, Stew."

"Thank you. And now that you've said that, I think I'm going the same way—commercial."

"Something wrong with the jet?" asked Stephanie, sounding concerned.

"No. I'll talk to you about it later. So we'll see each other Saturday night? Sunday morning?" Stew eyed Geneva in the distance.

"I can have Barbara arrange it so my connecting flight is in New York. I mean, if you want."

"Whaddya mean, if I want? Don't you know how bad I want to see you, girl?" Stew turned away from the crowd and looked at the statue in the fountain. "Don't you know how much I . . ."

"How much you what, Stew? *Stew?*"

Stew turned back toward the crowd. Geneva was forking up a chunk of food into her mouth. Stew imagined it was a strawberry from the fruit salad. The way she did that . . . how she put it in her mouth without touching her made-up lips . . . how she pulled the food off with her teeth in that way. It was so sensual. And then Geneva's eyes turned toward Stew.

"Stew! Answer me! You're making me fucking *crazy*! Say it! You say it *now*, Stewart Gregory! You say what's on your mind or I'll . . . I'll . . . I'll *kill* myself!"

"Don't be silly," said Stew. "I just wanted to ask you something."

"What?" Stephanie said with frustration.

Stew winked at Geneva. She blushed.

"I wanted to know how you feel about . . . well, about us having a friend."

"How? You mean, like, in bed?"

"Yeah, well . . . that, but more, like, bigger than sex. I mean something serious."

"Something serious; meaning you, me, and someone else?"

"Exactly."

"Sex, I don't care about, Stew. I always want you to have your thrills. But love? Is *that* what you mean? You want something bigger, like love? Stew, you can't even love *me,* how can you say you wanna love someone else?"

"Don't say it that way, Steph."

"Well . . ."

"Well what?"

"Well, then say it. Say it now. Not a coward, are you?"

"Watch your mouth, Steph!"

"Then open your goddamn mouth, Stew. Speak your heart."

Geneva was chatting with Pricilla, glancing at Stew now and again. Stew felt the pull on his heart, like a tug-of-war. He had Steph on the phone, and Geneva on the other side of the garden.

"Stephanie, you know how I feel about you."

"Not good enough," Stephanie said. She sniffled into the phone.

"*I love you, damn it!* Is *that* what you wanna hear? Okay, you *heard* it. Now how about answering my question?"

There was silence, then whimpering sounds.

"Stephanie?"

"Yeah."

"You alright?"

"No, Stew. My life is twisted, wrapped, and dependent on you. You *know* that. I'm not alright because I know that I can't have your heart. I know that you belong to others. God-damnit, I have to share you, Stew! How crazy is that? I don't share my toothbrush, my hairbrush, my underwear, or my tampons. I don't share any of that stuff, but I have to share you. And that means you're not mine. Call me selfish, but I *dream* about you being mine, Stew."

"You're being unreasonable, Steph. You know I am—"

"I do."

"So stop being so possessive and enjoy the ride. I realize you love me, that you have a heart. But we're both young still. We're having the time of our lives, right?"

"I guess." Stephanie sounded uncertain.

"So then take the connecting flight in New York. Barbara will give me the details. And fix your face, Steph. I'm gonna give you paradise one day."

"Yes, Stew."

"Gimme a smile, Steph. Tell me you want the best for me."

"I do. I do."

"Good. I have a surprise for us."

Stephanie hung up first.

NINETEEN

Pop had a long couple of days assisting Timmy. The two men were busy installing a force of men from around the country who were fit enough and experienced enough to handle the job of protecting so many women at the various website branches. Besides that, he learned as much as he could about the Platinum Dolls empire and how it made money. There had been phone calls from police detectives and investigators from both Seattle and Malibu, both of which he took the responsibility of responding to. Pop also spoke with detectives from the Forty-fourth Precinct regarding the incident at the Concourse.

There was little information to be had from the individual incidents, but much damage done to the business of this one. The women who had died were all working for Stew, and Stew had told Pop they weren't all love interests. In fact, Stew had been sexually involved with only one of the dead girls—Trina. So this wasn't likely revenge for any type of love quarrel.

The fires had been set by amateur arsonists. Both had been set somewhat simultaneously, but the Concourse fire was apparently accelerated by gasoline that had been siphoned underneath a door to one of the penthouses. There was no doorman at the Bronx property, so the perps probably got hold of a key or pulled the old "delivery" trick; claiming to be delivering something for someone in the building. No doubt the guy had probably pressed every buzzer, until someone let him in.

In Seattle, the doorman recalled the face of a man who had been there to deliver flowers, but he couldn't pick him out of a mug book. More important, there was evidence of forced entry and, after an autopsy, evidence that Sparkle had suffered a concussion from a blow to the head with a blunt object. The arsonist had also used gasoline on the bed where Sparkle—likely laying unconscious—was burned beyond recognition. MaryAnn had been on Chambers Street at work.

But as ghastly as the fires had been, the Malibu killing was by far the most intriguing. An empty casing had been found. Inspector Elliot had explained that the shooter had to be good, *real good*, to hit a target from as far away as the shoreline of the beach.

Pop made it clear that he'd be out to Malibu in a matter of days. All his son had explained was that the hit—the execution—had to have been a high-priced one. It was probably the work of a mercenary. For all those reasons, Pop had called on Porter for help. If there was anyone who knew the game of the sniper, it was Porter. Maybe Porter would even know some likely suspects.

All of these ideas had been filling Pop's mind as he sat in his Pelham Manor home. He was up early, maybe too early, and he should have had another cup of coffee. The one he had earlier wasn't keeping him awake. Sitting in his study, with his notes on the desk before him, Pop laid his forehead down to catch a few z's.

At 11:00 A.M. he got the call. His blue Chevy had been pulled out of the Hudson River, down in Greenwich Village. It had been nearly demolished in some puzzling assault. Two monster garbage trucks had been seen barreling into the vehicle. Pop quickly jotted down some details and slammed down the phone. He had to find out what had happened. Porter had borrowed his car.

Marvin and Leonardo were jogging, as they did every morning, from their studio apartment on Christopher Street, up the West Side Highway, against the flow of traffic, when they witnessed the garbage trucks smashing into the blue Chevy sedan. They had just reached the southernmost edge of the parking lot when the loud crash blew through the morning air. There was already the sound of car horns, the grinding of car brakes, and the squawking of seagulls in the air. It was an average summer morning, but the crash overwhelmed all of that, virtually vacuuming the attention of the two joggers from way across the stretch of asphalt.

The two stopped short, about half a block from the act, both of them with their hands on their hips and absolutely astonished at what they were seeing. The two garbage trucks mowed the car down and off the edge of the lot as though it were a five-ounce toy. The car dropped into the river, and then the big trucks pulled off.

Marvin and Leonardo looked at each other with their mouths agape and their eyes fully dilated. *Of all the nerve!*

"Someone is *in* that car, Marvin."

"They are *not*," replied Marvin, as if such a thing wasn't possible.

"Are too."

"Are *not*!"

"I've gotta help," said Leonardo, already pulling his tank top over his head, exposing a muscular chest with a nipple ring and a tattoo that read SUGAR AND SPICE.

"Oh no you *don't*!" ordered Marvin, his neck rolling like an agitated woman.

But Leonardo was already side-stepping along the railing, attempting to get a better view of where the car went.

Marvin had his eyes stuck on the garbage trucks, lumbering past them, and he had to shake himself out of the spell to go after his boyfriend.

"Leonardo!" Marvin shouted, without a trace of masculinity in his voice.

Leonardo ignored his boyfriend and hopped over to the opposite side of the railing, hurrying along the edge to get closer to where the blue Chevy was quickly being swallowed by the dark waters below.

"No, n-n-n-n-n-no . . . You are *not* on the cliffs or at the lake, Leo! This is *not* the Olympics and you are too out of shape to dive. *Leonardo!*"

That last dig stopped Leonardo dead in his tracks. "I've still got it, bucko," he said, clearly upset. "See, that's why I didn't bring the gold home. That's *exactly* why . . ." Leonardo pointed a finger at his lover to emphasize his point. "Because *your* had no faith in me!" he shouted.

"*Me?* What about your family? All of a sudden, *I'm* the bad boy? *I'm* the hater? What you lacked, *bucko*, was faith in your *damned* self!"

And with that, as a man sunk deeper into the Hudson, his life more threatened with each passing second, Leonardo, Olympic diver and silver-medal winner, made his decision. He took two steps, a short run along the edge, and then propelled himself, his body bouncing up as if catapulted and then hooking down gracefully into the water. On the edge, Marvin screamed like the bitch he was.

The Hudson River was a murky, polluted cesspool where used tires, shopping carriages, unwanted vehicles, and at least a thousand undiscovered corpses were submerged. This was home for it all. God bless the creatures that could still survive there.

Leonardo could only pray that he wouldn't hit any obstructions, things he couldn't see from above the water's surface. At worst, he thought, flinging his 180-pound body into a thirty-foot fall and hitting something head first would kill him instantly. There'd be no pain, maybe only a sudden sensation, then some blinding light, and then maybe a bunch of angels. Fairies, if he was lucky. Heaven. At best, he would be a hero. He'd be on the front page of the *Daily News*. The headline would read: "Olympic Diver Saves Victim." The story would have photos of him at the stadium where the medals were awarded, Leonardo with his silver medal. Then there'd be a photo of him just after his death-defying dive, and then another of him later, standing side by side with the person he'd saved, shaking hands. Marvin would be mentioned nowhere. No photos.

And that would *burn him up*. And Leonardo would get his laugh.

But there was no obstruction, just water as thick as glue. Leonardo tried to keep his eyes open as he held his breath, moving like a slick torpedo in the direction of the car's descent. He couldn't see the vehicle yet, only a film of what looked like globs of brilliant circles. As he got closer he realized those were air bubbles from the sinking wreck. And now he had something to direct and guide him toward where his help was needed. The deeper he glided, the darker it became; more haunting than he even imagined.

The Chevy had fallen into an embankment, which slowed the car's descent. Leonardo had been holding his breath for less than ten seconds, so he felt certain that he could be of help. He'd held his breath underwater for as long as a minute and five seconds in the past, but never in waters such as this. The fear alone would *surely* interrupt his rhythm. The weight of the Chevy was sinking the car deeper, as Leonardo swam up to the driver's side window. *Indeed* there was someone inside, just as he'd thought. His mind immediately flashed a message . . . a telepathic message, *Oh ye of little faith!*

Water was filling the cabin enough to cover most of the driver's body. His head and torso were hugging the steering wheel awkwardly, as though he were leaning up and into it. The man's head and face were bloody, and the front windshield was cracked, the water seeping in and filling the cabin even faster.

Leonardo was still comfortable with his preserved air, although he knew he not only had to finish what he could down deep, he also had to get back to the surface for a breath of life-affirming oxygen. He grabbed the door handle and yanked it, trying to jerk it free. It didn't budge. He tried harder by wedging his feet against the car and pulling again. The failed attempt was a quick reminder that he was not just pulling against the strength of the car, but against the power of the entire Hudson River.

Damn. I wish he were awake in there so he could roll down his window. Then I could just pull him out.

Leonardo began to have second thoughts. He wished he hadn't taken the dive. If only Marvin hadn't opened his big mouth. *What you lacked, bucko, is faith in your damned self!*

The thought of Marvin's scorn inspired Leonardo's energy. Somehow, Leonardo had to fill the car with water, gain entry, and pull out the man before his own dwindling air supply ran out. And then he'd have to get back to the surface with the added weight. The air began escaping from Leonardo's nose, then from his lips. There wasn't much time left. Not much strength either, or faith.

"So you having a little meeting?" Trent looked down at the gym bag in Lex's hand. "Or, uhh . . . have you just started working out?" Trent stood up against the wall, his arms folded and his feet crossed.

Seeing Trent waiting there near his office door had startled Lex. *Did he hear the call?* Lex wondered nervously. "Ahh . . . yeah, as a matter of fact, a little of both," Lex said.

"Mind if I come along?" Trent uncrossed his arms and feet and started heading toward his office. "I'll get my car keys. Lemme drive."

"No, no, don't bother," Lex said quickly. "This is kind of a . . . how should I say . . . *exclusive* engagement."

"Is *that* so?" Trent eyed Lex suspiciously. Something was going on and he wanted to know if it was what he thought it was.

Lex nodded, his eyes diverted from Trent as he answered. "Yeah, that *is* so. Now, if you'll excuse me, partner." Lex pushed past Trent. He had no intentions of explaining anything any further.

"It was you, wasn't it," said Trent accusingly.

Lex froze in his tracks. He didn't turn around; didn't want the evil in his eyes to show. He didn't want Trent to see the acknowledgment of the truth.

"The withdrawals, the money block . . . that money there in the bag . . . This is all some cockamamie scheme of yours, isn't it?"

Lex stood still. The resolve in his eyes was clear. He'd

been discovered, but it was nothing that he couldn't handle. Nothing he couldn't fix.

"Isn't it, Lex? Or maybe you think I'm a dummy; that I'll fall for anything."

"We'll talk when I get back," Lex said through clenched teeth. He still hadn't turned around, but he knew he'd have to handle this situation. Trent would not stand for this. *I am not going back to prison!* Lex told himself, and then he stormed off.

"Good morning, Mr. Roland," the driver said, as he opened the door to let his passenger in to the rear of the stretch. Wall Street was bustling with suits and taxicabs and messengers and overnight delivery services.

Lex didn't answer, he only smiled that practiced close-lipped smile and then slipped into the car.

Along the way to Brooklyn—over the Manhattan Bridge, down Flatbush Avenue and Eastern Parkway—Lex thought about Trent Morris. Lex had few black associates, and only one whom he called a friend. That was Trent. Lex had met his fill of con men and hucksters behind the prison fences. There were bank presidents, congressmen, and even mayors who were sent away. Some were able to keep their businesses afloat, while others, it seemed, who maybe were denied such resources because of their IQ or skin color or class, were stripped of even the most practical and smallest resource.

Lexington Roland saw this over and over again during his skid bid in the federal penitentiary. And that was partly the reason why he decided to join together with Trent. Lex felt that while he had inherited the good looks and convenient skin color, Trent was the one who was hungry, his background rooted in dispossession, racism, and the slavery of his ancestors. Trent was someone that Lex could build and teach and nurture . . . a sort of project—like Frankenstein's monster—who was to do as he was told.

No more check or credit card schemes. Lex told Trent that those activities were for common criminals. He told him that he—a man who grew up around the banking industry—would help him so that he'd be set for life, with all the credit and all the access to any amount of money he desired. All that Lex had wanted in return was a man to do the legwork for him while he was still completing his time. Trent was that man. He left prison six months before Lex. Trent followed his instructions to the T, and the two became partners the moment Lex stepped off the bus in New York, his new home for his new ventures.

And now, years after the frustration of prison, after the hard work they'd both put in to make this successful, Trent was his biggest threat. Just as Trent had helped Lex set this all up, Trent could tear it all down with one phone call to the FBI, Secret Service, or to any of New York's legion of attorneys. Porter had been Lex's most difficult problem, virtually holding a gun to his head. But Trent, he'd be a cinch. And once the problem was solved, Lex would be a fifty/fifty partner with Stew.

The limousine eased up to Salvatore's Spicy Pizza at the edge of Coney Island Avenue in Brooklyn. Tony Forman jumped in the car, while Bobby Forman stood under the canopy of the pizza shop, looking up and down the avenue for signs of police presence.

"Good job, Tony. I saw the news."

"Yeah."

"The man's on life support and not expected to live. . . . They called the tragedy unprecedented and the type of activity only seen in the movies. They said the garbage trucks had been hijacked, and that the assailants got away scot-free."

Tony smiled that proud smile. It was reminiscent of Ralph Kramden, *The Honeymooners* character who didn't know how to take a compliment.

"I guess a man's godda do what a man's godda do," said Tony. "How 'bout da money?"

"Oh, of course, here it is. The balance, plus . . . I put in a little somethin' extra."

"Extra? You mean more than the five hundred large?" Tony's eyes widened.

"I need you guys again," Lex said.

"Yeah? Hold on." Tony pressed a button. The wrong window lowered. He pressed another. "Aye-yo! Bo-bby, c'mere!"

"So tell us, Mista Wall Street"—both brothers were in the limo now. It was a new environment for them—"whacha got for us?"

"He's an easy target. Here's the picture. Name's Trent. Trent Morris."

Tony turned to Bobby, both of them with their crooked toothy grins.

"And you won't need garbage trucks for this job," Lex said. Then he smiled, too.

Pop spent the whole afternoon and half of the evening at the New York Medical Center on Eighth Avenue, just three blocks from New York University, The Blue Note Jazz Club, and the blitz of small stores, boutiques, and restaurants, all of it accounting for the sensational electricity that made Greenwich Village the magnet that it was. He had spoken with two police officers and a detective regarding why his Chevy was down in the Hudson River and about who that man was in the driver's seat.

"It's simple. I loaned out my car," he'd told them. Nothing more; nothing less. Charles Porter was a friend. They didn't need to know anything else, as far as Pop was concerned.

It was almost 7:00 P.M. and Pop was waiting for a miracle. If not a miracle, then at least a goddamn explanation. Did Porter actually go after a hunch on his own, without backup? If that was the case, Pop couldn't wait for Porter to get well . . . so he could beat his ass and put him right back in Intensive Care. The more Pop thought about it, the more sure he became that what had happened that morning was just too ridiculously coincidental to be an act of random violence. *Somehow, some way, this is connected to Platinum Dolls.* He would bet his life on it.

Pop sat there, grinding one hand against the other. Each hand absorbing the extreme tension of the other, until they were red and well exercised.

"Mr. Andrews?"

"Yes," Pop said, his tall, muscular build towering over the young male doctor.

"I know you've been patient and I've decided to let you see Mr. Porter. However, you need to know that he's in a bad way. . . ."

Pop was somewhat aware of the two freaks who were standing nearby, leaning up against the wall and stressing to hear what was being said. He'd been told all about the young man's daring rescue, how he'd risked his own life, and that he was a hero. He'd also seen the two men kiss and it almost made him vomit the chicken-salad sandwiches he'd eaten from the hospital cafeteria.

Wait'll Porter finds out who gave him mouth-to-mouth, Pop thought wryly. He tuned back to what the doctor was saying.

". . . he's hooked up to the respirator now—maybe the only thing keeping him alive. His lung has been crushed, there is extensive bleeding—internal bleeding—as well as the severe head injury. I don't know what else to say."

"Can I see him?"

"Follow me."

The two walked down the hallway, its tile floor glistening, its bright fluorescent lights making everything look more sanitary than it probably was. The walls were white, the nurses were white, their shoes and hats . . . the sheets on Porter's body. There was enough white to make it feel like Heaven. But why then did Pop feel like this was Hell?

Pop heard a low whirring sound, which had to be the respirator that the doctor had spoken of. And damned if that wasn't Porter with all that stuff hooked up to him as if he was a bionic man. *Jesus*. Porter was heavily bandaged about the head and face. Only one eye was naked; and it was partially opened as if he'd been doped up. Porter's arms were both in casts. One hand was bandaged and only a forefinger free. Pop wondered if that was the *only* part of Porter that was in good health.

"Has he said anything? Or . . . uh, has he *moved*?" Pop

had to catch himself. There was no way Porter could speak with that mask on his face.

"Not at all. I thought that this might be the last chance you'd see him alive," the doctor said grimly.

"Jeeze."

"I'll leave you alone for a minute."

Pop approached the side of the bed and waved his hand over Porter's eye.

"You there, buddy? It's me, Pop." Pop took hold of Porter's finger, perhaps the only evidence of life, besides those waves rising and falling on the respirator and the beeps from the other contraption beside it.

"Fuck, Porter, I got a mind to wup your ass right now! If you don't talk to me, I . . ."

As he was talking, Pop felt Porter attempt to curl his finger in Pop's hand. Pop pulled away at first, as if he'd been pricked by a pin. Then he realized that this wasn't a mummy, it was Porter trying to communicate.

"Scared the goddamn shit outta me, Porter. *Jeeze!*" Pop took hold of his friend's finger again. "I don't even know how to talk to you, man . . . all fucked up like this."

Porter squeezed twice.

"Shit, Porter, I don't know any SOS. How you feelin'? Uh, squeeze once for *I'm gonna live forever*, and twice for *I feel like shit*."

Porter squeezed twice.

"Jeeze . . . I guess that's bad. You're in a bad way, Porter. Tell me who did this. It's got somethin' to do with the Platinum folks, don't it?" Pop thought quickly. "Squeeze once for *yes*, twice for *no*."

Porter squeezed once.

"Jeeze! You found the perps, huh? *Just* like I thought! That's the goddamn reason I called on ya. And look where you are now. It's all my . . ."

Porter interrupted him, squeezing four, five, six times. He wouldn't stop squeezing.

"What, what, what?" Pop asked frantically.

Porter squeezed twice. *No*.

"No what?"

Porter's finger was still for a time. It worried Pop, until he realized the eye was still open; still twitching slightly.

Porter used his finger to stretch out Pop's hand.

What an idea! "See, that's my boy. Smart as ever, broken or not. Okay, okay . . . Now write me some. S . . . Okay, okay, *damn* . . . We're talkin' here!"

Porter spelled out S-O-R-R-Y.

"For what?" Pop asked. "For going after the preps alone? Aw, shit! Porter, I was just kiddin'. I'm jealous, *shit*. I wanted *to be there*!"

Porter poked the center of Pop's palm. Then he went on to spell again. M-A-L-I-B-U.

"Yeah, yeah, of course, the shooting. These were the guys who did the shooting. Even I know . . ."

Porter spelled out M-E, and then his finger drifted off Pop's palm. Porter's eye closed. There was a tear there.

Sorry? Malibu? Me? Pop frowned. What was Porter talking about? It didn't make sense. But before he could ask his friend anything else, a loud beeping sound filled the room.

"Doctor!" Pop shouted at the top of his lungs. In a matter of seconds, a small army of attendants pushed past Pop.

"Sir, please." A nurse urged him to leave the room. She had a hand on his arm. Shaken, Pop looked down at the nurse's hand on him. She immediately removed it. Everything was happening in slow motion now. The doctor's voice sounded distant as he issued instructions. The door closed Pop out of the room, and he stood there helpless.

Nothing seemed real. The P.A. system and some mellow voice announcing, *Dr. Gross, paging Dr. Gross to the ICU stat . . .* ; the queers in the hallway—one of them holding Pop's arm where the nurse had held him. Pop, again, with a look of granite. It all paraded around him like a warped collage, and he, the zombie, moped around within its boundaries.

Sorry. Malibu. Me.
The words would haunt Pop for a long time.

While Charles Porter—hit man for hire—was falling into his final state of rest, Stew was doing the town with Geneva Daniels. He had stayed the night in Scarsdale, after a delicious formal dinner, and early the next morning, with nobody to see him, he woke Geneva from her sleep, convinced her to get dressed, and they crept out of the house into a town car. The motor was already running, Timmy and Sammy sitting in the front seat. Sammy was large, Stew noticed. He wondered if the man had ever wrestled, and Stew asked him.

Sammy looked back and said, "Wouldn't *you* like to know what big Sammy is cookin'."

As the car pulled out of the driveway, Brianna Thompson stood in her bedroom window watching between parted curtains that were almost as sheer as her nightgown. She inhaled, then exhaled, then she wagged her head; a certain wisdom in her clever, fluttering eyes and a slight grin on her lips. *What am I ever going to do with you, Stewart Gregory?*

Since it was early, Stew took Geneva to breakfast in Manhattan, where they enjoyed a four-course meal of cheese omelets served on a bed of onions, green peppers, and tomatoes; cantaloupe-fruit salad; turkey bacon and blueberry waffles with a choice of raspberry, boysenberry or strawberry syrup; and champagne and English muffins with blackberry preserves.

"Now, do you eat this way *every day*?" Geneva asked.

"If I make the time, I do. Or, if there's a special occasion." Stew's voice sounded silky. When he spoke, it tickled her in places that were still virgin to any man's touch. "And you, Geneva, are a *most special occasion*."

Geneva's head lowered some and she looked down at her food. She didn't know what to say to such a compliment.

After breakfast, Stew and Geneva walked down Fifth Avenue. He bought her a dinner dress at Saks, a diamond bracelet at Tiffany's, and an array of intimate hosiery, lingerie, and brassieres at Victoria's Secret. It was Geneva's idea to model some of the intimate apparel at Victoria's, where there was a side room with mirrors and chairs in order for him to comfortably make his assessment. Stew had to cross his leg over and keep his hands folded on his lap in order to hide his erection.

"You like?" Geneva came from behind the folding wall, wearing a see-through nightgown and matching panties. One of the straps was falling off her shoulder as she posed with her hands at her hips, thumbs forward, and her head turned up and away. It was a step short of her saying, *See me, love me!*

Stew could've melted, she was so beautiful. Her nipples were defined and her breasts were supple and perky. Her curves were hourglass perfect, and the area below the navel had its fuzzy strands of hair. Geneva waited for an answer.

"Geneva, you're an angel. A naughty, naughty angel," he said with a smile.

Stew left his phone off all day, vowing that he'd enjoy these moments for all they were worth. *I deserve this.* All the while, Timmy and Sam kept their distance, going unsuspected and ever alert for any danger or threat.

At noon, the couple grabbed pizza and rode a horse and buggy through Central Park. The ride afforded them an intimacy that was a breath away from being a fairy tale. They snuggled during the ride, and Stew gave Geneva that first kiss. It went on for just a few seconds, before she pulled away and blushed. It wasn't so much a rejection as it was her humble demeanor. But she didn't close up too far inside her shell because when Stew made another attempt, she welcomed him and she slowly began to feed him back. The buggy ride seemed to last forever.

At 8:00 P.M., the couple attended a concert at Radio City Music Hall and then dinner at Showmann's in Harlem, where a jazz diva accompanied by a piano player was taking requests from the audience. Stew tipped them a hundred dollars and requested "You Must Believe in Spring" and "My Funny Valentine." After dinner, Stew told Geneva that he had rented the penthouse at the Plaza Hotel. He asked her if she believed in fate.

"I really can't answer that, because . . . well, I'm embarrassed to say, I don't *know* what fate is."

"Oh that's alright. I guess, what I mean is, do you believe that what is supposed to be is supposed to be?"

"Okay. You're saying, like, if there's a car accident out there in the street right now, do I think that was supposed to happen?"

"A little cruel," Stew said, "but something like that."

"I've wondered about that sometimes. You know, like where did the sun and the moon and the stars come from . . . that kinda jazz. I mean, I *know* there's a God. I can't see God in person, but I sometimes think that God is the stars in the sky, the flowers and the water and the earth."

Stew was stuck. He had been working toward making a point, but Geneva just threw him way off with her opinions about the world. He was mesmerized by her. "Wow. So how would we know if you and I are supposed to be together?"

"How?" she asked.

"Sure, since you're the philosopher."

Geneva smiled and her eyes widened. "Maybe some kind of miracle; a signal maybe." Her own idea seemed to excite her.

"How about this," Stew bargained. "I'd give anything in the world to make love to you tonight, *but* the universe might not go for it. We might not be made for each other. Do you agree?"

"I . . . I guess. If you say so," she said warily.

"So I'm thinking, let's take two pieces of napkin. We'll rip 'em . . . like . . . so. There. You have a pen?"

Geneva gave Stew a strange expression. *Of course not, silly!*

"Of course you don't. Okay, on this piece I'll write a Y for *yes*. And on this piece, an N for *no*. Okay. Now, I'll take both pieces and close them in my hands. . . ." Stew put his hands under the table and was mixing things up for Geneva to choose.

"Wait a minute. I've seen this trick before. You've written a Y on both pieces of the napkin before we started."

"What? That's outrageous!" Stew said with mock disgust.

"Tell you what, here . . . Why don't I do the choosing then, and *you* hold the napkins?"

"Okay."

Stew put the balled-up pieces of napkin into Geneva's hands and she put her fists under the table to scramble the papers. Finally, she pulled her fists out and placed them across the table. Stew picked the left hand. He also took the other napkin from her right hand and dropped it into a glass of water.

"Listen, before I open this napkin, I just wanna say that you don't have to do this if you don't want to."

"Oh, but I do, I *do* want to, Stew. This would be like God reaching down and giving us his blessings, or . . . he could be saving us a lot of pain and misery."

"I don't know. I'm not sure. . . ."

Geneva reached over the table and grabbed Stew's hand. It was a first. "Please open the napkin, Stew Gregory."

"Well, Geneva Daniels, since you put it like that." Stew unraveled the napkin.

The penthouse suite of The Plaza was considered the crème de la crème of penthouses. Presidents and their wives had been there. Sultans and princes and princesses and ambassadors had stayed there. Hugh Hefner and his bunnies had also been there. And now it was Stew's turn. The napkin trick had been just to lighten up the mood; to let Geneva know what was on his mind. Sure, he could've come right out and told her that he wanted to fuck her pretty brains out, but that was something he did with hoes he knew, or with those who would go the limit to prove something.

Geneva was a different kind of woman. She was nineteen. She was a sheltered girl having grown up in Rye, New York. She finished high school, but rebelled when her parents made demands about college. They wanted a lawyer or a psychiatrist for a daughter. All she'd wanted to do was spread her wings. Stew figured that he could help her with that.

Geneva was nervous. Standing in the bathroom, she looked at herself over and over in the mirror. She wondered if she was appealing enough in the sheer negligee that she had on. Appealing? *He can see everything! I'm not appealing, I'm naked!*

"Stew," Geneva called out to him from the bathroom.

"What's up, G-G?"

"Umm . . . can you, like, turn off the lights out there?"

"They're already off, sweetness," Stew answered, sensing her nervousness.

"Thank you," Geneva said. She stood there trying to psyche herself up. *Okay, I'm gonna go out there. I'm gonna act like I know what I'm doing. And he's gonna fall in love with me.* Geneva took a deep breath, she turned off the bathroom light, and she went to be with Stew.

It wasn't as dark as he could've made it. Stew could've closed the curtains, shutting out the glow from the moon, its reflection on the terrace, and the millions of twinkling lights throughout the city from all those high-rises, skyscrapers, and landmarks reaching into the night. But he'd decided not to. Stew left the gaudy curtains open, and just a flimsy white one to blur the impact of the cityscape, which now seemed to serve as an audience to whatever activity was about to take place in the penthouse bedroom.

The *last* thing Stew wanted was to frighten Geneva. Everything about her was unblemished by time or age, not burdened by a list of lovers or dark experiences of her body being taken for granted. *Yes,* Stew determined, *Geneva is someone I want with me forever. I'll make sacrifices if I must. I'll compromise what I have to.* She was going to be his, hopefully, in whatever way he wanted.

Stew could see Geneva as she emerged from the bathroom. Her every feature was clear: her doll face, her spirited curves, and her innocent eyes. She took soft barefoot steps to where Stew sat on the side of the bed. That in itself was out of the ordinary for Stew; to be sitting up waiting with bated breath. No, normally he'd be lying back against the pillows. He'd be arrogant, with his arms up and hands clasped behind his head. Ordinarily he'd be demanding, but not this time.

Geneva felt a chill shoot through her when Stew smoothed

his hands from her thighs, over her hips, and up to her breasts. He reached under her negligee, and she followed the natural urge to raise her arms up so that they dropped into a fold behind her neck. His hands felt so good molded to her, cupping her. She didn't want him to stop, but he did. She stood between his legs, purring and trembling at his every touch—her back, her behind, her underarms—until he eventually pulled up the sheer fabric and undressed her. She wanted to tell him, but she was too overwhelmed.

"You are the most beautiful woman I've ever met in my life, Geneva," Stew whispered softly. He helped her down to the bed so that she was lying against the pillows. All was exposed under him but for her privates, since she still had her panties on. He hovered over her.

Geneva stared back up at him. She wanted to say it, but she was caught in the fix of his gaze, tantalized by his limbs and the weight of him against her. Then he adjusted her arms so that they were stretched back into the pillows. When he lowered his face to the side of hers, and she felt his warm breath in her ear and on her neck, she shivered. The words were stuck in her belly.

"Sweet Geneva . . . with you I'll never want again," Stew whispered. He let his tongue explore her earlobe, and then slid it down along her neck, toward her shoulders. The feeling was electric, and Geneva shivered all the more. "Stew," his name almost burst through her lips. And once he reached her cleavage, she nearly lost her mind.

"Yes, sweet Geneva."

Her breath was nearly gone. "I have to . . ." She pulled her arms in front of her, and her hand took hold of his face. She swallowed. "I have to tell you something."

Stew stopped short and came back up to face Geneva.

"What . . . What is it, baby?" Stew studied Geneva. Her eyes were glassy with wonder. They promised dreams and fantasies and destiny. They were stars unlike those in the galaxy—these were his. They were focused on him.

"I think I'm . . . I'm a virgin." Geneva pulled her arms to her breasts, feeling naked and unmasked.

Stew chuckled, trying not to hurt her feelings. "What do you mean, *think*, Geneva? You either are, or you aren't. There's no halfway."

"But that's what happened. It was my first boyfriend. He . . . he *did* go halfway, like, this much." Geneva indicated an inch with her forefinger and thumb. Stew thought that this was cute, her being nervous about *this much*.

"Oh. So if it *was . . . this much . . .* then you just might *be* a virgin. Why did you have to stop and tell me that, G?"

"Because that's why we—he and I—stopped, because it hurt too much. It was very . . ."

Stew put a finger over Geneva's lips. "No more words. Your, uhh, boyfriend? He wasn't a man, Geneva. I . . . am a man. And I assure you, the last thing in the world you'll feel tonight is pain."

There were tears in her eyes, and one rolled down her right cheek. Stew kissed it and then put his mouth to hers. He warmed her up again, her tongue slowly enjoying his. It was an approval. She was giving him permission to move on. *Take me.*

Stew moved from her mouth down her chin; his tongue was like a paintbrush, stroking her, familiarizing himself with the taste of her body. Geneva shivered once Stew reached her nipples, his tongue and teeth teasing and taunting her with pulses of both silken affection and exciting stings, while his hands hugged her breasts fully, leaving nothing unsatisfied. He spoke in broken murmurs.

"Never hurt you . . . the best a woman can be treated . . . the tenderest loving care I can manage." *Was that a word? Tenderest?* And Stew went on like this, relaxing her, exciting her and pushing and pulling at her senses, until he reached her navel . . . her belly . . . her soft strands of pubic hair. Stew lifted Geneva's legs so that they were upright, and he pulled off her panties.

"Now I know no other man has done this for you, Geneva. . . . So you just hold on tight and let me give you pleasure from out of this world."

Geneva had no idea what he meant exactly, but he was already doing that—giving her incredible feelings that were causing her body to stir inside. Feelings she'd never felt before. For one thing, she'd never been in *this* position before. Stew had her legs suspended and crossed at the ankles. His hands held them like that as he kissed her calves, the back of her knees and then her thighs. He instructed her to hold her legs there for him, and she did so. He planted wet kisses along her behind and he moved inward, toward what her mother had told her was *a woman's world*.

Stew began to tease Geneva with light kisses so close to her center that she thought she'd die. "Are you ready?" Stew mumbled.

But Geneva couldn't answer. She was whimpering and sighing and shivering in response. She didn't need to answer, since he was already *there*. Already kissing her wet folds, and she felt both of his hands there as well. She felt his tongue smooth from the top to the bottom of her opening, *her world*, and at one point he inserted his tongue, in and out, causing her to cry with pleasure. His mouth covered her fully and his tongue flicked at her outer walls. He inserted a finger as he did this, his other hand massaging the areas around her wetness. Geneva's body locked stiffly and a rush zoomed from her bowels to her brain. Geneva screamed, a piercing scream that drifted off into nothingness.

Stew had made sure to insert two and three fingers so that when he mounted Geneva, the only difference would be in her mind—her knowing that this was it, that this was when she'd become a woman. After her scream, Stew let down Geneva's parted legs and easily slid inside of her pussy. He consumed her mouth with his so that she would taste what he'd tasted, what he'd eaten. The suddenness of it all, he guessed, would serve so many thoughts and emotions that Geneva would be in a state of surrender. Her body was but a group of muscles that needed attention in the effort to relax and accept him entirely. And Stew's intention was to take it to those extents. He'd do it gradually and there'd be total satisfaction.

Geneva felt a strain at first, the penetration causing some

stinging sensation within her walls. Stew's body was not too big for her to enjoy the full weight of him, at least she didn't think so. He hadn't gone there yet. He wasn't flat against her or all the way inside yet.

She felt comfortable bending her legs back to the sides of his waist, and she intuitively clasped her heels behind his back. It allowed her to accept more of him. She kissed Stew deeply. Geneva could taste the difference on Stew's lips and tongue, and suddenly knew that these were her own juices that she tasted. It was another first for her, but it didn't matter. With Stew things were different. She felt she was under his control and she was willing to go along, wherever he wanted. She felt safe.

Stew slid in and out of her, farther than she'd ever known, and farther than she probably realized. Stew moved steadily, saying nasty things in her ear, keeping her excited, while his thickness pushed up inside of her.

"Oh, Stew." Geneva sniffled and the tears began. She was somewhat conscious of the burn between her legs, but it was acceptable. She could take this, the good and the bad. For the want and desire and the need to reach that . . . that ocean of pleasure again, Geneva clawed at Stew's back. It was enough to make marks but not break skin. Stew responded by giving her more and more, reaching deeper and deeper. Geneva's screams captivated him and turned him into a wild beast. She pulled at him. She *wanted* his aggression and his power. She *wanted* to be taken entirely. And then there was the jolt to his spine and the spasms that overwhelmed his senses, and he let go. Abandon moved through his body like a river of pleasure, and he, too, turned stiff and hard until he slumped down onto Geneva and realized his might, his will, and his power had all been surrendered—all of it spent until he was breathless with the consequences of a man who didn't know the concept of limitations, or the difference between lust and love.

TWENTY

In his robe, just another Plaza Hotel accommodation, Stew stood outside on the penthouse terrace sipping warm tea and looking out over the summer landscape—New York City becoming the Bronx, the Bronx becoming Westchester, and Westchester becoming the infinite point, the horizon.

There was so much out there for a man to conquer, whether man-made or God-made, and Stew knew the secret wasn't just money. The power belonged to the man who had control over both money *and* women.

Women could empower men or they could cause their downfall. That was all there was to it. And while power was the greatest aphrodisiac for man, a powerful man's aphrodisiac was women. A woman could inspire and motivate a man's productivity. She gave him reason. She also absorbed his tensions, frustrations, and anxieties.

Stew had learned this over the years. He lived by it. And as he had these thoughts, as he knew them to be at the heart of his success, he turned to look into the bedroom. The patio doors were open, the curtains parted, and Geneva was inside, asleep with a smile on her face.

"Why you?" Stew asked in a hushed tone. "As far as I've come, why is it that *you*—just another woman, *still a girl, even*—have weakened me?" Stew felt almost as if he'd lost his mind. It didn't even make sense. He had women in different parts of the country waiting breathlessly for his phone call, for his presence . . . for him just to breathe their way. And yet, this one girl, someone he barely knew, just came along and swept him off his feet. He couldn't understand it. In a way, he *didn't want to*. Knowing would complicate things too much, and Stew liked things simple.

Stew pulled his phone from the pocket of his robe. He had a call to make. "Brianna? It's Stew."

"Stewart, how nice of you to call," she sang. "Say . . . I was wondering. . . . Would you happen to know the whereabouts of one, hmmm . . . I believe her name is . . ." Brianna paused, allowing the sarcasm in her voice to sink in.

"She's right here, Brianna."

"No shit, Sherlock! *Oops! Did I say that?*"

"Sorry, Brianna, I just—"

"No explanation needed, Stewart. But you know, all you had to do was ask. You know I would've handed her over to you on a silver platter. No need to sneak around, boss, or should the appropriate title be *super lover*?"

"I guess I felt a little . . ."

"Shady? Uh, low-down? Or were you thinking cradle robber?"

"You sure know how to dig into a man, Brianna."

"Hmmm, sometimes I wonder. If I had my choice, you all would be wearing dog collars. But *that's* another conversation. How is she? Did you hurt her?"

"Actually, no, she's lying there asleep, with a smile on her face."

"Is *that* so? Well you *are* a good man, Stew, despite the fact that you're a *weak* man. You're still a *good* man."

"Maybe that's why I called you, Brianna. I'll be *damned* if I called to apologize for snatching up this prize catch, but I'm wondering, is it *okay* for a man to be weak? I'd really like the perspective of an educated woman."

"Is it okay? You mean, how do I perceive it?" Brianna took a deep breath. "I don't think it's okay for *you,* Stew. And I'll tell you why. You and I are young still. We have our whole lives ahead of us. Because of that, we must make careful decisions. We must think first, before we act. Some mistakes we can't afford to live with for the rest of our lives . . . mistakes that may limit us. Shackle us. A mistake could be developing feelings for someone when you're not prepared to see the union through to some definite end. . . ."

"I'm listening," said Stew. He'd just pulled the patio doors closed and now he was looking over the city again, in Brianna's direction.

"Now you, you're a hell of a businessman, Stew. Look at all you've accomplished, putting food on so many tables at twenty-eight-years old. That's almost unheard of unless you're some superstar, ball player, rapper, or actor. And you should agree with me that you wouldn't have met me, *or* Geneva, if it wasn't for your company. True?"

"True."

"So there. Your business is important. And what does it take to run your business? You! Stew, without you, none of us would be where we are. Sure, we'd be doing something else, but not *this*. Not living like princesses in estates and penthouses and beach houses across the nation. So your top priority in life, first and foremost, should be you: *your* health, *your* well-being, and *your* peace of mind."

"I hear you," said Stew. Her words were sinking in.

"Now here's my big question. Does Geneva help you in any of that? And if she does, so be it. You're the winner. If she doesn't, if for some reason she's just added baggage to you . . . just another girl to call yours, then that will be your problem. They say that to sail big ships, you've got to go where the waters are deep. But, to that I add, that no matter how big the ship is, it can handle only so much weight. Otherwise, Stewart Gregory, the ship will sink."

Nothing was said for a time. Stew could see down into Central Park where joggers were like moving dots and cars were as small as paper clips.

"Something to think about, huh?" Brianna said finally.

"Sure is."

"How's Stephanie, Stew?"

"Oh fine. Remember I told you she's up in—"

"Transylvania," Brianna interjected. "I know *all about* Canada, Stew. That's *not* what I was asking. I mean, *how* is Stephanie? Are you both still soul mates?"

Stew chuckled. "I like how you put that, Brianna." It sounded like she insinuated that they were married.

"Well? You looked like soul mates when you both stopped by here earlier this year. Have I mentioned the soiled sheets that you left in the guest cottage?"

Stew laughed aloud. "O*kay!* Go ahead and throw the whole guilt trip on me."

"Oh, trust me . . . I'm not the one who's guilty."

"You know what I meant, Brianna. Stephanie and I have some rough edges, a few, to be more precise."

"Let me guess. You don't give her enough quality time. She gets beside herself when she finds out about the next woman, *especially* if she's not included. Oh! And I can't forget the big whopper; she wants your love, huh? I bet you haven't even told that woman you love her yet."

Stew remained silent.

"And after all she's done for you. What . . . you don't love her?"

"Well . . ."

"Do you appreciate her?"

"Of course."

"Is she one of your best friends?"

"Yeah."

"You'd go to every extent to see that she's happy."

"I would."

"And one more question. Does she satisfy you? In bed."

"No question."

"Then, Stewart, my friend. You not only *love* her, but you're *in love* with her. Stewart, you may not be a one-woman man, and of all the men who are like you, you may be one of the few able to afford that playboy lifestyle . . . and I mean a *genuine* playboy lifestyle. But you'd better start making some commitments somewhere along the line, otherwise, jewels like Stephanie are gonna drop off your jewel tree, never to return."

"It sounds like I'm being disciplined," said Stew.

"That was our last conversation the other day. We know *that* didn't sink in. I hope this one does. . . ."

Stew didn't say a word. There was nothing more to say.

"Oh, Stewart?"

"Yes, Brianna."

"Do deliver Geneva back to where she belongs . . . that is, when you're finished with her."

Brianna hung up. The conversation was beating around in his head like a penny in a tin cup. He thought about everything she'd said, and about how intuitive she was. Once upon a time, when he'd first set eyes on Brianna, he had wanted her. But there had been that look in her eyes that said, *I will not be any man's toy. I will give myself to the one man who will have me as his queen. There is no other way.* And Stew accepted that. He admired her integrity. She knew who she was and what she wanted in life. And that's the way it was.

Stew was only *thinking* about bending now, but back then, he was just as determined as Brianna. *I don't love them hoes.* But this was different. Geneva wasn't a . . .

"Stew?"

Stew turned around and saw her standing by the patio doors. "Hey, gorgeous. Good morning."

"Hey," she answered, her voice groggy. She snuggled up to him. "I heard laughing," she said.

"It was Brianna. She said I stole you and that I should have you back before my limo turns into a pumpkin."

Geneva giggled. "You alright? Last night. Wow!"

"Yeah, wow," Stew agreed. "You're not hurting or anything?"

"Are you kidding? I can hardly walk!"

"I can fix that!" Stew swept Geneva off her feet and carried her back into the bedroom. Her shriek of delight amused him. He carefully placed her on the bed. "You look crazy-guilty," he said.

"I do? I'd hoped you'd see something else."

"Like?"

"Stewart Gregory . . ." Geneva reached out to Stew and

pulled him down on the bed so that he was partially on top of her. "I'm in love with you."

Stew had no chance to respond. As soon as the words came from her lips, Geneva covered his mouth with hers and fed Stew her tongue in such an aggressive way that he had to work just in order to keep up and avoid being swallowed. They kissed until the robes came off, and within minutes he was inside of her again.

"Are you *sure* he's not available? Maybe he's locked in a bedroom with—"

"Mr. *Morris*. Sir, if you'll excuse me for saying, I've never heard you like this in all the years I've known you. You usually have more control, more reserve."

"You're absolutely right, Barbara. I'm sorry. Please excuse me, but I *must* speak with Stew! This is a matter of life and death!"

As Stew's executive assistant, Barbara had heard these types of pleas before. So many folks wanted to speak with him, yet so few were given the chance. Trent Morris was indeed one of those few. And considering the tragedies that had befallen Platinum Dolls over the past few weeks, Barbara had every reason to believe Trent's claims. But she was being truthful. She had not heard from Stew in almost two days.

"I can promise you I'll keep trying him, and the moment I get through, I will have him call."

"Thanks again," said Trent before hanging up.

This was unlike Stew. Barbara always had access, even if it was *she* who needed to hear his voice. She thought quickly and then dialed Timmy's cell phone.

"Yes."

"Timmy, it's me, Barbara. I'm sorry to bother you, but this is a little unusual. Have you seen Stew?"

"We're in New York, Barbara, at The Plaza. He's in the next room."

"Would you mind letting him know I called? Umm . . . there's a call for him that seems to be extremely urgent. From Mr. Morris, also in New York."

"Uh, sure. As soon as I see him, he'll get the message."

Timmy didn't let Barbara know one way or the other what was occupying Stew's time, or why he chose to stay out of touch. He just spoke to her in a business-as-usual tone. Barbara had no choice but to accept whatever Timmy said.

"No problem. Thanks."

Timmy was beginning to feel as secluded as Stew had chosen to be. But this was only a day. He had Sammy to keep him company, to talk about guns and to play cards with. Stew would get over this new chick soon enough, just as soon as he satisfied his appetite. Timmy rose from his bed and grabbed the remote control. He wasn't a big fan of TV, since he knew that almost everything was designed to brainwash the naive couch potato. Everything had ulterior motives. A pretty face sold everything from laundry detergent to cars, and the news was more sensational than informative. But that was the American way.

He flicked on a channel and found a news program. A tow truck with a crane was pulling a car out of the Hudson River. The car was heavily damaged, and a ton of the Hudson's grimy water was pouring out from where the windshield used to be. Timmy raised the volume as two joggers appeared on the screen. The camera zoomed in on only one of the two, as he was being interviewed.

"So how's it feel to be a hero?" the interviewer asked. His microphone had the Fox logo branded where the television viewer wouldn't miss it. Meanwhile, the jogger-turned-hero spoke into the mic.

"Frankly, I'm happy just to be alive. And that it's summertime, because during the winter I may not have survived such a dive and rescue."

"Yes, and if I may, you are an Olympic athlete, I'm told."

"Yes, I brought home the silver medal for my country. It was three years ago, but I think I've still got it."

The images changed as the hero spoke. The camera shifted to a photo of him with the silver medal hanging around his neck, then back to the diver as he was today, then to another shot of the crane lowering the dripping wreck onto a flatbed. A bunch of police hovering over the calamity were also shown at the scene. A different newscaster picked up the story.

"Police say that the garbage trucks were abandoned just blocks away and that their drivers were seen running off to the nearest subway. So the case of the blue Chevy, the garbage trucks, and the dead driver are just the latest in a list of New York City's famous mysteries. . . ."

Timmy yawned and flipped the channel. On *Good Morning America*, the guest was an author who had written a few dozen books while she was incarcerated. *Cute*, Timmy thought before switching channels again. He flipped through commercials selling everything from dishwashing liquid to tampons. He continued past reruns of *The Beverly Hillbillies, I Love Lucy, All in the Family,* and *The Jeffersons.* Timmy flipped the stations a few more times and eventually settled on Bravo. An old interview with Larry Fishburne was on. He was explaining why he chose to be called Laurence. Timmy watched with interest as the bearded professor who was interviewing Fishburn proceeded through his twenty questions.

"What's your favorite curse word," he asked.

"Mothafucka," answered Fishburne with a laugh.

Timmy smiled and cut off the TV. He wondered how far his father and Porter had gotten with their own investigation. He started to call Pop but then decided to go check on Stew instead. They were in the next room over, a short hallway separating them. Timmy eased up to their door and just before he was about to knock, he heard the girl.

"Oh! Ohhh! Stewart, yes! Oh, God, yes!"

Timmy made a U-turn, went back into his room, and headed for the shower. His expression never changed. This was nothing unusual.

Pop Andrews got the superintendent to unlock the door to Charles Porter's apartment. He had been living close to Pop in Tuckahoe, a small suburban community whose stretch from Mount Vernon to Yonkers was wider than it was long. It was one of the few neighborhoods that could still be considered suburban, whereas so many others had become cities.

"Thanks, guy. Don't worry, I'll let you know before I leave so you can lock up."

"Will you be long, Agent Andrews?"

"No, sir. And that's *former* Agent Andrews, sir. But people call me Pop."

"Alright then, Pop," the superintendent said. He smiled and then left.

Pop turned to face the unbearable. He switched on the light to help brighten things, and to scare off the one ghost he knew would be here. He saw the trophies, at least a dozen of them, sitting on the windowsill. Pop picked up a pile of bills off the table. Con Edison, New York Telephone, and the car note for his Isuzu Trooper. Pop noticed there were at least two or three overdue notices from each one.

He threw the envelopes back down on the table and strolled farther into the apartment. There were half-eaten boxes of Chinese food in the fridge, alongside a box from Gino's Pizza. It looked like he had been living on fast food, living the fast life. Pop grabbed a Budweiser. He figured Porter owed it to him. He shut the fridge and went into the living room. The *Daily News* was spread out on the couch. The *New York Post* lay underneath it. Both papers were open to the feature sections, the two-page spreads in each one showing the fire up in the Bronx. Photos of the arson in Seattle, Washington, were also shown. There was a publicity photo of Stew Gregory, and underneath it, photos of the dead girls, including Trina, the girl shot in Malibu.

Sorry. Malibu. Me.

Pop walked over to a study desk in the corner of the living room. He sat down in a tall-backed chair in which he knew his friend had once sat. On the wall behind the desk, there was a corkboard with a photocopy of the Platinum Dolls family. Stew Gregory was standing beside the dark Japanese woman Timmy had told him about, and a few other people were standing to the left and right of those two. Pop wondered where Porter had acquired the photo and why he had it up on his bulletin board. Pop reached up and took an ad from the board. It read simply, "Merc for Hire." There was a number with a 212 area code. Pop jotted down the number. He began to pick through other papers. They began to paint a picture. There were some tear-outs from *Hunter* magazine. High-priced rifles that Pop knew well, all of them over ten thousand dollars. There was also a flier for the Northeastern Hunting Association's Twentieth Anniversary Hunting Competition. *I guess it'll be just me and Timmy this year,* Pop thought.

Pop took a deep breath and dug further. There were more bills, and a receipt from Springfield Rifles. Pop scanned a Visa statement and found that Porter had less than two hundred dollars of available credit left on a card that had a limit of twenty thousand. The statement showed at least seven charges for gas. There was also a five-hundred-dollar charge for a night-vision scope, and a ninety-dollar charge for ammunition. Porter had bought water-resistant camouflage gear and gloves as well. And then Pop found a charge of nine hundred sixty dollars for a round-trip ticket to LAX. Pop shook his head and reached for the phone. He had a hunch, and he wanted to call that 212 number. The line was dead. *Of course the line's dead. He hasn't paid the bill in over a month!*

Pop got up and went into the bedroom. The room smelled musty and the bed was unmade. He pulled open a closet door. There was a stockpile of hunting gear. There were outfits, vests, and jackets on hangers, and holsters and hats hanging on hooks. There was also FBI gear, stuff that Pop had gotten rid of long ago. His hand ran across a blue windbreaker with FBI in bright white block letters on the back. Porter also had a DEA and an ATF jacket. *But he was never . . .*

Pop bent down to look into a knapsack. He couldn't believe his eyes. He pulled out the leather bag and poured out its contents on the bed. There was money, loads of it, neatly packed in amounts of ten thousand dollars. Pop counted fifteen packs; one hundred fifty thousand dollars. He checked the bills individually, just to be sure. He was in total disbelief. As far as he could tell, they weren't counterfeit.

He realized that the bills were slipping out of the wrapper of one of the packs. Pop took it out and counted it. They were all hundreds, but there were only ninety bills. Nine thousand dollars; did Porter take the other thousand?

Pop wondered about the contents of Porter's pockets when they'd found him. He'd have to check that out. He looked around a little more. *What is that?* He turned back to the closet and looked at the suspicious bags. *Was there more money?* Pop opened the bag. It was a Springfield A1A; a custom-made long-range weapon that could take out a pigeon, a turkey, or a human being, depending on the ammunition used and if there was a muzzle suppressor attached. You wouldn't want to use it on a turkey if it was intended for Thanksgiving dinner, and you didn't want to demolish the head of a fifteen-point buck if you wanted it stuffed as a trophy for your wall. The taxidermist could never fix *that* kind of damage.

Was it just coincidence that I called on Porter and that he was somehow already aware of this attack on Platinum Dolls? Or worse, was he involved in some way? The puzzle was coming together slowly but surely. First, Pop had calls to make.

Trent Morris was through with Lex's shenanigans. He had been in the dark about a lot of things, but he knew the difference between right and wrong, and he knew about the withdrawals from the L.T.S. account. And there was no mistaking the phone call he'd overheard.

"It's done! It's fucking done!" A young, excited male voice had shouted into the phone. Trent had picked up the call in error because Lex had been on another line. But he'd put the phone down gently so as to not be caught. No, he didn't know exactly what his partner was up to, but he knew that it was grimy. He knew that he wanted nothing more to do with Lex, and as far as he was concerned, L.T.S. was no more. Fuck the Wall Street office and the resources that Lex

had set up—associations with big banks, brokerages, and investors. Fuck the company limousine—Trent could get around just as well on the subway or by taxi. And furthermore, fuck Lex, too—his friendship, the partnership, *and* the money.

Trent was clear on a few things. He'd saved a bundle of money thanks to Platinum Dolls. He'd gotten himself into a nice midtown Manhattan high-rise, complete with a doorman and a view that showed him some of the East River. And there was a cute waitress who worked over at The Blue Angel Restaurant, who'd gone out with him enough times that it was turning serious. Things were *happening* in Trent's life; a stretch from the life of an ex-con who continued to dabble in crime, or who felt that he had no choice but to do dirt, to con and deceive and victimize others just to survive.

This was the first time in his life that he was happy, and nothing or no one was going to spoil it. It didn't take much to make Trent happy, but it took even less to put someone like him back in prison. Trent was determined to toe the line. He was absolute in his objectives to achieve, but he would *not* compromise when it came to doing the right thing. He would do the right thing even if it hurt. Even if he had to start over from scratch and struggle to get to where he was today, he would do it, because Trent Morris was *not going back to prison no matter what*!

He was in a cab that had just turned onto the Forty-second Street exit ramp off FDR Drive. He didn't wait for Lex to come back and talk to him as he'd said he would. Trent didn't want to fall for any more of the guy's smooth talk. He figured he'd reach out to Stew. He'd explain things in detail. He'd show Stew how to dissolve the L.T.S. partnership without losing ground in his company goals. All that Trent wanted was a job, a position in a company that he believed in, which he helped build. Trent hoped the least Stew could do was apologize for not finding out about Lex earlier. He'd help Stew protect Platinum Dolls from Lexington the Great, before the man destroyed something so profitable . . . so promising.

Trent considered all of this as the cab turned off Forty-second Street and down Madison Avenue, heading toward Fifty-seventh Street. It was a beautiful summer's day, and not even Friday's traffic could take that away. And things would change once he saw Stew. The day would be a new one. Barbara had returned Trent's phone call. Yes, she had found Stew. No, she had not spoken to him.

He's asleep, I guess, Barbara had told him. *That's how he gets when he's at those swanky hotels. Especially the ones you have in New York. I expect to hear from him shortly. . . .*

Trent had thanked Barbara wholeheartedly, and then he made a run for it. All he took was the framed photo he had—the waitress from the Blue Angel—and his attaché case, all stuffed with important documents regarding Platinum Dolls. Trent knew Stew's taste. He'd seen profit and loss statements, receipts, as well as all other financial data having to do with Stew's company.

Stew would be staying at one of only five places while in New York: the UN Plaza, The Helmsley Palace, The Four Seasons, The Waldorf-Astoria, or The Plaza. During the cab ride, Trent called information and got the numbers of all five of the four-star hotels. The Plaza was finally the one to transfer Trent's call when he asked for Timothy Andrews.

This was what would be considered inside information; to know that Timmy was Stew's personal bodyguard and that hotel rooms were generally reserved in his name. It was a safeguard to protect Stew's privacy. It was something that was evident on the hotel receipts, which Trent had access to, as a partner in L.T.S. The cab was at Fifty-seventh and Sixth, just a block away. *Today was gonna be a good day*.

Tony and Bobby Forman were as high as high could be. It wasn't a drug-induced high. It was the money. Lexington had given the two a million in cold, hard cash for the job on the extorter in the blue Chevy. Shoving that car into the Hudson with those twenty-plus tons of iron and steel had been easier than expected. And to think they'd gotten away with *murder*! Then all of a sudden, the Wall Street dude wants another job done. And badda bing! He gives 'em another five hundred smackers up front. Tony and Bobby felt like they'd come upon Christmas in June.

And so they'd gotten hold of two beat-ups, a black Impala and a green Grand Cherokee. They parked outside of Lex's Wall Street office and waited for the black man with the black shirt and the yellow polka-dot tie and yellow blazer. He'd also be wearing black pants. When Lex described Trent's outfit, Tony had laughed. *Whadda we gonna be shootin' at, a goddamn freak from the Ringlin' Broddas Circus?* he wondered. But it didn't matter. The bright gear made this guy an easy target to locate and follow.

The Forman brothers—Tony in the Impala, and Bobby in the green jeep—were two vehicles behind the taxi that was carrying Trent. They easily tailed him from Wall Street, up the FDR, and now across Fifty-seventh Street. All they'd need was for this moulie to be out in the open somewhere. They'd shoot him down like a lamb, ditch the cars, and maybe hightail it down into the Sixth Avenue subway line. It was only a matter of time.

This must be what love is all about, thought Stew. That sense of abandon, when you gave your mind, body, and soul to another person unconditionally. That feeling when you poured your all into the experience without cares or worries of the repercussions. Love. It now seemed laughable, how Stew had ignored it all these years. How he'd rejected the proclamations of those who loved him. How he'd called them hoes right to their faces—and they didn't mind. *What the hell was I thinking*? It was as if some door was closed in his mind; one that wouldn't *allow* him to love, to let go, or to express his true feelings. Instead, he had been thinking negatively about women. He wondered how could he love himself if he couldn't love the ones who loved him?

So much pain and agony he'd gone through to get to where he was today—Detroit, Malibu, Seattle, New York— not to mention the struggle to be a black man at the top of his game. He'd gone through all of that and yet missed out on one of life's incredible luxuries.

Geneva had opened that door. She opened it wide so that all the light in the world seemed to pour in. It was a wonderful and sensational light. It was an incredible feeling; one that he never wanted to let go. Suddenly, Stew began to see the greens, the blues, and the yellows of life. He finally saw other colors besides black or white or red. It seemed like hours ago, when he'd been looking out over the city from the terrace, that he'd seen only what could be conquered and what could be overcome by power, money, and influence.

But now, walking hand in hand with Geneva, taking a wayward stroll through Central Park, Stew could see the light blue sky peeking down through the fully bloomed trees. He could see the lawns of green grass where the children skipped and played, the squirrels worked to prepare for the fall, and the pigeons fluttered their wings. There were butterflies and flowers and lovers. Everything seemed to feed that energy, that warm summer excitement. There was love in the air, and Stew breathed it in, as much as he could in the attempt to cleanse his soul. Stew was so caught up in the moment that the four million dollars he was supposed to pick up at the bank were forgotten. *Today was a good day* with incredible revelations.

"Why do you always look at me like that? I don't know whether to feel scared or excited. It's like you're in another world or something."

"Trust me, Geneva. I'm in another world—one it would take a million years to understand, or explain. . . ."

"Do you see the butterflies?"

"Oh, I see 'em. I see butterflies, and stars, and white doves . . . all of it surrounding my beautiful angel."

Geneva giggled and her face reddened.

"Oh stop, Stewart! You say all the nicest things. Look, there it is."

"What?" Stewart asked, oblivious to anything but Geneva.

"The butterfly I was talking about, silly."

Stew turned to look at the black butterfly gliding over the

grass behind the park bench where they were sitting. It was close to where the two sat, as though it was putting on a show.

"Bet I can catch it," Geneva said.

"Bet I can catch it before you," Stew said.

And both of them hurried around their respective sides of the bench to catch the black butterfly. It wouldn't surrender. The butterfly weaved and circled and fluttered through the air, just within reach at times, and easily evading the two even as they jumped or lunged for it. The creature would not be caught. It would tease them, playing their game, and it would continue to win. It would always fight for its freedom.

At one point, both Stew and Geneva jumped at the butterfly and crashed into each other, Stew absorbing most of the pain from Geneva's elbow. Stew fell to the ground, feigning agony and torment. He bellowed and twisted on the ground, hiding his face from Geneva, who immediately ran to him.

"Stewart! Are you okay? Ohmigod! Stewart!" Geneva bent down to where Stew was curled up on the grass, and in the next instant he reached out to grab her.

"Boo!"

He wrestled Geneva to the grass, burrowing his face into the crook of her neck and her bosom. She screamed with rapturous joy as he did this, and then as he tickled her sides and pinned her down. The two were entangled, their lips and tongues doing their own wrestling match, their own dance. This went on for as long as they could stand it, as the two lay in each other's arms on Central Park's lawn.

"You know something, Geneva?"

"Hmmm?"

"I don't think I've ever known love before now."

"No? Me neither," she replied, snuggling into Stew. "I can't wait to bear your children, Stewart! I can't wait to be your loving wife. Picture it . . . Mrs. Stewart Gregory. Me!" Geneva laughed. "Stewart Gregory, I want you to take me, right here on the grass. Make me your slave for all the world to see! Let's make the butterflies jealous!"

Stew was frozen. The words children and wife got stuck in his mind like glue. He hadn't quite thought about all the sacrifices that would arise as a result of his new friend. The tumble in the grass wasn't just a revelation, it was a shocker.

Timmy was sitting alone on a park bench all the while watching the two of them. He was enjoying this, too. It was like a movie. Stewart, the porn king, all lovey-dovey with some young thing he'd just met. Hmm . . . what else was new?

But somehow Timmy thought this could be different. He'd never seen Stew like this, separating himself from the world—his world—for so long. Especially not just for one pretty girl. And if Timmy didn't know any better, he'd swear that Stew was getting in heavy with his Geneva-girl. *Miss Westchester*. A looker she was, too. If Stew was gonna take a dive, he sure seemed to choose the right one. She was young, ripe, and more than willing.

The two were now sitting about a good three hundred feet from Timmy. Both of them were on a bench, probably talkin' shit. Timmy thought about Pop again and decided to make use of the dead time. He pulled out his cell phone and poked in the Pelham Manor number. As he waited for an answer, he could see Sam way on the other side of Stew and Geneva. Sam was also sitting on a bench. He had a newspaper open and was wearing dark sunglasses, just as Timmy had on.

"Pop. What goes?"

"Hey, Timmy, where ya been?"

"Oh . . . out with the boss. I'm in Central Park right now."

"Oh, hmmph . . . must be nice. Uh, Timmy, have you even seen the news?"

"No, Pop. You know how I am. See no evil, hear no evil, and don't believe the press."

"Well, I hope you believe *this*. Porter's dead."

"*What*?" Timmy shot upright on the bench.

"That's right. Some young punks railroaded him offa the pier . . . a parkin' lot, more or less, down in the Village. . . ."

Timmy recalled the images he'd seen earlier. The tow truck, the crane pulling the car up out of the Hudson, the Olympic silver-medal guy, he remembered now. He realized that all that had been about Porter. Timmy put his free hand

and forefinger to his other ear, as even the summer breeze and the chirping of birds now seemed too loud, blocking out all sounds so that he could hear his father clearly.

"Remember my blue Chevy?"

"Pop! I saw that on the news today. It was yesterday that this happened, wasn't it?"

"Yup, totaled the Chevy," Pop confirmed. "Some diver dude rescued Porter but . . ."

Timmy was listening to Pop, but he was also watching Stew. Stew and Geneva were running now. They were merrily trying to catch something. It looked like a butterfly. He listened as Pop told him about the events in ICU, about Porter's deathbed confession. He saw Stew and Geneva both jump for the butterfly, and Stew falling on the grass. He was in the fetal position on the ground. Timmy stood up and so did Sam.

"Hold on, Pop."

Timmy watched Geneva crouch down over Stew, and then he heard her scream as Stew pulled her down to the ground with him. Timmy sighed relief and sat back down. He gave Sam the thumbs-up sign, and Sam picked up his newspaper and sat down, too.

"Sorry, Pop. Go on about Porter and Malibu."

"Son, I think our friend Porter was a hired hit man."

"You are fuckin' kiddin' me!"

"Timmy. I went to Porter's place. I saw the ad he placed in a magazine called *Hunter*. It looks like he did this for a living. Or at least he was just startin' to."

"Pop, I can't believe it. I *won't* believe it! Porter was FBI. He was one of your best friends."

"You're right, son. He was *one* of my best friends. I have a few of those, ya know. I was gonna call on Farrintino, Jupiter, and remember Quell?"

"Yeah, I remember, they're all hunters, all agents."

"Yeah, but I couldn't reach 'em at the time. Porter was the first one to get back to me. So I pulled him in for the Platinum job."

"Okay, so how does that make him a hit man?"

"Timmy, at Porter's house there was some paperwork. He

had a voice mail service in the city . . . some 212 number. I called it. *It was his voice, Timmy!* I'd know his voice anywhere. Been around that man for more'n a decade . . ."

Pop explained that the name used on the recording was Steele, and the ad said "Merc for Hire."

Stew and Geneva got up off the grass. They had been down there kissing for at least twenty minutes. They sat back down on the bench. Timmy noticed a black man entering the park, about four or five hundred feet away. He was moving along the path toward the couple. The man seemed harmless, all business. Timmy figured he was probably a club promoter or something. Timmy eyed his outfit. Had he not been busy listening to Pop, he probably would have laughed.

Timmy continued to listen to Pop break it all down. The bills, the fast-food life, and the laser-printed photograph of the Platinum staff. Pop told him about the jackets from all the agencies, and all the money.

"And there's something else I never told you, Timmy. . . ."

Timmy never digressed. He'd never stopped doing his job protecting his boss. It didn't matter if a tornado hit, he'd be on the job. Sure, he was shocked by what Pop was telling him, but the man with the yellow blazer was only twenty or so feet away from Stew. He was headed right to the bench where Stew sat. Timmy was on high alert.

Stew heard his name, which shook him out of the spell Geneva had on him. He turned and saw Trent Morris. It was hard to miss that loud yellow jacket. Stew chuckled. Trent always was an attention grabber. He'd always liked Trent. It was Lex that . . .

"Trent?"

The two shook hands and there was a buddy-buddy hug. Trent let out an exhaustive sigh, happy to be welcomed.

"Stew . . . I am very sorry to interrupt you, but we *must* talk. It's very, very important. Beg your pardon, ma'am," he said, acknowledging Geneva's presence.

Stew could sense the urgency in Trent's voice. "What's up? Talk to me."

Trent did just that.

Timmy and Sam had gotten to their feet again. They strolled cautiously on either side of Stew's bench. Just in case. Timmy had asked Pop to hold on. He lifted his hand and pretended to scratch his cheek, as he spoke into the mic on his wristwatch.

"No threat right now, Sam. But just in case, ya know?"

"Never can be too sure," Sam replied. Both men were within sight of each other, but still a good distance from Stew.

Stew's visitor sat down beside him. The man had an attaché case, which he placed on his lap and opened. From the two-hundred–plus feet away, Timmy thought he recognized the visitor. He could swear he'd seen him before, but then Stew knew so many people. Timmy heard Pop's voice on the cell phone.

"Yeah, Pop. Sorry, just busy doin' my job, like you taught me." He kept an eye on Stew examining the items from the attaché case. Timmy figured it had to be business.

"So what does it mean, this R.T.?" Pop asked.

"You said it was on the credit card statement? American Airlines? Ahh . . . of course, that's round trip, Pop."

"Well, you know me, Timmy. Last time I been in the sky . . . Anyway, the last thing I wanted to tell you about was the pad on Porter's desk. There was a name there. . . . I had to use a pencil to call up the impression cuz the paper with the message was nowhere to be found."

"What was the name?"

"Lex-the-twerp."

"Lex-the-twerp?" Timmy asked, trying to make sure he'd heard correctly.

"That's what it said, Timmy. I'm lookin' at the thing right now."

"Listen, Pop. I got a situation here. Lemme call you back." Timmy shut the cell phone and stuck it in his pocket. He lifted his wrist to his lips and simultaneously reached around with his other hand to take the nickel-plated .45 automatic from the small of his back.

"Sam, you see the green Cherokee at four o'clock?" Timmy was closing in on where Stew sat. Sam came back in his ear.

"Cherokee? Shit! I'm lookin' at an *Impala*, black, behind you at eleven o'clock!"

Timmy's eyes grew electric with disbelief. "Oh *shit!* We got trouble, Sam. The Cherokee's on the grass!"

Timmy moved faster. He swung his head from left to right and back again so he could see both vehicles. The .45 wasn't visible yet, as he held it in the pocket of his windbreaker. Just then he heard the roar of a motor. The black Impala had climbed over a curb, and was plowing through the grass. Timmy knew his boss was in danger. The Cherokee was on the lawn as well, negotiating around a tree and picking up speed in the direction of Stew and the two others on the bench, none of them aware of the forthcoming danger.

"Stew! Get down!" Timmy shouted, when he realized that the driver in the Impala, the vehicle nearest to him, had a firearm pointed toward the trio. The window was down and the driver was working to get a good shot.

Timmy fired while he sprinted. He was about twenty yards from the vehicle, moving parallel with it, firing at the front and rear tires to stop the car from getting closer to its target. The car was the greatest threat. If the shooter couldn't get close, he couldn't get his target. *Shut his power down!* Pop would say.

A tire blew out, but the driver got off a number of shots. The peaceful park suddenly turned deadly. Pigeons scattered turbulently into the air. Squirrels scurried to and fro. There was a high-pitched woman's scream.

Sam could hear his breathing and his quickening heartbeat. Both sounds were fighting for attention in his head, as he leapt over a park bench to move in on the Cherokee. He cleared the bench like a hurdler and ran at top speed, catching the jeep by surprise.

Sam was running along the passenger's side, but he knew that he could still take down the jeep. No tires, no progress.

Sam fired six shots in two seconds. He heard other shots across the way, and he heard a scream and wondered if anyone had been hurt. The six shots riddled the Cherokee's door, a side window and a tail light. It wasn't easy to hit a bull's-eye while moving so fast. Sam unloaded two more shots. The driver had begun to fire a gun out of his window. The Cherokee spun out of control and began to careen toward a great oak tree. Sam didn't have to fire another shot. The jeep slammed head-on into the tree, the crash sounding less incredible than the damage that the vehicle and its driver sustained. Sam noticed that the driver's head had smashed through the windshield.

The Impala made a ninety-degree spin, the driver's gunshots running wild now that the car was redirected, and the shots were flying toward Timmy. But he was committed, his body moving like a rocket toward the Impala. A bullet hit him on the right side of his chest. Timmy took a dive and rolled Rambo-style until he was in a spread-eagle position on the grass with his .45 pointed and firing until it was empty. Bullets penetrated the vehicle's windows and exterior.

Timmy was sure he scored. He rose up on one knee and pulled open his windbreaker. Then he ripped the Velcro to free the Kevlar vest. He could feel the burn on the right side of his chest, and he pulled down his T-shirt to check the wound. There was nothing there but a red mark.

His attention was back on the Impala within seconds. He pulled a full clip out of his ankle pouch and hit the release on the .45. The empty magazine fell out and Timmy quickly smacked the fresh clip into the weapon's well. He rose slowly to his feet, feeling somewhat reborn. He already knew he had hit the perp, he just wasn't sure how bad. He approached the driver's side door and snatched it open. Then he pulled the victim out onto the grass where he lay lifeless.

"S-S-S-Stewart . . ." Geneva's voice was a plea. She looked up at Stew, who was kneeling down by her side, only now realizing the extent of the injury. "I've been shot?" Geneva's face was one of total disbelief. There was incredible fear in her eyes, and her lips trembled.

"Timmy! *Ti-mmy!*" Stew shouted with all his might. He heard a grunt behind him. Trent had been hit in the shoulder and was laying there staring up at the sky. He looked like he'd seen a UFO. But Geneva was the priority now. Stew was fine. Shaken, yes, but not shot. He stared at the red stain just over Geneva's left breast. Her hair was disheveled and her face was tearstained and turning pale.

"Ti-mmy!" Stew shouted again.

"W-w-why, Stewart? Why us? *Why?*" Geneva cried.

"Hold on, baby, just hold on, everything . . ."

"I'm cold, Stewart. . . . It hurts. . . ." Geneva's voice was weak. She shivered in his arms.

Timmy had finally made it over to where they were. He was on the phone. "Yes, in Central Park! Close to The Plaza Hotel . . . the south-side entrance. Hurry! Two people have been shot, one critical." Timmy listened for a moment and then answered in an irritated tone. "No! I'm not a cop, I'm a bodyguard. Timmy Andrews, got it? Andrews! Please get help here *quick!*"

"The other dude's finished, Timmy," said Sam.

"God-*damn!*" Timmy shouted. He wanted to slam his cell phone against the pavement. As far as he was concerned this was his fault. This was not a time to say, *Who knew?* He was supposed to be in complete control at all times. *At all times!*

"H-H-Hold me, Stewart. Stewart? Am I gonna die?"

"Of course not, of course not." Stew's eyes dripped tears onto Geneva's blood-stained blouse. "You're so pretty, Geneva. Nothing could *ever* happen to you." Stew turned to look up at Timmy. Tears blurred his vision. His lips quivered violently as reality took hold. He held in the violent sobs that filled his chest. His angel was slipping away.

"Stewart . . . I . . . love you," Geneva said, her own tears wetting her face. "We . . . were . . ." Geneva choked. "Almost there." She shook uncontrollably. Her body seemed possessed, taking on a life of its own. Her jaw locked and she coughed up a glob of blood. Her body collapsed in his arms, her eyes still open and looking at Stew, but no longer seeing him.

Stew squeezed his eyes closed. He threw his head back and screamed into the sky, "Noooooooooo!"

The cry was heard throughout the park, as joggers began to gather, cars along the drive had stopped to get a look at what had happened, and a siren was heard approaching from afar.

A twist of fate
Roses are there
It's not too far
Each and every time
Could come today
Wherever we are
Right where you are
If we open our minds.

Could be designed
We may be fooled
This ain't our show
But the truth won't hide
Reach for the sky
It's the naked truth
Cuz you never know
That beats a well-dressed lie.

Timmy instinctively went to Trent's side. "You're fine . . . aren't you, Trent?"

"Y-Yes," Trent answered, trembling. "I'm bleeding."

"It's clean, Trent. Shot didn't even hit the bone."

"You mean, I'm gonna be okay?" Trent was S.T.D.— Scared to Death.

"Come on," Timmy said, sounding tired. "Get up." Sam helped Trent up. They seated him on the park bench. They left Stew to mourn. It was best. He had to get past the shock and live with the reality.

"Trent, what happened here?" Timmy asked. "Who is after Stew? Who's trying to sabotage the company?" Timmy was fitting the puzzle together. Pop had said Lex-the-twerp.

Lex was Trent's partner. Both of them were Stew's partners. *Why would Porter have been involved with Lex?* Porter, the hit man. *And how many hit men were after Stew's dynasty?*

Timmy listened to Trent while Sam stood watch over everyone, the living and the dead. And to think, this had started out as a good day.

TWENTY-ONE

The confusion started all over again. The emergency vehicles, the sirens, and the spinning red and white strobe lights. All of it had recently become a way of life for Stew, and within a short period of time, a sedate, leisurely park was transformed into just another busy part of New York City. Just another manic Friday morning, and an atmosphere where travelers tried to get somewhere, or get away from somewhere, all at once. And then, of course, the press came.

The homicide squad from the Thirty-second Precinct came out in full force. It had been awhile since a person had been killed in Central Park. Sure there were joggers who were foolhardy enough to come out at night, and there were other bodies that had been dumped there (just a place to get rid of them), and there were even the one, two, or three homeless souls who froze to death in the winter, but that was all *expected*. That was part of park lore and had been since its opening. What did the officials expect, with all those trees, all that grass, and all those shrubs planted right in the heart of the naked city? It was like building a jungle in the center of a Monopoly board, and there in the jungle lay the predators, the lowlifes, and the thieves. All of them lurking in the dark, waiting for their next victim.

No. This wasn't the average. There was nothing typical

about this. This was some gangland shit, and in its wake were two dead shooters and one dead girl. It was a case of being in the wrong place at the wrong time. Then there was the cat in the black and yellow monkey suit, and a black-and-yellow polka-dot tie! And all of this madness took place in broad daylight! Boy, oh boy, was the homicide squad gonna have a ball with this party.

By noontime many of the questions and answers had been tossed around. The EMS trucks had gone. The coroner took away the bodies, and the medics treated Trent's bullet wound. The bullet that went through him had been so hot, it virtually sealed the wound as it entered and left his body.

Slowly the park was getting back to some normality. The flatbeds were loading up the two bullet-ridden vehicles—the Impala with most of its windows and tires shot out, and the Cherokee scrunched up like an accordion by the big oak tree.

All sorts of photos had been taken of the crime scene, and then the tourists arrived and were marveling at the idea of some poor schmuck losing control of his car. They were all over the place, just outside of the yellow police tape and right alongside the media trucks, which were commandeering the lawns of Central Park as if the soil and grass were asphalt. As if the reporters had permission from Mother Nature to mash her soft earth with their heavy rubber tires.

The principles were up in the penthouse. Detective Fuentez and two of his subordinates, Trent—with his bandaged shoulder—Timmy, Sam, and of course Stew, who was numb, worn, and in a stupor.

Lex was at his desk, sitting upright in his executive chair. He had been a nervous wreck since meeting with the Forman brothers. All he wanted to hear was that it was over. Or, *It's done! It's fucking done!* as they had exclaimed after the job on Steele.

Janice was there to help Lex. She was down on her knees, most of her body under the desk, and her face bobbing up and down in his lap. She relaxed him this way, sucking at all of his stress and tension, making him feel invincible—so the coward inside could remain hidden. It was a blow job that helped Lex fool himself. And then the phone rang.

"You are not speaking with God, what can I do for you?"

"It's me."

"Who's me?"

"It's Steele, you twerp."

"I don't know what . . . *Wait a minute!* But you're—"

"Very much alive is what I am.

"Stop it, *stop it*! Get out of here! Go in the bathroom or somethin'—go suck on your thumb. *Go on!*" Lex had his hand over the mouthpiece of the phone as he ordered Janice to leave his presence. She got up off her knees and trotted into the bathroom. This wasn't the first time Lex had lost his temper. "Sorry, Steele . . . Uhh, we, uh . . . had a deal. . . . I was, uh, there. . . . I was late, but I did come. . . ."

"Sure you did."

"But the garbage trucks! The police! The news! I thought you were *dead.*"

"You thought wrong, twerp. You *set me* up!"

"No, no, *no*! I did nothing of the sort. I didn't even know those guys—"

"What guys? How did you know about that?"

"Well, the news, the . . . Steele, you gotta believe me, we had a deal. I had the money. I *still* have it. I can bring it to you now. Now! Immediately! Just tell me where. I can have a messenger—"

"No. I want you. *You* bring it."

"Okay, okay. Where?" Lex picked up his pen and jotted down the information.

Fear was worse than death. It was a slow torture. It was the vulture hovering above, waiting for the right time. The prey down below was as good as dead if it became slow, somehow incapacitated, or if it fell asleep. The living prey was no worse than a carcass. Lex was feeling like prey, and if he didn't follow directions . . . if he didn't satisfy the vulture, he would indeed become that carcass.

After the phone call, he immediately went to the bank to withdraw the money he'd put back, but when he arrived, he received disturbing news.

"I'm sorry," the bank manager said, "the L.T.S. account has been closed."

"Closed? How can it be closed? I'm the only one with the power to close the account!"

"Well, according to our records"—the bank manager tapped some keys on his computer—"you did close this account. As a matter of fact, it was done from our Fifty-sixth Street branch, just twenty minutes ago."

"Twenty minutes ago? I was in my office getting a—"

"Mr. Roland, please control your temper. This is a bank where we conduct business with professionals." The manager waited for Lex to calm down. "Now I see here that you gave your partner legal rights to—"

"My partner?" Lex thought about Trent and Stew.

"Sure. Mr. Trent Morris, is it? Yes. He presented the necessary documents that made him executor over the L.T.S. account." The bank manager looked closer at his computer screen. There were notes that had been added to explain the termination of L.T.S. "I see here that, well, it says that the principle partner on the account . . . Mr. Roland, I'm afraid my computer screen says that you *died*."

"What?" Lex reached over to violently shift the bank manager's computer monitor so that it was facing him. "That's impossible!"

The bank manager looked over Lex's shoulder at two security guards who stood watch, arms folded.

"Trent! That bastard!" Lex looked up at the gentleman. The rage was waiting to lash out at someone. Anyone. But Lex quickly realized that the two weren't alone. He turned to see the two armed guards peering at him. Lex apologized and left the bank.

Outside of the bank, Lex stepped toward his limo. Martin was standing by the door.

"Sir?"

"Take me uptown, Martin."

"I'm sorry, sir, I can't do that. I just received a call from my boss—"

"Your *boss*? I'm your fucking boss! I've been using your service for over eight goddamn years!"

"I'm sorry. If you like, you can talk to him. . . ." Martin reached in the window and pulled out the car phone. It didn't give much room to maneuver, so he had to hunch his head close to the car window to hear. "Boss? It's Martin. I'm here with—"

Lex pushed Martin out of the way. He hunched over and put his ear to the phone.

"Vinny? What's the meaning of this?"

"Your account's been closed, Lex. But I thought you were dead?"

"Dead? Now what kind of bullshit is *that?* I'm right *here*! Alive and . . . kickin' the side . . . of the . . . fucking car door." Lex kicked the limo three times. Martin stood back, his head turning this way and that looking for help. A police cruiser was crawling with the traffic along Water Street.

"Now you listen to me, Vinny. Whatever money you need, I got. But you can't just stop my day by shutting the account!"

"No problem, Lex. Just plug me in with your bank. Give me an account number, a bank manager . . . *something*. I'm sure we can—"

Lex dropped the car phone so that it hit the side door as it hung out of the window. He went and flagged down a taxi. The radio in the cab gave him news about Central Park. Now he wanted to kick himself in the ass. Why had he hired two meatheads to do a professional's job? Steele *was* a professional. Lex knew him before he even began his Merc for Hire business. *Hell*—it was Lex who even suggested that he begin advertising in the first place. And then he had to go and betray him? Try to kill him? *What was I thinking?* And now that Trent was trying to—and succeeding at—sabotaging L.T.S., Lex needed Steele more than ever. *I've gotta fix this. I need Steele to help me. Obviously, the meatheads couldn't do the job*.

Lex had the taxi stop at an ATM on the way uptown. He

needed to get hold of whatever cash he could. Of the five bank cards he had, he figured he could pull down at least five thousand. Just to keep Steele happy. Just until he could clear up Trent's attack on L.T.S. *You just wait, Trent. I've got somethin' real nice up my sleeve for you!*

"*Shit!*" There was a limit on each card. He could withdraw only five hundred per card, per day. The last card he used was the L.T.S. Corporate Visa. The ATM ate his card and he got a message to, "See bank representative."

Lex cursed Trent and took the two thousand in cash back to the cab. Fifteen minutes later, he was knocking on the door of the penthouse suite at The Plaza.

"Who?" a deep voice asked on the other side of the door.

"Steele, it's me, Lex. Open up."

Stew waited a few seconds so that Pop could get out of sight, along with the others. He then opened the door, knowing he'd solved the big mystery and captured the man behind all of the mayhem. Stew had a volcano's worth of pent-up rage in his heart, but he had to control it. He had to stick to the plan.

"If it ain't Lexington." Stew gave Lex a broad smile and he cocked his head back.

"Shit! Stew? What a surprise! I . . . I must've come . . . to the wrong friggin' door," said Lex, making up things as he went along. *What's this, a trick? Coincidence?*

"Might as well come in." Stew reached out to shake Lex's hand. Not an ounce of threat in his eyes. The handshake served as a vise grip, pulling Lex into the penthouse like he was a long-lost relative. Stew shut the door behind Lex then patted him on the back.

"Gee, Stew . . . didn't know ya were in New York. I thought you had somethin' smokin' up in Canada?" Lex looked around.

"Yeah, yeah . . . Well, some other things came up. You know, with the fires 'n all. Have a seat, Lex. I'll order up lunch. The food is fan-tastic here. I'm livin' like a king!"

Where the fuck is Steele? Are they workin' together? "Gee . . . *you're* in good spirits. Wow . . . and you'd think after all the damage that's been done, you'd be down and out. K-friggin-O. But nahh . . . you're amazin'. You keep on truckin' like a dog-um juggernaut 'er somethin'," said Lex, stalling, trying to figure things out.

Stew called room service for lunch. "Yeah," Stew jumped right back into the conversation. "A guy has to get used to this type of tragedy. It helps the heart grow strong. Really." Stew winked at Lex.

"Wow, Stew. You're *amazin'*. So you, ahh, don't have any hard feelings about them girls who died? What about the funerals 'n such?" *Is this guy for real?*

"Are you *kiddin'* me, Lex? You know how I do. . . . You meet one bitch, you've met 'em all." *And you're the biggest of all.*

"Good thinkin', buddy. I was thinkin' the same thing. I mean, what's a few dead bitches? It makes room for the fresh meat." *So Stew and I were on the same page all along.*

Stew laughed out loud and Lex joined him. "Oh, you're a riot, Lex! Fresh meat!" And Stew laughed some more. "And who the hell is thinkin' about funerals, huh? *Shit.* I pay them bitches good. Let 'em pay for their own funerals!" Stew's face froze, waiting for Lex's response. And, of course, Lex was in stitches, a joyful tear forming at the corner of his eye. Stew laughed along.

"Pay for their own funerals! What a joker!" Lex laughed until he nearly fell out of his seat. "So, Stew, you seen Trent lately?"

There was a knock at the door.

"Oh, *that* was fast," said Stew, getting up to let room service in.

It was one of Detective Fuentez's subordinates. He had The Plaza uniform on, pretending to be a waiter. "Lunch is served," the actor proclaimed. He wheeled the cart in and pulled the hood off two plates with club sandwiches. Then he stood by waiting.

"Thank you, sir," said Stew. "That'll be all."

The waiter didn't move. All three men traded looks.

"Oh, I'm sorry. Don't know where my head's at." Stew

pulled out a ten-dollar bill and shut the door behind the joker. "These clowns will hold you up for money every chance they get."

"I agree," said Lex, the sandwich already wedged into his mouth.

"So where were we?"

With a mouth full of food, Lex uttered, "Trent. Seen 'im?"

Stew shook his head. He had a salty look in his eye. "Do I need to face that guy again? Shit! That punk gets on my nerves. Sometimes I wish there was just you and me, Lex. I mean, how'd that dude get an equal out as it is? Who is he?" *He put the lid on your coffin, that's who he is.*

Lex shook his head, trying to finish the food in his mouth so that he could say something.

Stew told himself that this guy was the absolute pig. *How did I ever get to doing business with this fool in the first place?*

"Listen, that's just what I came here to talk to you about. Okay, so you caught me. I knew you were staying at The Plaza all along, so I kinda came to catch you before Trent did. . . ." Lex swallowed. "Sorry for the intrusion. See there's somethin' I should talk to you about, regardin' the shootin' and the fires 'n stuff."

"Don't tell me. It was all Trent! *He* was responsible for all of that? *Damn.* Maybe I was wrong about him all along! The guy's a genius! I mean, the first hit on Trina was a no-brainer! Who knew? The TV, the newspapers . . . we hit CNN! *Imagine that!*" Stew was up on his feet putting on a big show—all of New York was behind him, out there beyond the patio doors. "And now *Entertainment Tonight*, the *Ed and Dre Morning Show* in L.A. . . . and *Access*! Fucking *Access*! I mean, who fucking knew, Lex? All the press just sucked all of America's mind . . . made 'em all flock to the website. Over a dead bitch! Not even a pretty dead bitch. Just some hoe outta some hood somewhere . . ." Stew was carrying on.

Meanwhile, Lex was sitting back. Pride on his face. Legs crossed. And now he was pointing to himself. Both hands were suspended out in front of his chest, and he was pulling his thumbs back and forth like a hitchhiker, only he was poking at his chest. Stew was reminded of a car's hazard lights. That continuous signal.

"And man . . . we made so, so, so much *money*! The viewership on the website grew forty percent! That kinda money can buy me all the bitches in the world!"

"Ahh . . . but what about the fire?" Lex asked, his hands in his lap now. "The Bronx site wasn't making the kind of money we expected. The penthouse was expensive . . . plus all those salaries."

Stew stood there spellbound. His eyes fogged up. He tried to read Lex's mind. "Oooooh *shit*! Of course! The fucking *insurance policy*! How did I ever forget!"

Stew had plugged in the final pieces to the puzzle. Lex had wanted to cut expenses where there were losses. Get full value on the insurance policy—some ten million dollars— and maybe, he thought, Stew would forget about that branch of Platinum Dolls. Maybe Lex thought that Stew would accept his losses and stick with the branches that made money.

"And Seattle, what a waste of money to pay for MaryAnn's penthouse," Stew continued. "After all! Honey's not in her *own* place in North Carolina. Brianna's not in her *own* place up in Scarsdale." There Lex went again with the thumbs again—the hazard signal. "Daisy lives on the ranch in Texas, and Leslie in Malibu. What was I thinkin'? MaryAnn should've been happy there on Chambers Street. Who the fuck is she?"

Lex was looking up at the ceiling while he continued to point, this time using his forefingers. Lex made a sound like a doorbell ding-dong.

"What . . . what . . . Trent's not a fucking genius? We don't owe all of this to him? I think you're mistaken."

"Wake up, Stew! Wake up, buddy . . . *pal* . . . *partner*. . . . It was *me*, Stew. I did all that. Trent knew nothing. In fact, I kept him in the dark about everything. The shooting—even though the hit man wasn't supposed to kill the bitch—I think he missed or somethin'. But hey! That was *my* plan. *I* hired the dude. It was this guy I knew back in the day. He suddenly wanted to become a merc."

"A merc? You mean, like, a mercenary?"

"Yeah. It's just one 'a those terms, ya' know? Like in the money business we call a merger, a merge . . . or a proposition, a prop. Well, mercenaries call themselves mercs."

"I still don't get it. What's a mercenary do?"

"Hey, *dingle berry* . . . they do professional *hits*. They get paid, they do a job . . . end of story."

"So it was your bright idea to hire this guy?"

"Every bit of it. And the *fires* . . . Oh, that couldn't have worked out more beautifully. The Bronx penthouse . . . a friggin' dinosaur! The Seattle penthouse . . . she wasn't worthy." Lex had his arms open, as if he was conducting a board meeting.

Stew thought about Sparkle in Seattle and the six girls who'd died in the Bronx. He wanted to be sick.

"And like you say, money can buy all the bitches *in the world*."

"Wow. I've gotta bow down to you, Lex. You are a genius."

"Come on . . . finish your food. There's so much we need to discuss."

Stew was all out of energy. All the activity of the morning, the loss, and now this. It tapped every bit of his strength.

"See, this is how I been lookin' at it from a few weeks ago. Remember we talked about the second quarter? Well, I wanted something bigger, Stew. I wanted a friggin' guarantee, and nothin' makes more money than free publicity."

Stew sat there staring at Lex. He listened to the fool hang himself.

"But you haven't heard the last of it, partner. It turns out the merc wanted more money. So I tried to do him—"

" 'Do him,' " Stew repeated, unemotionally calling for an explanation.

"Yeah. I tried to hit the hit man."

"Wow. Isn't that dangerous though?"

"Not if you're smart like me."

"A genius."

"Exactly. I had two meatheads do the job, but it turns out they fouled things up."

Stew wondered how. *Keep talkin', twerp.*

"Did you hear about the garbage trucks pushin' that car into the Hudson?"

"No. I've been busy. . . ."

"Well, it turns out the guy might not be dead—anyhow, this is where you come in. We're gonna resolve L.T.S. and start out fresh. It'll be just you and me—*S* and *L*." Lex did the pointing. Stew pretended to be interested.

"Sounds good, but what about Trent?"

"Well, those meatheads I hired are supposed to take care of him. They might've even got 'im already—I don't know. But Trent will be history soon. Then it'll just be you and me."

Stew imagined Trent in the other room, seething behind the door, while the others listened and recorded.

"I can see us now. . . . We'll buy the top floors of the Empire State Building. The observation deck, *yeah*? And we'll sit there with lines of women who can't wait to suck our peckers."

" 'Peckers'?" Stew repeated.

"Oh sure. That day may be right around the corner. . . . And I even got somethin' else up my sleeve, Stew. Somethin' to grab more headlines."

"No shit?"

"Yeah, I got a couple of girls planted in Malibu. They're waitin' for my instructions. When the publicity dies down about all the girls dyin' and what not—bang, we kill off two moe."

"How? Shoot 'em? That's played out, Lex. We been there, done that."

"Oooh, I like your attitude, Stew. But nah. I'm gonna have these whores poison a couple'a bitches."

"No shit. Whores?"

"Yeah. A couple'a dykes I picked up on Eleventh Avenue—right here in the city. Hungry whores they were. But I wouldn't let 'em suck my pecker. I convinced 'em to do a job for me. They were all for it, too. Seems they both got criminal records. And the Korean whore! Whoo-eee! She's a hot number. She killed a John in cold blood."

"Wow. And when should we make this happen?"

"We save this one. Next time it feels like a bad quarter comin', ooops . . . there goes another ho!" Lex laughed.

Stew chuckled. "Tell me . . . any more tricks up your sleeve? Don't leave *me* out."

"Relax, relax. We'll come up with some creative techniques. Keep the police goin' crazy. The media will love us. The website will be flooded with visitors. We'll keep re-placin' the—"

Stew couldn't take any more. He lifted up the table and everything fell onto Lex's chest and lap. Lex was a mess. "Stupid mothafucka!" Stew kicked Lex in the ribs and he fell back onto the floor. Then he reached down and grabbed the collar of his business suit. He held him up. "You're a disgrace to the human race . . . worse than rat shit!"

"But I thought—"

Stew didn't let Lex say another word. Before everyone flooded out to stop him, he thrust the twerp through the windows of the patio door. They shattered and Lex was on the terrace floor, shaking out of the daze.

Trent shouted, *"Get 'im, Stew!"*

Pop admonished Trent. Timmy was the first to grab Stew before he was about to throw Lex off the terrace and commit murder. Stew was shouting at the top of his lungs, as Timmy and Sam led him away. Detective Fuentez and his homicide squad would handle things from there.

Atlanta, Georgia

TWENTY-TWO

Conclusion

The monthlong whirlwind that had taken its toll on Stew and nearly drove him crazy had finally come to an end. Pop called Inspector Elliot out in Malibu, and Lisa "Me So Horny" Wong and Kim Weathers were quickly apprehended.

Stephanie appointed a business manager for Transylvania, and met Stew, Timmy, and Sam for the connecting flight to Los Angeles. Sitting in first class, they discussed the four turbulent weeks and what it would take to tie up the loose ends. There were the funerals, first and foremost. Malibu, then Seattle, then back to the Bronx and Westchester. Stephanie wondered if she had enough black outfits to keep up with the formalities.

Stew was all cried out after Geneva dying in his arms, and he kept the same sullen expression at every funeral, almost as if it had been practiced. He gave no speeches and made no statements to the press. He merely rode the wave of misery, doing his best to uphold a certain dignity through it all.

A blizzard of images filled the landscape of his memories. All the many faces he'd seen throughout the years; the ones who stayed, the ones who left, the others who perished. The personalities stretched for miles as though on a conveyor belt, all of them sitting in sensual positions and smiling, frowning, or crying, being carried along behind Stew's eyes, so that what seemed to be his present reality was all an illusion.

He hugged and comforted MaryAnn in Seattle, Sharon in the Bronx, and Brianna in Scarsdale. He uttered his sorrow, his kind words, and his incredible guilt. Throughout the ordeal Stew heard the sounds of his employees sobbing their testaments, crying for answers, and one or two who screamed their hate for him. There were the flowers, the dark clothes, and always the small heaps of dirt waiting to be shoveled back into the ditches to cover the deceased in their coffins.

When the burials on both coasts were completed, Stew and Stephanie found themselves alone in a limousine, with vehicles to the front and rear of them. The entire motorcade of Platinum Dolls' business managers, executive assistants, and personal security streamed from Atlanta's Hartsfield Airport, down I-85, then along the countryside until they reached the twenty-foot wrought-iron gates that parted so the vehicles could enter Stew's seven-acre estate. A wave of activity suddenly interrupted the summer air. Stew and company, close to two dozen in all, spilled out of the luxury vehicles and into the seclusion of what, to Stew, was finally going to be home sweet home.

For now, the website operated in autopilot mode—same as it would on New Year's Eve, with no staff available. There were major issues to address, major problems relating to the company's well-being. Many women had packed up and left. Many others were frightened that they might be the next to die. Despite the fact that the perpetrator and catalyst of these violent crimes had been captured, and that he would likely never see freedom again, the fear still remained. That one person could penetrate an organization and so easily claim lives left the feeling among the women that they were bait in a lion's den.

As important as the troubleshooting was, and would be for some time, Stewart Gregory decided that this was a time for seclusion, for mourning, and for calm. The company wasn't broke or hopeless. It hadn't turned over and died. Now was just the time to rest, relax, and regroup.

July fourth came and went. August brought on Atlanta's heat wave. And by September, Stew Gregory approached his business with renewed energy and spirit.

His houseguests during this time were many. There was Yvonne, who managed the Atlanta home, along with the twenty-eight girls who'd remained during the bad press—only seven had departed. There was Honey, who managed the North Carolina farm, where the Southern belle theme was sold as part of the Platinum Dolls site. There was Justine, who managed the Washington, D.C., branch. And Leslie, who had been relocated from Malibu to Seattle. MaryAnn vanished after the funeral for Sparkle, and nobody knew how to reach her. Barbara and the new business manager, Amanda, were there along with Suzie, all of them from the Malibu site. Brianna and Sharon were there from the Scarsdale and Bronx sites, and Daisy was there from Houston, where the farm girl theme was designed for the Platinum Dolls website. Kelly came down later from Transylvania.

The girls who stayed back at the various homes around the country also used the time to relax. Close to three months of reading, keeping in shape, and doing hobbies such as painting, song or poetry writing, or taking Internet courses. In North Carolina they swam in the lake on the property. In New York the girls from the Bronx and Scarsdale got to know one another better, and went to the movies, or roller skating, or to Six Flags.

In Washington, D.C., the girls formed a topless car wash enclosed under a large tent; three of the girls did the advertising and collected the money. Congressmen poured in. In Seattle the girls spent time refreshing the interior of the loft and indoor park. They painted. They tended to the indoor plants. Then Andrea came up with the idea to decorate T-shirts by painting their nude bodies and making those impressions on the fabric. The shirts would be sold once the auction would be up again.

The Malibu beach house was business as usual. Twister, tanning, swimming, volleyball, and beachfront barbecues. It was as if they'd never felt the pain of it all. In Houston they rode horses and attended rodeos. Transylvania was complete. The dark dungeons, with their shackles and chains and virtual spider webs, were finished. The fifteen girls to be employed were eager and hungry enough to help out whenever they could. The violence in America never mattered to them anyhow.

So there they were—the force behind the Platinum Dolls brand. Everyone was committed to see their end of the network through, to reach an ultimate goal. During the preceding months, the women were to prepare for a late-night meeting on August thirty-first to discuss their plans. Stew had already designed the big picture. Now it was time to dig into the integral parts, the areas that mattered most.

Timmy and Sam had help down in Atlanta, where Brian and Butterball oversaw the home security along with a small team of Dobermans that roamed the perimeter of the main house at the forefront of the seven acres. All four of the men were outside now, like sentries to the fort, making small talk, while the executive board—of a sort—was inside and the long-awaited meeting about to begin.

Side by side, Stew and Stephanie walked into the large study, which Stew used as his office when he was home. Just behind them was a special guest, his good friend from Detroit, Ashley Sinclair, his friendly competitor who had flown down earlier in the day. Ashley looked radiant, with her short blond hair and sinewy shape and wearing a cocktail dress. In Ashley's eyes and demeanor a sense of wisdom and confidence was evident. She immediately tugged every woman's attention. She was someone they wanted to know.

"Thanks for waiting, ladies," Stew said. He stood before them, his weight leaning against the huge red-oak desk, one leg crossed over the other, and his hands clasped below his waist. There were studded leather chairs positioned here and there, and two matching leather couches in an L-shape by the floor-to-ceiling pane glass windows. There was also an extensive wall library of over twenty thousand books, and to the back of the room, by the large oak double doors, was an eight-foot-high fireplace. The chairs in that area, two La-Z-Boys, had been repositioned so that they would face forward where Stew was now standing. Some of Yvonne's top girls stood back and listened.

On the wall behind Stew and his desk—accessorized with a laptop, a bank of phones, and the Pimp Hard teddy bear— was a portrait, a commissioned painting, of Stew's mentor: the shrewd, successful, late-billionaire, Reginald Lewis.

To Stew's left was Brianna, sitting on the arm of a chair. In the chair was Sharon. Behind the chair was Barbara. All of them had clipboards, organizers, and pens, awaiting crunch time to begin. Yvonne, Honey, and Kelly were farther to the right, sitting in separate chairs and already comparing notes. Justine, Leslie, and Amanda were seated on the L-shaped couch. And Suzie chatted with Daisy near the fireplace, on the La-Z-Boys.

Stephanie and Ashley were also on the couch, anticipating Stew's next words.

"Seems like forever since we've had a chance, all of us, to sit together as one and discuss business. Fortunately, our business is conducted over the Internet, so Platinum Dolls is still intact. Our face is still smiling at the world. But you know, and I know, that the time has come . . . Our rest is over. It's time to go back to work and regain our position in this game . . . in the marketplace. You know, since the end of June, when we all came through those gates together, I've had a chance to put my own priorities in order. One or two of you know exactly what I'm talking about." Stew gave a side-long glance and locked eyes with Brianna for a split second. And then he turned to Stephanie. "I've also had an opportunity to speak to each and every one of you on an individual basis, and I must say that I truly have some interesting, charismatic, and devoted friends to help me steer this ship. You all are incredible in your own ways, and, as much as I wanna swallow you all up as my own, I know that in order for the company to survive—in order for Platinum Dolls to reach its pinnacle—I must keep my selfish ways in check.

"Maybe it would be easier if I were a woman. Like Ashley Sinclair, my friend here. Some of you have talked with her already, and you'll hear from her shortly. I often wonder if I'd be as focused on pleasure seeking, if I were a woman in charge of Platinum Dolls. But another side of me wants to believe that it's *because* I'm a man that our company has grown as it has. Who knows? I *do* know this: I'm happy enough with the blessings around me that I can stay forever young. I can continue to be happy and secure and self-confident enough to achieve my goals . . . *our* goals. And isn't that what everyone wants? To be happy, secure? To achieve our goals?" He looked around at their faces.

"Well before we get knee-deep into the details of how our company will once again reach the top, I have a special announcement." Stew cleared his throat. There was a dramatic silence. "I'm going to be a daddy soon. . . ."

Squeals and applause and "You go, boy" filled the room. The chatter began. Stew cleared his throat. "Ahh . . . there's a little more to it, ladies. . . ." Stew looked at Stephanie. She winked back at him for encouragement. "Actually, I'm going to be a daddy *three times over. . . .*" Now the noise *really* broke out in the study. It was suddenly a party atmosphere.

"Who's the lucky girl, boss?" someone called out.

"Don't you mean *girls*?" another asked.

"Well, why don't I just embarrass the hell out of them in front of everybody," Stew joked. "Come on up, ladies." Brianna was suddenly by her chair alone as Barbara and Sharon stepped up. Stephanie was already by Stew's side, kissing his check. All three women were pregnant by Stew. Stew gave the three hugs and kisses and sent them back to their seats. Brianna gave Stew the evil eye and he blew her a kiss back. Ashley pumped her fist in the air and Stew saw how excited she was for him.

"So I did all of that to let you know that life has gotten *pretty* serious all of a sudden. There will be children running around this house pretty soon, and I'm gonna need plenty of money to take care of 'em. So let's get to work." Stew reached out and took from Stephanie a list of issues that he wanted to discuss.

"First, I want to give everyone an assurance. Of the three hundred girls we had in early June, there are now a hundred and fifty left. There may even be a few less by the time we get back to work. But it's just as well. We need *believers* in our company, and that's what we've been left with. Wait a minute . . . don't be alarmed. See that pretty blonde over there? Well, she does basically the same thing we do. She's the lady responsible for the Detroit Playhouse. She's also been at this longer than I have. *And* she's here to help. Ashley? Wanna tell them?"

Ashley stood up and began to speak. She was immediately authoritative. "Sure, Stew. Ladies, I admire this man and the empire he's built. He's struggled. And he deserves every good fortune he's got. Number one, the women are *not* a problem. I have a hundred talented girls just ready and waiting to play doctor with your Internet visitors."

There was laughter and giggles.

"That means they'll act like cowgirls for you down in Houston, Daisy. They'll also do the Southern belle thing for you, Honey, with tasseled umbrellas, bonnets, and prairie dresses *at* the *ready*."

Honey gave that bashful smile of hers.

"And Justine, we can get D.C. in shape and quick, but don't worry about that. Ladies, there are thousands—I mean *thousands*—of girls out there who want to perform for men on the Internet. They *want* to make money. Trust me. It may be a matter of going out to recruit. And that might mean money.

"Number two, I've committed to investing twenty-five million in this company. So what can stop this? The answer is *nothing*. Not . . . a . . . thing. So, Stew? Please commence with your decision."

"Are you married, Ashley? Because if you're not, I . . . I digress."

Stew shook his head.

"I just get goose bumps to know that this woman, who is my friend, has so much damn *power*! When I grow up, I wanna be just like you. Okay. So the talent concern is covered . . . and I guess the money is, too." Stew smiled.

Stew went down his list to discuss the quality of the various branches, whether it was the costumes and attire of the performers, the atmosphere as seen by the viewer, or the attitude of the girls. They must stay in character, whether Southern Belle or Chickenhead. "That's the stereotype being sold, so that's what the girls must stick with."

Stew went over security briefly and then the concern of performers going beyond the call of duty. "If we let our girls get *too* involved with the client, we'll lose them. We're selling a *fantasy* here. Not *pussy*."

Stew brought up insurance concerns and medical benefits for the girls, as well as physical and mental fitness and proper nutrition. He offered scholarships for those girls who stayed with the company for more than two years, and incentives if they stayed on longer. Finally, Stew spoke about the overall self-esteem of the company and of every single employee.

"We must be unified. We must all be on the same page, reaching for the same objectives. Family is important. Teamwork is important. And the company will go the limit to treat each of its employees like a million dollars. We don't wanna lose a million dollars. That's something we take very good care of. Something we want to keep."

Every member of the Platinum Dolls managerial staff offered proposals during the meeting. Brianna wanted to install a toll-free line that exclusive members would be able to call to speak to her girls. Stew approved. Daisy thought it would be a good idea if her Studio A could be out in the barn instead of in the house. She wanted to do this in the warmer months only, complete with hay and pitchforks on the set. Daisy didn't think it would be a bad idea if horses, chickens, or goats looked on while her girls performed on-camera. The room erupted with appreciative laughter at the suggestion of animals on the set. It was the kind of creative thinking Stew was looking for. And he approved.

"You know us Southern girrrls, Stew. . . . All we want is some pretty dresses and some more of them Victoria's Secret unmentionables, and we'll be fiiine," said Honey, her southern accent dripping from her lips.

Justine wanted to have part of the D.C. studios reconstructed to simulate the Oval Office. One of her performers had suggested how captivating it might be, how controversial it might be, to have two or three girls in action right on the president's desk. Controversy. Stew loved it.

Stew approved everyone's concepts, even Sharon's Friday Freak Sessions. She said that Stew knew what she meant, so she didn't need to explain. The room nearly fell apart from laughter when Sharon winked and licked her lips for Stew.

There was no idea too nasty or too controversial or too laid-back for Stew not to accept. It all spoke of the renewed spirit that would give the company the polish it needed. And now with the Web's WiFi increasing in order to allow more than just still shots and video streaming, it wouldn't be long before each of Platinum Dolls studios would show live activity, no different than what was broadcast on the evening news or *Monday Night Football.* It was clear to everyone in attendance that the company's destiny and Stew's ultimate dream would live on to become more than a venture and more than just another brand. Platinum Dolls would become an institution that would not be afraid of change, and it would not side-step its challenges.

Four months had passed since that midnight meeting. It was New Year's Eve and Stew was now twenty-nine. His lovers were well into their first trimesters of pregnancy. The third quarter proved to be profitable, and Trent Morris was now the senior vice president of S & T Ventures—Stew and Trent.

Lexington Rowland was being held without bail, after having pled guilty to the murders of two women. For the seven other murders in New York, the district attorney was proposing the death penalty. Deliberations and negotiations were still ongoing.

Pop had spent twenty thousand of Porter's cash on the funeral and saw to it that the ex-agent was buried in style. The remaining sum of a hundred twenty thousand went to Stew to help with the expenses for all the other burials and funeral arrangements. No expense was too great.

Pop was down for the festivities as well, along with Timmy, Sam, and many of the other elite bodyguards that the company employed. All of them were on duty, in tux and tie, ensuring the welfare of everyone present.

In all, there were over five hundred guests who were there for the year-ending gala. Many of the faces were new, women who had been ushered into the company by Ashley, and others who had been newly recruited. There were the business managers, the office workers, and there were a few Internet technicians there for the party. Betty, the accountant, flew in from New York, and so did Charlene, whom Sharon appointed to take her place since she now called Atlanta her home.

Sharon and Barbara were glowing at the center of a throng of girls, all of them asking questions about their arrangements and touching the pregnant bellies trying to feel the babies.

Just like Sharon and Barbara, Stephanie was shining with joy and color, and added pounds. Stew had finally professed his love. Stew, ever the politician, made his rounds, remembering Andrea, Sandy, and Vickie, and June and Tina, with whom he had shot the last movie in Seattle. He ran into Misty, and they hugged and kissed. Misty whispered something in Stew's ear, and he declined gracefully. There were Cheryl, Octavia and Jordan, who all were Platinum Dolls from the Bronx. Brianna was there with her champagne glass in hand, introducing her suburbanites—Delores, Pricilla, Elizabeth, and Francine—to the rest of the guests. Judy and Jessica, star entertainers from the D.C. branch, haggled for Stew's attention, and Maria and Patty took turns dancing with their boss. Dream, Salt, and Tonya all had camcorders and were conducting mini-interviews with anyone they could convince, all in the effort to have memories to look back on.

The great halls, dining areas, living rooms, and indoor patios were all filled to capacity. Red and black balloons floated everywhere with their strings hanging overhead. The indoor pool was covered with a hard floor so that the room would be suitable, a ballroom for everyone to congregate at near-midnight. Twenty-five waiters served food and drinks. Music of various kinds filled many parts of the house, from classic soul to jazz to hip-hop to Top 40. Noisemakers sounded continuously in anticipation of the countdown.

The women all wore party hats or tiaras, which looked either silly or elegant, and sensuous evening gowns, some so sheer their style teetered between fashionable and erotic. So much cleavage under one roof, it was impossible not to overindulge. The hairstyles, the sequined fabrics, the glitter on the skin, the thighs and calves and stiletto heels, so many sets of full lips, saucy expressions, and so much mesmerizing perfume in the air. It was all enough to drive a man insane with desire. But that was another Stew Gregory, some other place and time.

"Stew?" It was a familiar voice, and then a tap on his shoulder. He turned and a sudden fear shot through him. He wondered if Timmy was watching this. He swore she had a gun behind those flowers and that she wanted revenge. *Oh my God! This is how it's gonna end!?* Then Iris lifted up the bouquet to give to Stew.

"I come in peace, to congratulate you."

Stew took the flowers and swept Iris off her feet. He breathed with relief. "I'm sorry. I'm so sorry, Iris," Stew said wholeheartedly.

"Are you kidding, Stew? My brother is gonna get everything he deserves. And I won't shed a tear. I'm just happy that *you're* the winner and that you came out on top, *alive*."

"Oh, Iris, it's been so long. . . . I've been so busy. I never got to reach out to you. Never got to *thank* you. It's because of you that I got here today. You . . ." Stew finally put Iris down. He realized that had he ruined the flowers.

"That's okay. It was the thought," she said.

"How did you get here? I thought you moved back to Detroit?"

"I had a friend's help." Iris stepped out of the way so that Stew could see. It was Candice.

Stew let up. "I didn't think you could make it!"

"You're out of your mind if you think I'd miss this," Candice said, already swept up in Stew's embrace.

"Wow. How'd you find her?"

"Long story, buddy, another time."

"It's almost time, Stew," Stephanie said, then greeted the other two. Candice and Iris both congratulated Stephanie.

"Come on, ladies. It's time to welcome in the New Year."

And they did. And for sure, this was the start of a really good day.